To Ken
Enjoy the Yarn!

THE

PRODIGAL

FATHER

Karl F. Manke

Karl Manke

author of *UNINTENDED CONSEQUENCES*

Alexander Books

Alexander, N.C.

Publisher: Ralph Roberts
Cover Design: Ralph Roberts
Interior Design and Electronic Page Assembly: WorldComm®

Editor: Ralph Roberts

ISBN 978-1-57090-271-0

Alexander Books—an imprint of *Creativity, Inc.*—is a full-service publisher located at 65 Macedonia Road, Alexander, NC 28701. Phone 1-828-252-9515, Fax 1-828-255-8719. For orders only: 1-800-472-0438. Visa and MasterCard accepted.

This book is also available on the Internet at **Amazon.com**

THE
PRODIGAL
FATHER

In memory of
Floyd Bennett
and Don Hornus

CHAPTER 1

THE POOL HALL
"A man had two sons."   Luke 5:11

"I sure as hell can," asserts Gibby Geiberson.

"You may be able too but it's stupid," reiterates his older brother Dillon.

Not satisfied with his older brother's high mindedness, Gibby tries to further stimulate his brother's interest.

"I'll bet you twenty bucks," taunts Gibby, not willing to be ignored.

"It's a dumb stunt Gibby," says an ingenuous older brother.

Gibby and Dillon Geiberson are the sons of Norbert and Joan Geiberson. Dillon, is a well-built and handsome man. Accessorized by cut features and short- cropped, auburn hair, he resembles his father. He conducts himself with an air of confidence and maturity beyond his twenty four years.

He has taken on much more responsibility than is really expected of someone his age. He manages most of the day-to-day responsibilities of the Geiberson family's Circle G, a 13,000-head cattle ranch covering nearly a million acres.

The younger of the two boys was given the name Marlon at birth. As a two-year-old, unable to say Geiberson, he would pronounce himself as Marlon Gibby. Eventually he became just Gibby Geiberson. It stuck.

At twenty years old, he's many years younger in maturity and responsibility. Nonetheless, to his credit he possesses an adventurous spirit his elder brother has never developed. But not always to his credit, his

adventurous spirit has no set boundaries and he is often foolhardy. Today is such a day.

Norbert has had roofers all week re-roofing his hip-roof barn. A mechanical high-boy has been brought in to lift bundles of shingles, each
weighing around 50 pounds, up the 20-foot side walls. It's been left unattended with the keys in the ignition. Across the roof on the other side
of the barn is a conveyer used to lift bales of hay into the loft. It's also
unattended.

The positioning of each of these conveyances has given Gibby an
overwhelming idea. His modus operandi is to ride his dirt bike off the
roof of the barn, leap from its bottom edge onto the conveyor, then ride
its twenty-four inch wide, belted incline down to the ground.

More often than not, Gibby takes his destiny into his own hands. He
neither seeks permission nor questions the wisdom of his decisions. He
simply moves foreword meeting each challenge as it rolls out.

He suddenly appears cresting the barn roof, riding his dirt bike across
its peak. Apparently he has employed the high boy to raise himself and his
bike to the roof. Giving a war whoop, EEEHAAA, and then in one fluid
moment, he charges down the gables toward the conveyer belt. Reaching
the bottom edge of the barn's summit, he gives the handlebars an upward
jerk, causing the entire front wheel to rise up in the air, while the rear
wheel lands squarely on the conveyer.

In all of five seconds,and still riding on only the rear wheel, he lands
safely on the ground, displaying his smirky "I told you so" grin. Dillon
has met this smirk before on many, many, occasions. Being the more responsible older brother, he's tried to prevent Gibby from self destructing,
now he's met once again with his brother's same fiercely independent and
uncompromising grin. Gibby is sitting back on the seat, his arms folded
and one leg resting on the ground to balance the bike, the other on the

clutch as though it's some kind of mechanism for launching a missile. "You wanna try that one big brother," mocks Gibby. Without comment Dillon turns and walks away, shaking his head. "Maybe not him, but I'll bet I could" comes a mellifluous voice behind him. It's the self-estimations of Jed Lander's daughter, April. Jed is Norbert's senior cow boss. He's been with the ranch since Norbert's father hired him years before. He lives on the ranch in a tenant house provided by Norbert, along with his wife Karen, and his twenty-two-year-old April.

"In your wildest dreams April," shouts back Gibby.

April, at her full 5'10"'s gives herself a statuesque like appearance. Tossing her short, reddish-blond hair, she peeks her hazel colored eyes through bangs that force her to tilt her head to one side. Then with one thumb hooked in the back pocket of her tight fitting cutoff jeans, she follows the other across her forehead pushing her provocative bangs out of her eyes, simultaneously giving her head a slight whip to help them along.

"If you teach me how, I know I could learn," is her sonorous reply as she playfully pokes her finger into his chest.

Gibby has more of the Mielke features from his mother's side of the family. He's tall, blond, blue eyed, and slight of build. He gives the impression that he has more growing to do. He's at an age where he may have a cigarette in one hand and a computer game in the other; not quite a boy, yet at the same time, not quite a man.

Hormones have forced their way into his life in some new and uninvited direction, often leaving him unwittingly frustrated. April is well equipped to bring on this kind agitation in Gibby. He's overtaken by just her presence alone, and, now especially, by her bewitching display of female equipment. He finds this experience to have components that cause him a strange discomfort, but at the same time welcomes an element brought out of it that's strangely alluring.

When they were young children they played day after day together. They were friends as well as competitors. Her being a "tomboy" and him being a young whippersnapper didn't cause any tension. They rode horses together, and on hot summer days swam together in Strang Lake. All through these adolescent years Gibby had always been able to impress April with his bravado. He would spend an inordinate amount of time designing daring feats he knew she couldn't perform. Lately it's been her turn to impress him.

Gibby has been more occupied with the new and different endowments she possesses. It's a strange, new, distinct power she is discovering that she suddenly has over him. It's a power that she has never experienced before. It is quickly becoming her new best friend. She flirts with him in a way that's calculated. It's obvious she's enjoying her feminine cleverness. He fights it by trying to marginalize her effect on him. In the past, April has always defended herself by aggressively using her trump card – being two years older. Now, also adding to her credits, is this mysterious control she has over his hormones. Gibby finds this all disconcerting.

April's flirtation toward Gibby, has for certain, not gone unnoticed. Dillon has carried a secret crush on April since she was in eighth grade. Because of his reticent nature, he has never put forth the effort to make his feelings known. His hope has always been that she will be drawn to his manliness. After all, he is twenty four years old, two years older than April, and has been told many times how mature he is for his age. Dillon has always found the power that adulthood offers attractive, while often finding it frustrating to have to deal with an inferior, immature younger brother. For Dillon, being hard working, attentive to duty, forthright and obedient, is the kind of behavior he hopes will be rewarded.

For all his hoping, April is seemingly unimpressed. She has not embraced his penchant toward responsibility, and for the most part, finds him boring. Her actions make it quite clear that the tune she is choosing to hum along with is the free spirit of his younger brother.

Recently Dillon's attitude toward his younger brother has taken a new turn. For this nubile young adult it's an awful, awkward turn at that. Rather than merely being unimpressed with Gibby's playful irresponsible ways, he now finds himself envying the attention April showers on this younger brother *because* of his goofy behavior. It's a tangle of emotions he finds difficult to sort through. His way is to ignore these feelings, to never admit they exist, not even to himself.

Nonetheless, envy will not be ignored. It simply morphs itself into a negative behavior. What Dillon has always considered stupid and non-threatening about Gibby is turning on its head. Gibby has become some-one he has to compete with. He finds this new development disturbing. Rather than deal with it, his way has always been to withdraw into him-self, displaying behavior that can only be described as, a pout.

At first glance, one would expect Norbert to fawn over his eldest son, who in so many ways, is similar to himself; diligent, hardworking, responsible.

Norbert loves both his sons equally, on the other hand, he would concede in an argument that he reacts differently to their personalities. The old saying "the squeaking wheel gets the grease" applies to how he behaves toward their behavior. He usually meets Dillon's course of action with quiet applause. Albeit, Norbert, undeniably has always had a twinkle in his eye for Gibby's shenanigans, and is much more demonstrative in his attention toward this young rogue than he is toward his older, more responsible sibling.

He has given Gibby, many a pass where he has held Dillon account-able. The result being,, and much to the chagrin of Dillon, is that in the instances he finds his younger brothers behavior beyond annoying, his father meets it with forgiving patience.

Nonetheless, Norbert sees something in this younger son that more than occasionally puzzles him. This boy is like a perpetual motion machine, always in full throttle. Anyone who has encountered this young rogue cannot help but be impressed with his open vigor and zest for life. When he was a little boy, his parents found it amusing to watch his energy propel him in unpredictable directions, while fully expecting him, as Dillon had before, to enter his teen year's by putting away his adolescent antics. In kindergarten he had been diagnosed with an attention deficit disorder. It's now apparent he is not growing out of this derangement. As a matter of fact, he awards himself for his, seeming fearlessness in the face of danger.

Before retiring for the night, it has become Norbert and Joanie's habit to spend their private time discussing the day's happenings. More often than not, Gibby,"the squeaking wheel", gets more of their attention.

"I don't know what I'm going to do with that boy, Joanie." Not waiting for her reply, Norbert continues. "That stunt he pulled today is about all I can take." Norbert is pacing around the bedroom, occasionally going to a window, peeking through the curtains as though he expects to find Gibby lurking somewhere in the darkness.

"The only one impressed with him was April. She acts like that old bird dog we used to have, once she went on point it was near impossible to rein her back. I think she's got quite the crush on him."

Joanie, in complete agreement, adds, "I get the same feeling. One would have to be blind not to see what she's up to."

Joanie pauses for a moment to let the full impact of this problem work its way into her psyche. "Gibby's too young for this kind of pressure. I almost wish she'd discover Dillon."

Norbert has put on a pair of pajamas and has taken his place next to his wife. Their bed is fitting for the ranch house. Norbert's father had it imported from the old country. It's a large bed with a high head board. Joanie has propped two large pillows behind her back allowing her to sit up while working on her crossword puzzle.

Norbert is comforted in Joanie sharing the same concerns for Gibby that he has. Then listing one more, he adds "I'm not certain Dillon could handle her."

There is no hiding the amount of attention Norbert pays to his family. His wife and boys give meaning to the ranch. Without them, his success would hold little significance. Their prosperity, at least in his own eyes, is reflected in his family. To him the continued success of the ranch is a testament to the harmony in the home.

As mothers have done since the beginning of time, Joanie has developed a strong protective shield around her boys. Mothers and daughters don't seem to have the same relationships, but then sons don't pose a threat to their mother's fading beauty like young daughters seem to do.

Joanie and Norbert recognize their differing roles, as well as differing approaches to child rearing. At best, they are able to support each others decisions, and if they can't, they try and stay out of the others way.

With this thought in mind, Joanie flops down her crossword puzzle, abruptly leaving the bedroom. In a matter of minutes, she returns. She has scooped out a large dish of vanilla ice cream covered in chocolate syrup. With a wry little smile, she plops it in front of Norbert.

Looking up with an exaggerated smile, Norbert pats her on the behind. "Oh baby you just spoil me."

Knowing where this can lead Joanie swats his hand away. She's not done with this conversation. Joanie is still mulling over April and Gibby. She wants Norbert's attention and is now even more determined to keep him on track..

Finally, with a sense of frankness, she blurts out, as many parents do when they become aware of their powerlessness, "Norbert, we're going to have to put a stop to their nonsense." Pausing for a moment, "After all, she's two years older than Gibby."

Silence.

Norbert is whipping his ice cream around and around his bowl producing something that looks like chocolate soup. He considers her question for a moment, licking some of his contrivance from the back of his spoon.

"I think we should stay out of these affairs. For all your concerns, we realistically can't control with whom they develop their relationships. After all, they are adults."

More silence.

Frustrated over this changing family dynamic, Joanie is trying as best she can to relinquish her motherly grip on her boys. She is suddenly absorbed in an ardent memory where this kind of impassioned concern for her sons welfare, served her family well. "I just don't want to see Gibby get hurt."

Norbert continues to circle his spoon around the inside edge of his dish, scooping the balance of his concoction into his mouth. Looking directly at his wife of 25 years, licking the spoon clean, he says, "Joanie, what makes you think we have that power."

Waiting for an answer, he continues on with a questioning expression.

Joanie takes his empty dish and spoon and heads for the kitchen. Looking back, she says "Well, we have to do something. I don't think we should sit by and watch our son being manipulated."

Returning to the bedroom, still muttering, "I know that girl knows what she's doing." The worry reflected in Joanie's eyes is the kind only a mother with a vulnerable child can understand.

Norbert is careful not to dismiss his wife's concerns. On the other hand, he is more concerned with keeping Gibby alive -- at least until he has enough sense to keep himself alive. The foolhardy risks Gibby takes makes Norbert wish he could just take a carefree, nonchalant attitude toward his son's haphazard immaturity. The problems Gibby may be having with girls, at least in Norbert's eyes, pales in comparison.

The cruelest part of both these enigmas is how powerless these parents feel. The reality is no matter how much they discuss the problem, Gibby will continue to chart his own course.

Soon the night has its way and they both fall into a calming rest.

The next morning arrives on schedule. Norbert feels refreshed enough to meet his day with his normal air of confidence. Standing in front of a window illuminated only by a mercury yard light, he attempts to form an idea, that has recently come to him, into words. He's wrestling with the thought of giving Gibby more responsibilities. Thinking back to time when he was Gibby's age, he remembers how his father promoted him to cow boss and how eagerly he had looked forward to these new responsibilities. These are fond memories. His hope is that this attitude will find its way to Gibby. Somehow, he denotes that a different response may be waiting than the one he's hoping for. *"Hope for the best but be prepared for the worst"*, is the mantra Norbert lives by.

His thoughts are quickly interrupted by a familiar voice with familiar call. "Come and get it while its still hot."

Joanie's been busy in the kitchen putting together a thrashers breakfast of eggs, bacon and pancakes. Watching her multitask all of these entrees as they come together, is as entertaining as watching an experienced conductor control an orchestra to end on the same note. Once her men leave for the morning chores she knows she won't see them again until lunch time. She's determined to have them well nourished.

Entering the kitchen, Gibby is still stretching and yawning, never,

ever having quite enough sleep. He has spent most of the previous evening partying with friends.

Sitting together for meals is still a tradition in the Geiberson family. It's been alive for the entirety of their married life. Sometimes it's boisterous, sometimes it's quiet. Either way, it provides for family interaction that isn't available any other time.

Norbert is unusually quiet this morning as he eats his breakfast. Not making eye contact with anyone, he's calculatedly keeping his head down, appearing as though his main concern is separating his pancakes from his eggs.

Both boys react accordingly. Recognizing their father is not his usual self, they make small talk between themselves.

Dillon, never missing an opportunity to censure Gibby's life style, chides him with, "Have another rough night, Gibby?"

"No, not really" he returns. Gibby is trying to horse down enough bacon and eggs and get out of there before the questioning attracts the attention of his parents.

Satisfied this questioning will, indeed, arouse a response from his mother and father, Dillon's eyes peer over the top of his cup as he takes a prolonged sip waiting for the expected result.

As expected, Joanie's attention immediately shifts from her fussing with a paper towel used to soak up bacon grease and directly onto her youngest son.

"Gibby what time did you get home?" Not waiting for an answer, Joanie pressed him "I know it was after 2:00am because I was awake and your truck wasn't here yet."

When his family begins to question what he does in his private time, he inadvertently postures himself much like a trapped animal would, looking for a way out. When that fails, he begins to fight back.

He's still in the "looking for a way out" stage when Norbert, finally breaking his silence, senses "a way in". Wiping his hands on a napkin and looking directly at his youngest son, "Gibby, when you graduated from high school two years ago your mother and I agreed to allow you some time with friends. We're aware that this is the last you're going to see of many of them, as you all move on with your lives, and now is the time that you also need to begin to move on with yours."

For most of his life Gibby has been given a pass around the ranch. This is the first year he's been expected to pull his share of work.

Gibby's eyes are fixed on his father, not really knowing where this conversation is going. One thing he's sure of is, it can't be over fast enough, and he can't get out of here fast enough.

Meanwhile, Dillon is enjoying his brother's twisting, and especially now that it's under his parents scrutiny. He's struggling to control a smile. On the other hand, its always been his feeling that his parents are too easy on Gibby. If it were left to him, Gibby would be given some hard ultimatums.

Continuing his line of thought Norbert stays the course. "Fred Mc-Donell retired this spring, and as you know, he was in charge of the machine shop which accommodates at least a 100 pieces of equipment. Fred was a darn good manager, he sure knew his stuff. I hated to lose him."

Gibby is getting a sense of where this may be going. He had worked in the shop with Fred ever since he could handle a wrench.

Dillon also senses where this conversation is going. His smirk has quickly been replaced with a frown.

Norbert continues "I need a replacement and I think you can do it. You want to give it a try?"

Norbert's ethos has always been to encourage his boys to take responsibility for fixing their own vehicles. This began way back with their bicycles. He feels this builds a proper kind of self reliance. Early on, Gibby has shown a particular proficiency toward everything mechanical and has proven his talent in fixing anything broken. His father has taken notice and feels quite confident in passing this management responsibility to Gibby.

Gibby is at a loss for words. Yesterday he's hanging out with his buddies, now he's being challenged to leave his boyhood for the responsibilities of an adult.

Dillon's reaction is a deeper frown. After all, it's only been in the last six months that his father has given him a manager's spot. He has always thought of himself as "The good boy", having *earned* his father's trust. He proudly accepted the position. Now his father is seemingly compromising his long -held principles by rewarding Gibby's bad behavior with a promotion.

Now there is a silence, only lasting for seconds, but seems like it's way too long. Gibby clears his throat. It's obvious he's trying to form some words.

"Dad I don't think that's what I want to do."

These are not the words a father, who builds a ranch in the hopes his sons will carry on his legacy, cares to hear.

Again a pause. Norbert looks searchingly at Joanie. Gibby's words cut him deep. The hesitation, the obvious disappointment reflected on his face portray a quality not commonplace with him. With an unmistakeable reluctance, but also with noticeable patients, Norbert measures his words carefully, "If I put you on the spot Gibby, I don't mean to. Maybe you could give it a couple days to think it over." With that, Norbert settles back in his chair, trying to smile and reassure himself that the wand of trust he is passing on to this less than enthusiastic son, will not come back fruitless.

During this discourse all eyes have been on Gibby. Nobody notices Dillon has gotten up from his unfinished breakfast and left the house.

The conversation remains cool as breakfast is finished. With only a few congenial platitudes Gibby silently kisses his mother good bye, making his way out of the house to the machine shop.

So far Gibby's life has been his own. He has come and gone at will. Free to lead his cavalier life, leaving a sense of responsibility toward anything or anyone, other than himself, to someone else. He is, for the first time in his life, experiencing a feeling of being trapped. He's exacerbated by his father's proposal. Instead of finding safety and contentment in his familiar surroundings, he now finds discontent. His mind whirls leaving a sick, unsettled feeling that is quickly becoming his worst enemy. The ranch has a suffocating choke hold on him creating a panicked need to escape.

Not anywhere near ready to break his tradition of hanging out with his friends, he finishes his tasks for the day, cleans up and heads for town. With a heavy flow of dust billowing up behind his truck, he shakes off the pressure of the ranch. Finally reaching the highway, he enters a different world, a world created by himself and for himself.

Ed's Pool Hall offers a relief from the rigors of the ranch. It's comprised of males best described as non-conforming and edgy. The smell of stale cigarette smoke, male sweat and beer almost overtake the smells emanating from a musty and dysfunctional toilet located down a narrow stairway.

Pete Simon is three years Gibby's senior and a permanent fixture at Ed's. He's of Jewish decent, small in stature with a wine red birthmark on the left side of his face that he attempts to conceal with pancake makeup.

"'Sup Gibby?"

"Same ol' shit, different day."

"Hey dude I got some killer weed, you wanna go outside for a hit?" says a grinning Pete, feigning a left hook to Gibby's jaw.

"I think you're onto something" says a smiling Gibby grabbing Pete's left hook with his own left hand.

Gibby finds Pete alluring. Pete possesses an aggressive personality that can best be described as brazen. He fancies himself a gambler and a gangster, playing high stakes poker. He also carries a 9mm pistol, holstered under a jacket. What he lacks in physical stature, he tries to compensate for by presenting himself as crazy, therefore becoming the wrong person to mess with. He's a fast thinker, usually outwitting any opponent by intimating a bizarre form of violence toward anyone daring to cross a line. He has been heard warning one would be assaulter "Ya, you may beat my ass, but you're going to be one awful funny looking dude walking around with no nose, cause I'm going to bite that son-of-a-bitch right off."

Pete is equally attracted to Gibby's spirit of adventure. Gibby possesses a deeper commitment to the daredevil life than Pete. Pete's is mostly talk and living vicariously through those who are actually men of action. Pete's idea of manliness comes through the pungent aroma of Old Spice cologne, carrying his pistol, and talking a lot of bravado. In spite of their differences, together they present a formidable foe. What one of them lacks, the other complements.Once in the parking lot, they climb into Pete's baby blue vintage 1958 Lincoln Continental. It's a rare antiquated model with a retractable hard top. Gibby messing around with his radio annoys him as he simultaneously swats at Gibby's hand while attempting to roll a joint."Keep your frickin' hands off my dials. You'll screw em up."

A mocking Gibby retaliates by waving his fingers in Pete's face "whoo, whoo ya gonna break my hands, Petie?"

The bantering ends as soon as Pete lights the reefer. Struggling to keep the abrasive smoke in his lungs without coughing he passes it to Gibby. "Here" says Gibby giving "here" that sucking coarse sound that can only be made by an inhaling marijuana smokers. Within seconds of the first hit Gibby feels its full strength lifting the hair on his temples. "Wow!" says

Gibby sucking in yet another lung full of it' potent vapors. All he can say is "wow." "Where did you get this shit?" Not waiting for an answer Gibby continues his diatribe "This shit is dynamite." His eyebrows shoot up and his eyes take on a watery blank look.Grinning from ear to ear Pete says "I can get all we want." Leaning forward his face returns to a more somber appearance. "How'd you like to do some business with this stuff?" he asks as he takes another hit.

"Whatta ya mean?" quips Gibby with a pot-induced grin.

"I mean, the guy I bought this stuff from is willing to cut me a deal on a kilo." Pete's voice is taking on a new excitement. "I know between the two of us we can easily get rid of a kilo and still have enough left for ourselves. You know what that means. We get ours free!"

Pete has let the car windows down. The night air is cool. Gibby shivers a bit, partly from the coolness, and partly from the excitement of this new endeavor.

With or without the drug influencing his thinking, Gibby says "Consider me in.."

Pete lights up another joint. Continuing to laugh and act reckless as they bully their way around Powellville. The glass pack muffler snaps and roars with e acceleration. If the pot isn't enough, Pete has a bottle of cheap wine under the seat. This is enough to bring out an even more careless attitude toward everything and everyone. In spite of the normally calming effects of the drug, Pete begins to imagine himself a race car driver. His favorite trick is to depress the gas and brake pedal simultaneously then release the brakes quickly, leaving the gas depressed. The result is a patch of burnt rubber for at least 20 feet, followed by hilarious laughter.

Managing to stretch time into the wee hours of the morning, they soon notice they are the only car left in town. Now there is no sense in being out. The whole idea of the evening was to see and be seen. The type of life each of them yearns for is to live e day as though it were their last. They both imagine they would then die happy. Both go their separate ways promising to get together and work out a plan with the dope dealer.

CHAPTER 2

BILL STRANG'S CABIN

5:30 a.m. always comes too early for Gibby. He awakens to the sounds of his father's usual thumps on his door while yelling at him to "Wake up and piss. The world's on fire."

His mouth feels like it's full of dry cotton as an even dryer tongue tries to make its way around parched lips. Driven by thirst and a simultaneous strong urge to urinate, he walks stiff legged across the room to a waiting pair of jeans hanging on a hook in his closet. Stumbling, he somehow manages to get into them as he maneuvers himself to the bathroom down the hallway.

Information about the night before is competing for his attention as it begins to make its way back into his frontal lobes. This is not an unfamiliar experience for Gibby. Throughout his young years, he has experienced many, many similar experiences. He's learned, that if he patiently waits, any blanks in his head will eventually fill up.

Dillon has a disdain for Gibby's lack of responsibility,and doesn't pull any punches in openly criticizing his brother's ongoing life style.

"Gibby you act like a dumb ass. When are you going to drop this rock and roll bullshit and act your age? You're almost twenty-one?"

"Why don't you just worry about yourself, Dillon? You can start by keeping your nose out of my business," counters Gibby.

Dillon can never let things rest, as the elder brother, he always thinks he has to have the final word.

"I don't know how dad thinks you can handle managing the machine shop when it's obvious you can't do much to handle your own life, much less, anybody or anything else."

Having Dillon in his face is considerably rougher than his parents have ever thought of being. Gibby knows at times like this, he'd rather slug Dillon, on the other hand, he also is aware that Dillon is much larger, outweighing him by at least fifty pounds and a couple inches taller. He'd need a board, a club, something to make sure Dillon didn't get up right away. For now he's deferring revenge, yet certainly not without a resentment. For the time being he's going to have to resign himself to his brother's self-righteous anger. On the other hand, Gibby knows enough of his older brother buttons to push that he is equally able to annoy him. "Dillon,the reason you don't like my life is that you're too much of a tight ass. You couldn't handle it. Don't you realize that the difference between us is that God has endowed me with gifts he didn't give you? Hell Dillon, I can piss right into the wind and not even get wet," says Gibby mocking his brother's piousness.

It's been said of some folks that they don't possess enough character to lose it, or that some don't have enough courage to do neither a good art nor a bad one. Gibby envisions his elder brother fits in both categories. Dillon has always considered himself to be the "good boy" and his younger brother to be the "black sheep" in the family. It's difficult for Dillon to understand why his father doesn't just boot Gibby out. Instead, he speaks quietly and patiently to his ever-growing concerns over his brother's behavior. Dillon's festering hate around Gibby is growing worse e day, moreover, it is now spreading to include his father.

It hurts Norbert to his soul to have his sons at odds with one another.

Dillon is even more intense in his dislike for Gibby when Norbert tries to assure him that Gibby will eventually figure it all out.

"Dad, he's just pulling the wool over your eyes, and you and mom fall for it. Just don't expect the same from me, OK.?"

Norbert feels his son's frustration with his younger brother. "It's not like that son, we know Gibby's up to things we don't approve of. He's not fooling anybody. All I'm asking of you is that you don't hate him" says Norbert quietly, without getting loud and defensive.

Dillon looks at his father in disbelief. Shaking his head in disgust, he then turns and walks off.

Norbert lets out a long sigh, saying a silent prayer for both of his sons.

Dillon gets frustrated when things aren't going his way and goes into a pout. It seems to him that Gibby is rewarded for bad behavior, while he in turn is ignored for his diligence. His thoughts meander around as he enters his office. *"After all, aren't I the one who makes sure the ranch runs smoothly, and what thanks do I get?"* Never seeing himself as a selfish, calculating manipulator, rather he envisions himself as a no-nonsense business man, who justifies attacking anyone crossing him.

"After all, aren't I the youngest president the Kiwanis Club has ever initiated? Aren't I the head warden at the Anglican Church? Don't I manage my finances responsibly? I never would be in the successful position I am today if I had indulged those assholes who opposed me," he thinks to himself.

His view of his world is seen more and more through the lens of resentment. He finds he's becoming an alien in his own family. Even though he has chosen to be an oppressor in order to enforce control over his would-be enemies, he has made himself a victim. His resentments toward his family are taking more of a life of their own and damn the consequences. *"That little punk is going to be out of here if it takes e ounce of energy I have."* These thoughts are exhausting and incendiary, nonetheless, Dillon will not give them up, instead, he succors them, taking great delight in his ripening bitterness.

Each of Gibby's infractions are more and more, molding themselves into the fabric of his brother's sensibilities, each carefully categorized, and they all are damned as intolerable.

It's mid-morning on a September day in British Columbia. Joanie is wearing her white cotton socks. She already feels the heat of summer giving way to the coolness of fall. Being a woman of great energy and determination, she quickly adapts to most new developments in her life. She is in the throes of furniture rearranging when Dillon walks in for his mid-morning coffee break.

"Dillon, honey, will you give me a hand with this couch. I want to move it against the wall away from the window so it doesn't get direct sun. It's starting to fade!"

Without a word, Dillon lifts his end of the couch and moves it as directed by his mother, afterward, continuing his mission toward the bathroom.

His silence and demeanor perplex Joanie. She knows her sons well enough to know when things aren't right.

On his return, she's waiting with her maternal instincts in high gear. "Dillon you look troubled."

He shrugs his shoulders, shaking his head. "Well mom there's nothing going on," he says trying to deny his mother's mindfulness.

"Dillon, don't try denying it. I know when something's troubling you." His look continues to perplex her. "So let's hear it." Dillon can't misinterpret his mother's concern, he's experienced this kind of probing his entire life. As many times as he has gone through this close questioning from his mother, he continues to try to sidestep her. He always does this when taken by surprise.

"I don't have any problems Ma," he snaps back. The sarcasm in his voice tells his mother otherwise.

Never having been intimidated by either of her sons, she presses him further.

"Listen Dillon, this is your mother speaking. I *know* when things aren't right with you." She pauses, still continuing her gaze, "So let's sit here for a minute and talk about it. "

"Alright, alright Ma. I know you're not going to let me rest until you get what you want." Losing control he blurts out ," It's that damn Gibby. He could be standing over a body with a smoking gun and you and dad would swear to God he didn't do it!"

Like any dam that holds back toxins, a weakness in its wall spells disaster. It doesn't take long before there's a torrent of poisonous contaminants pouring through the breach. Dillon's contempt for his younger brother seems to have no boundaries.

Used to Dillon's contentiousness toward his younger brother, Joanie tries to dismiss it as normal sibling rivalry.

"Don't worry about Gibby fooling your dad or me. We're fully aware of your brother's 'Tom foolery," assures Joanie.

Hearing his own carping, Dillon soon disappoints himself. It's more of an accounting than he wants to let out, but then his mother has always been able to get more out of him than he is willing to give.

"Oh the baby!" he is first inclined to say of his own whiny behavior. Dillon has always regarded his coping mechanisms as mature, therefore he considers himself above any kind of outburst. Still, what more does his exasperation with Gibby say? Isn't it the thundercloud, the thundercloud that has been brewing under all his virtues all his life? The subtle fluids from his hate are brewing and now mutilating his soul. Jealousy, anger, pride, uncharitably, cruelty, sulkiness, self righteousness, all mixed into one-ill temper.

Dillon is sitting in his mother's kitchen, resting his cheeks in both his hands propped up by elbows, bent on the table. His eyes gaze out between his two pinched cheeks as he awaits his mother's expostulations.

It's obvious to both that this conversation is becoming uncomfortable. Joanie is trying hard to measure her words. The last thing she wants to happen, is to create hostility between herself and her eldest son.

"I want to talk to you about something else" says his mother in her more controlled voice. "It's about April."

Obviously she has hit some kind of nerve in her son. His eyes involuntarily blink, moving side to side while trying to maintain an unaffected demeanor. His brain strains to make the shift from Gibby to April. Right now both remain a challenge. This is definitely not a development he is going to be comfortable with, and his involuntary shifting around in his chair reveal it.

"Why would I want to talk about April" are the only words he can think of to say, as he fiddles with the salt and pepper shakers, rolling them between his calloused hands.

His mother's tone has begun to change. It now possesses an ominous bluntness. Dillon notices her eyes also have a serious matter-of-fact look about them. This always forewarns a no nonsense discourse.

Joanie continues to take the lead. "It doesn't take a rocket scientist to realize she's been flirting with Gibby. What I want to ask of you, is to keep an eye on her, and if at all possible, dissuade her. Gibby's much too young for her."

When the boys were little, Joanie had them convinced she could read minds. This is a residual thought in Dillon's head that this yet may be true. He carefully watches for any signs this is happening. Convinced that his crush on April, is, at least for the present, still hidden, he reassures his mother, "Ya, OK. Ma I can do that." He says.

Much to the relief of Dillon, they finish their talk. It's been his life-long experience that once his mother begins delving into an object of thought, she doesn't let it rest until she's satisfied its come to its completion. Even now he's not sure his mother may know more than she lets on.

On one end of the barn he's cordoned off a section creating an office for himself. Not able to rid his mind of the conversation with his mother, he sits behind his desk pondering his next move. She is forcing him to confront his feelings for April. The pressure he's under to deal with his strong, yet reticent attraction for April, is creating an even stronger resentment for Gibby.

The thoughts continue to invade his mind all morning. Thank God for ranch hands asking questions and the telephone ringing forcing the subject of his thoughts to change. Life never remains one dimensional for long.

Jed Landers is on the phone.

"Dillon, we've got a big problem. I'm here on the north pasture. We've got about 500 head of those organic grass-fed cows wandering around outside the fence."

There's a big market in Japan for these cattle. The last thing Norbert wants is for these animals to be in jeopardy.

This news brought Dillon to his feet. His head snaps toward the north window in an involuntary reflex.

"I'll round up as many men as I can. We'll be there as soon as possible," assures Dillon. To successfully run a ranch this size demands the agility to meet any crises. Dillon has proven to his father, time ,and time again, that he's capable.

"What is the situation as we speak?" Dillon further questions Jed.

"Right now we're trying to get ahead of the lead herd and get them stopped," replies Jed in his usual "got things under control" voice.

This is what makes men like Jed Landers the kind of cow boss a rancher wants. He's cow savvy, definitely knows his business. Men like Jed have a right to pride themselves in their unique abilities. Never once in his adult life has he thought of doing any other kind of work. He came to work for Norbert's father, proving to be an invaluable asset immediately. His ability to organize and manage a couple dozen young, hard-living, buckaroos has stabilized the Circle G, making his talents an enviable asset among ranch owners.

Jed's second phone call is to his wife Karen, explaining the situation to her and letting her know he may not be home until after dark.

This call has gotten April's attention. Sensing excitement, she inquires, "What did daddy want?"

"They've got a break in the fence up on the north pasture. He's called Dillon to round up the buckaroos."

April looks at her mother, obviously excited to join this venture, still, fully expecting her to try and pull her back. Recognizing this look on her daughter's face, Karen knows how high spirited her daughter is, and doubts much that she'll be able to sell her on another plan.

Contorting her face into a frown, realizing the danger to which her only child will be exposed, she shrugs her shoulders in an obsequious gesture, "I wish you wouldn't do this, but I know you're going to," acquiesces her mother. Pausing a second for emphasis, she adds, "for God's sake don't do anything stupid." April is already at the door heading for the horse barn. She gives her mother the words she wants to hear, but certainly giving them no more than lip service, "Don't worry ma, I won't."

If there is nothing else April shares with Gibby, it's their mutual attraction to edgy, adrenaline-driving adventures. Her mind races, with her thoughts going no further than the high she is getting from the mere anticipation of an adventure.

Much of the work on Norbert's ranch is done on horseback. Some is done by helicopter or dirt bike. The latter two are Gibby's domain. The million-acre ranch calls for any controls that successfully aid in manage-ment- nonetheless, the horse remains the backbone of this kind of operation.

For April, a familiar whistle brings her favorite quarter horse trotting to the gate. The horse gives an immediate approving snort, recognizing its bridle and saddle. April has never tired of the beauty this beast presents when excited. His snorting and prancing in place foot movements, only add to the action. With deft hands, she slips the bridle over the horses face and ears, quickly cinching the saddle. Within minutes she has joined the gathering buckaroos. Dillon, already saddled up, is beginning to shout orders when April makes her appearance.

He can't help but notice her feminine form, her tight fitting jeans, and her arched back as she sits in her saddle. It's a alluring attraction. Not wanting to be caught starring, he quickly looks away, feigning something else vying for his attention.

Purposefully, she rides directly to Dillon. "My dad says I can go along." Clearly she has fabricated this. As it usually goes with her interaction with Dillon, she's takes his blank stare to be a sign of hostility. If she only knew how his heart is pounding.

She hesitates a moment, returning his stare. Looking into his deep, almost black eyes, she must admit, he is a handsome man. Handsome enough to give him a small flirtatious side glance. Turning her horse, she quickly makes her way through the,still gathering buckaroos, not want-ing for attention from any of them.

The Geiberson ranch is situated in a lush, green valley of grass, vari-ous small glacial lakes, assorted species of trees, ranging from deciduous to evergreen. The snow-capped mountains that surround most of this area accords the prospect that one could reach out and stroke them. It's hard to imagine how the God of the universe would use the violence of continents slamming together, and the several ice ages clawing at the earth's surface, to leave such a beautiful valley.

The dozen of buckaroos making their way across the pasture are suddenly taken back by the whining sound of a dirt bike spooking their horses.

"What the hell is he doin'?" says a buckaroo.

"Bein' a horse's ass," says another."Ya, I saw him ridin' a horse one time, it took a minute to figure out who was Gibby and which was the horses ass," says another unimpressed wrangler. Buckaroos, being the business folks they are, especially when their on a mission, keep their words simple and to the point.

It's not Gibby's style to ride a horse. Instead he's riding a 125cc dirt bike, jumping a mogul as though his only purpose is to stay airborne. The Doppler effect left by his motor is soon fading into the distance, leaving only a soundless, leaping and twisting cartoon like contortionist.

Dillon knows exactly what to expect from Gibby. He's not even slightly amused by his antics. Nevertheless, he finds himself glancing at April searching for her reaction. She takes notice, not realizing why Dillon would take an unsolicited glance her way. Taking it as flirtation, she smiles and sends back her own approving gaze.

To April this only is a harmless flirtation, but to Dillon it only tends to intensify his tension. Never having had a girlfriend in his 24 years he's clueless when it comes to women and dealing with them in their many ways.

There are several 50-acre, glacially-formed lakes left from the last ice age on the ranch. The posse is making its way up on one of these. It's been called Strang Lake for as long as anyone can remember. The water is a blue, crystal-clear body encircled in a depression of rock and alpines.

The story is that old Bill Strang, a gold miner from the Yukon gold rush days, had struck it rich. He made it this far before his mules died under the burden of carrying his fortune. He built himself a cabin made of cedar before winter came, but then died himself before spring. His fortune, like most legends, gets embellished. It's now reported to be somewhere in the neighborhood of 8,000 ounces of gold dust and nuggets, some the size of chicken eggs. It has never been found, and yet to this day, is still believed to be buried somewhere around the lake.

The trail straightens out and then widens again allowing April to position her horse alongside Dillon.

Breaking the ice she questions him, "Do you think we can get all our cows back?"

Her question piques his interest in her but not quite the same way her femininity tenses him.

Trying to form a sensible answer in the midst of his mental paralysis, he finally answers question.

"We've got a lot of money in those cows. I'd hate to lose any of them."

Riding side by side, by what is amazingly left of Bill Strong's cabin, April remembers when she, Dillon, and Gibby used to ride out here as kids. They spent many hot summer afternoons swimming and looking for Strang's fortune. They always talked of fixing up the cabin. Being made of cedar, it definitely has outlasted many others and could still be revived with a little work.

Dillon is also having unsolicited memories. His head perspires as he adjusts his wide- brimmed Stetson, wiping his brow with a blue neckerchief. He remembers the last time the three of them came to swim. Even back then, it seemed she spent time goofing around with Gibby, rather than pursuing him in his silent romantic proclivity.

The cabin brings back too many familiar frustrations for Dillon. Taking a deep breath he wishes it weren't so difficult for him to express himself. The usual words finding their way into the ears of anyone within hearing range from him seem, most typically, to be angry words.

Gripping his reins a little tighter he shouts, "Let's pick it up, " he spurs his horse from a gait to a trot. The riders behind are aware that the horses they are riding will be the same animal they'll be riding back after they reach the north pasture. These critters are a tough breed but no one wants them spent riding to the problem. Giving each other the look that questions the wisdom of their boss, they reluctantly pick up the pace.

Thuap- thuap- thuap announces the overhead presence of Norbert's helicopter. Simultaneously Dillon's cell phone rings. Knowing it's his father even before he releases it from its holster, his familiar "What's up dad" goes across the air waves.

"Take it easy on those horses, Dillon. We're going to need e ounce of strength they have to get these cows back behind a fence."

When Norbert gives orders like this, he seldom waits for a response. He always assumes it will be done. Continuing in a commanding voice he adds, "I'm flying up the river. I want to get ahead of the main herd and see if I can't stop them!"

"OK. dad," returns an Dillon, embarrassed because of his knee-jerk reaction to April's seeming flirtations. "We should be meeting up with Jed in about twenty minutes."

Hanging up with Norbert, he immediately has Jed on the phone.

"They breached the fence about 500 yards east of the Powell River," informs Jed. "We've got cows spread out from here to Rangoon."

Within minutes they meet up. The ground is pulverized, as 500 mindless cows have passed through. leaving only hoof prints and manure.

"Bill, you take a half dozen of these guys and see if you can't get out in front of the lead herd. Charley, you take another bunch, spread out and get the strays out of the timber," yells Dillon at the assortment of cowhands. "Jed, you stay here and broaden that fence hole out so we can get them all back through."

April has joined her father, deciding to stay with him rather than risk Dillon's aggressive leadership.

"Daddy, I hope you don't mind me tagging along with you."

"Not at all darling. You can help pull fence posts. We gotta make a hole big enough to get 500 head back through."

Both are busy trying to pull posts and wind barbed wire when Gibby appears over a small ridge pushing his dirt bike. It's obviously disabled with its bent front wheel and broken handlebars.

Looking in Gibby's direction, Jed, with a half a grin, asks "What the hell happened to you, boy?"

"I went ass over tea kettle," returned an also grinning Gibby.

"I guess you did," says Jed now with a more serious tone. "That's some gash you got," grabbing Gibby's head in both his hands, twisting it first in one direction then the other. "Looks like you're going to live," smiles Jed realizing Gibby's not hurt as bad as he first thought.

April has poured water from her canteen onto her neckerchief and is wiping the dirt and blood away from the cut.

"Hold still Gibby," says April feigning a testy voice as Gibby jerks back.

"Ouch," he shouts, "You're trying to kill me!"

"Oh hold still you big baby, I'm not hurting you," says April, not to be dissuaded.

Looking at Gibby's disabled bike and the open gash on his head, Jed tosses around the next move. "Gibby you ain't gonna do anybody any good here. I think you need to get back to the ranch and have that cut looked at. April honey you ride double and get him home," says Jed..

April gives Gibby a quick glance. Their eyes meet, both secretly savor it's embarrassing excitement, and seemingly waiting for the other to downgrade the affair. A nod by Gibby breaks up the moment. He mounts the quarter horse behind April, giving Jed a reassuring salute as April turns her horse in the direction of the house.

The ride is silent. Hot passion is often wordless. Both are lost in their own imaginations.

Gibby's arms are wrapped around April's waist. The smallness of her waist only serves to accentuate the weight of her undulating breasts. Being conscious of her buttocks slightly brushing against his groin in rhythm with the horses gait only adds to their already over-stimulated hormones.

April slows the horse to a walk, not sure where all this is going, at the same time, both are much in consort with the each other's every move.

Coming around a narrow part of the trail, the old miner's cabin appears. The two of them are aware of being alone with only the other.

"Look Gibby, there's Strang's cabin let's stop and rest my horse." Says April breaking the silence as she reels her horse off the trail toward the shack.

Gibby has never shared any of these kinds of feelings with April. He has always protected himself by viewing her as an adversary.

"Yeh, I think you're right," says Gibby clearing his voice, trying to get a handle on where these new feelings are taking him.

Dismounting first, and in an unpredicted move, he reaches a hand to hold the horse's bridle, the other assisting April.

"That's sweet of you Gibby," says a tense April trying to cover her nervousness.

Gibby does not let go of her hand. She in turn does not attempt to pull loose. They are standing in front of one another and aware they both are trembling. As if on cue, they draw the other to themselves, their lips meet in a passionate kiss. Their breathing is deep and rapid. Gibby's lips feel like rubber. He barely has enough blood left in his head to keep himself conscious.

"April, I have to sit down before I fall," confesses Gibby. His face looks ghostly white while April's is beat red.

They paw, kiss, finally struggling to the ground on a grassy area behind the cabin.

"Where are we going with this?" asks April, hoping Gibby will have an answer to rationalize their passion.

"I don't know," answers Gibby. His voice is tremulous. "Right now I don't want to stop and figure it out."

Both find themselves much in alliance with their lust. It's the reckless kind that only the young have for one another.

Again, drawing themselves into a deep kiss, they nearly devour each other. With one hand on the back of Gibby's neck, April fumbles with the other until she finds Gibby's hand and presses it to her now heaving breasts.

Tumbling around, not willing to release the other, they somehow manage to get buttons unbuttoned, with clothing being discarded in every direction. Neither has ever done this before and are surprised at how fast they are figuring it all out.

They are not pretending to be celebrating a long-term attraction. What they are doing is born out of pure passion, primordial and uncomplicated.

Her desire to have Gibby inside her is equally as strong as his desire to be there. Being chaperoned by neither parents nor peers they simply follow their fantasies.

Soon they lay naked beside each other in silence, not knowing what to say. This frolic began fast and ended fast. Their awkwardness is both innocent and yet depressing. This is often the grim reward paid to those who understand sex only in orgasmic terms. Without a component of love and commitment that is rarely found outside even long term marriages, they are aware something is missing. The unspoken missing element is that they failed to give, and that they only took from each other. The similar feeling each is experiencing is the same embarrassment had each been caught by the other masturbating.

April is first to talk. "Please don't hate me." Her voice carries a desperate plea that begs a justification for what she has done. It's the same desperate words spoken by many "Aprils" who have undone their virginity in a less than satisfactory course of action. It's a pitiful plea,- one that confuses Gibby. As is the case so many times within these encounters among the young, one party, but not the other, hopes the indiscretion can be justified by hoping and praying the act will provide a stronger bond than actually exists between them.

"I don't hate you April," he pauses for a moment, looking at the tears forming in her eyes and beginning to roll down her freckled cheeks, "but honestly April I don't have anything more to give you right now."

Gibby is not sure what he is feeling, still, he pulls her to him as he would any suffering creature. He doesn't know what love is, maybe it's pity he feels but he's not sure. Right now her hair is tickling his nose. It's a simple annoyance, yet enough to cause him to pull away.

April is pragmatic enough to understand Gibby's tardiness toward manhood. But at the same time, she is drawn to his helter-skelter living style, that's found only on that loony edge between adolescence and adulthood. Maybe it's because she has two extra years on him that causes her to believe she may have to wait until Providence pulls them together.

"Gibby does this mean *anything* to you?" whispers April pensively. She runs her fingers across his bare chest, hoping any playful gesture would be enough sharing to create even a simple bond. Maybe a weak one, but something. It's obvious April would like to engender more meaning, a deeper meaning to the past event. Her hopes remain that Gibby, in turn, will rise to the level of her hopes.

Gibby remains still, quietly thinking. *"April, I don't know what you want. This is a brand new experience for me. Besides what do I have to offer you anyway?"*

Gibby enjoys the attention he's getting from April, but still regards himself as young, single, and above all, free.

He likes her face, her body, he notices she has an openness he likes. Right off he can't think of anything he doesn't like about her. Taking another drag on his cigarette, he blows the smoke in the direction of the cloudless blue sky. The experience came on so fast, and ended so quickly, much of it is still a big blur.

Realizing the moment has passed, they try and make light of what has just taken place by making a quick inspection of the area, forcing a remembrance of some fun in their passed experiences with each other here. Looking out a window in ole Strang's cabin, with the sun forcing its way through its dirt-encrusted pane, indicates it must be about 4 pm. Time to enter back into the reality of the world they have momentarily left behind.

Together they have stepped over a chasm in their lives in which there is no bridge back. Things have changed forever. The panacea, the elixir of their sexual encounter, has brought with it a birth of new questions, new thoughts. It's as though both have written "fragile" across their foreheads, hoping the other will not ignore it. Neither are comfortable with the thought of any responsibility for someone other than themselves, but then, that's what youth grows out of as adulthood rushes toward them. Since nature abhors a vacuum, as one segment of growth exhausts its purpose, another charges in.

The ride back is silent. Lost in their own thoughts, they dismount back at the horse barn. What they have not spoken is heard in the silence of their gaze. For the present they are comfortable going in their individual directions.

CHAPTER 3

PETE

The buckaroos have finished turning the cattle around. Most have found their way back behind a mended fence.

Dillon leaves four men with the herd, promising to send back supplies for a night's stay.

"Bill, you Charlie, Louis and Bob plan on staying out here for the night," commands Jed.

"Keep an eye out for strays. There's nothing like a stray cow to wet the appetite of cougars, bears, and wolves," adds Jed as he mounts his horse to return to the ranch house.

The horns are purposely left on cows in this part of the country to assist in warding off an attack. The hope is, the price to pay from an unwitting predator, will prove to be to high.

Making their way back to the ranch house, they again pass by the old miner's cabin. A glance holds a recollection that causes Dillon an anxious memory. Even when they were playing together here as children, April was always absent to him. Dillon has a love-hate relationship with his feelings for the place. He loves it because it's the birth place of his feelings for April, but he also hates it because he knows that her love for him is only his illusion.

An unsuspecting Dillon catches an unexpected glimpse of a familiar looking neckerchief. He recognizes it as one Gibby was wearing earlier. It seems to be waving to him in a taunting sort of way. Still wondering how it got here, he dismounts. Bending over to pick it up, he can't help but notice the encrusted blood clinging to its fabric. Scanning the surroundings for any illusive explanation, Jed speaks up. "I'll bet he and April stopped here on the way back to the ranch."

This comment gives Dillon an even more perplexed look.

"I guess you didn't know," Jed went on to explain. "Gibby went ass-over-tea kettle on his bike. He bent the front wheel and couldn't to ride it home and he had a gash on his head. I ordered him to ride double on April's mare back to the ranch.

Dillon can't hide his anxiousness. "Ride where?!" he blurts.

"Well he cut his head on the spill he took" says Jed repeating himself as he motions toward the bloody handkerchief. "April rode him back to the house to have it looked at. He had a pretty bad gash. It may require a stitch or two."

Just the thought of Gibby and April being alone gives Dillon a shocking jolt of jealousy, all mixed in to form anger and resentment. This is by far, an extremely fatal mixture for any impartial thinking.

Dillon's face takes on the bland look of hopelessness, as jealousy steals its way into his thoughts. He hardly hears Jed as his explanation continues. His mind is being held captive by the same old pallbearers of character that have plagued him from his youth – his pride, his anger, jealousy and envy to mention only a few.

Arriving back at the ranch house as the sun is leaving the exhausted day, going through its reds and pinks, yellows and grays. Finally darkness. The buckaroos clean up their horses, bed them down for the night, then go their separate ways. Some climb in aged pickup trucks that have certainly seen better days, still others head for the bunk house to cook up a rancher's supper of beans and bacon. They don't require much more than a decent meal, a decent wage, a decent bunk, and occasionally a trip to town to blow off some steam at the local watering holes.

Dillon walks into the ranch house at exactly the right moment to hear his mother's announcement. "You're just in time. Supper will be ready as soon as you get yourself cleaned up." On his way to his room, Dillon passes by Gibby's open door. He stops, hesitating long enough to change into his prosecuting disposition. Pulling the neckerchief from his pocket, with a raised voice declares, "I found this by Strang's cabin." He tosses it on the floor.

Far from giving Dillon any kind of an explanation for any of his actions and now with a freshly bandaged head, Gibby gets up from his bed and with a simple "Thanks," retrieves the item from the floor and tosses it nonchalantly into a waste basket.

Far from being satisfied with Gibby's shrugging off any further explanation, Dillon attempts to give further chase. Continuing his stance in the door way to Gibby's room, he tries to pull himself together. He clearly knows what his suspicions are, but somewhere between hurt and paranoia his psyche remains conflicted. No words come out. He continues to stand and stare as though reluctant to move until Gibby confesses.

This in turn, causes Gibby to stare back, meeting Dillon's stare with the only question that can form in his mind. "What?" It's Gibby's only response. This only adds to further frustrate his brother.

Without a word, Dillon turns his back on his brother, walking out leaving Gibby alone to wonder how much of a connection between himself and April his brother has uncannily put together.

Following him into the house is Norbert. Giving Joanie his trade mark slap on her rear end, she smiles while feigning disgust, then turns giving him a kiss anyway.

"How'd it go?" she asks.

"Good," replies Norbert. "We managed to keep the herd together and get them all behind the fence."

Conversation during supper is sufficient enough between Norbert and Joanie, and with each of the boys individually, but the lack of conversation between Dillon and Gibby goes unnoticed.

Within moments of finishing supper there is a loud car horn. It's Pete Simon announcing his arrival, summoning Gibby. Gibby is up and out the door.

"What the heck is the matter with that guy? Doesn't he have legs? I don't believe he's ever done anything around here close to what could be called civilized," says Joanie. "You'd think he could just once walk to the door and knock."

Norbert remains silent with a knowing grin on his face.

This, as usual, is enough to set Dillon off. He graduated from high school with Pete and that's as far as any other similarities can be stretched.

"Dad I don't know why you don't put a stop to Gibby hanging out with that Pete Simon. He's nothing but trouble. He was an idiot in high school, and he hasn't changed a bit. Hes still an idiot."

Norbert quietly studies his oldest son. He doesn't doubt Dillon's assessment. It's accurate. What he's more concerned with, is Dillon's reaction to Gibby's seemingly harmless escapades.

"You're probably right, Dillon. I don't doubt your assessment for a minute," said his father with a deliberate pause.

Dillon takes a moment's delight in his father agreeing with him, as he relaxes for a second.

"But I'm more concerned with how you are reacting to your younger brother," adds Norbert with the same fatherly tone.

"What do you mean,dad? Am I merely supposed to kiss his little, pink ass and just say, 'Oh well, boys will be boys'?"

"Not at all."

"Well, what then?"

"I think we are all going to have to practice patience and tolerance until Gibby comes to his senses. If he doesn't, then we, as a family, have to be available to help him pick up his broken pieces."That's bullshit,dad" blurts out Dillon.

"I don't think so," says his father. "Oh and by the way," now looking intensely into the eyes of his oldest son, "I'll do the same for you."

Dillon knows his father well enough to not try and dissuade him from his moral, or spiritual convictions. At the same time, he can't help but realize how far short he falls from his father's ethics. It's not that his father is bad, it's rather that he holds a moral standard, that in Dillon's eyes, is too damn high. It rather reproaches him, leaving him with an uncomfortable feeling.

"Dad, I'm not you. I can't think like you," whines Dillon. This may be the only resentment he has for his father.

"No, I know you can't. At least not yet," says a focused Norbert, as he says these words to a son, he can only hope for the time being, to just love. It's become obvious to Dillon that his father is not going to say anything more about this matter.

Meanwhile several miles up the road the discussions between Pete and Gibby are taking a more business-like tone.

"So, what did you find out about these guys in Vancouver," questions Gibby.

"They definitely want to do business with us," reports Pete, while rolling his cigarette between his thumb and forefinger, slips it to his lips, inhaling.

Gibby plays with a little stubble of his goatee as he thinks through what Pete may be doing. He knows Pete well enough to know how much he loves to play the role of a big shot until things get a little thick, then he wimps out.

"So what kind of deal do they want to do?" presses Gibby.

"They say for two thousand bucks we can have a return of five thousand and still have enough weed for ourselves," says Pete, exhaling a jet stream of whitish smoke.

Still suspicious of Pete's fantasy to play a role he's not capable of fulfilling, Gibby presses for more clarity. "Where in the hell are you going to get two thousand dollars Pete, we barely can rub two nickels together," laughs Gibby sarcastically.

"We're going to have to work on that. I think I can come up with a grand if you can get the other thousand."

As the evening is taking on a much more serious dimension, Gibby is much quieter and certainly more pensive than earlier. He takes a long drag on his cigarette, his mind traveling at mock speed, digging through all the recesses of his recollection to produce the location of a thousand dollars. The fear of being left behind in a deal as edgy as this, drives him forward. This is the stuff he lives on.

Pete, on the other hand, is driven more by the flamboyance of the deal. He prides himself on being able to produce enough charm to compensate for his many other shortcomings. It's his big chance to be thought of as a big shooter.

The night wanes on with a myriad of drinking and weed smoking.

"Gibby, you got it damn good." Just the tone of Pete's voice indicates the buzz he has going has more than compromised his frontal lobes.

"Whatta ya talkin' about?" says the equally altered mind of Gibby.

"I've seen how your ole man treats you. You've got it made. I could have learned to stand on my head and whistle 'O Canada' out of my ass and my ole' man would have never noticed.

"You're probably right, Pete. My dad's been pretty patient with my B.S.," slurs Gibby.

"My dad dumped me at my grandparents along with my mother then he took off. Shit, Gibby I was only twelve. He used to come around once in a while when I was in my teens, but hell, I haven't seen him in years."

"That's pretty screwed up." sympathizes Gibby as only one inebriated friend can do for another.

"That's why I do what I want, when I want, where I want and piss on everybody." Pete's become a reckless contradiction to common sense. He doesn't realize how much he has become his father. It seems no matter how hard he tries to defy the laws of good judgment, the result is, he gets beat up. Never enough to kill him though, only hurt him.

In spite of all Pete's bluster, inwardly he needs an ally in Gibby. There is an attraction Pete has for something Gibby has. He doesn't know exactly its name. He's seen it surface in him several times. He admires its nameless components. It goes beyond a physical toughness. It's a toughness that's deeper than style.

Even in Gibby's altered state, Pete's words give him pause. On the outside Pete displays a tenacity, but his different reactions to new circumstances, is what is becoming questionable. Gibby's beginning to wonder just how much more there is missing in Pete's competence.

"You gonna be alright Pete?" asks an uneasy Gibby.

"Don't worry about me, you just work on getting that thousand," voices Pete defensively.

As the night finally concludes, Gibby makes his way home. The effects of the night are beginning to wear off just in time to be met by his mother. Her look is a mixture of frustration, disappointment and impatience. Wrapped in her red fuzzy robe, she is determined to make her point.

"Gibby I don't know what kind of game you're playing, but I don't care much for it. Your hanging around with that Pete Simon night after night can only lead to no good. I wish you'd think about it." Joanie feels she has substantial reasons for her distrust for Pete. Any encounters she has ever had with him have resulted in him blatantly patronizing her. "Mrs. Geiberson your hair style is perfect for you!" or "Mrs. Geiberson I can't believe your Gibby's mother, you look young enough to be his sister," or "Ms. Geiberson that outfit you're wearing makes you look like a model."

In spite of Gibby's own surveillance of Pete and some obvious cracks in his character, he jumps to his defense.

"Ma, Pete is my friend. I don't care if nobody in this family likes him, I like him" shouts a defiant Gibby.

Not to be outshouted by his defiance, she shouts back. "I know, and I believe you know also, he's shallow, bold, and cocky. He lacks a quality your father and I have tried to instill in you."

Gibby digs his heels in a little deeper. "I won't have anybody in the family picking my friends for me!"

Dillon is awakened by all the shouting. It only takes him a moment to weigh in against his brother.

"Pete thinks he's some kind of tough gangster, like he's a big shot. I don't know what you find so cool about him. He's always been a loser and always will be."

Whether right or wrong, the last thing Gibby is putting up with, is his brother's self-righteous opinions, especially when he tries influencing who he chooses for friends.

"Stay out of my world, Dillon" says Gibby with an index finger jabbing within an inch of his brothers' face. It's a finger that has a sign saying 'private, no trespassing or suffer the consequences.'

"Ya sure I'll stay out of your business as long as you won't expect any of us to bail your sorry ass out when you and your buddy Pete end upside down somewhere," pontificates Dillon.

"I'm not taking this B.S. from any of you for another second," spits out an agitated Gibby in disgust.

A slight smirk makes its way across Dillon's face. It's obvious he's taking great delight in having his brother against the ropes.

Gibby suddenly realizes that what he's hearing from his brother is not the normal rivalry they have always had because of their age difference. His brow furrows, puzzled at this new development. Dillon is taking their relationship to a new, low level.

Norbert has remained on the sidelines of their late-night confrontation. Swirling the last part of a glass of milk' pondering where this hostility in his family began, and even more significant where it is taking them. Placing the cold glass against his cheekbone, Norbert looks back to simple times when his boys were much younger. The only rivalry between them was who would be first in line to bounce on 'daddy's' foot. Life seemed much sweeter then. He remembers how he made them giggle and laugh as he rough housed with them. Now he's wondering whose children these two are. They have both undergone such a slow transformation, that this change sneaked in undetected.

There is a part of him who wishes that life could remain like it was in those simpler times. Catching himself, he swings back into the present. Being a pragmatist at heart, he has more than a little faith that the breach in his family's love for each other can, after all is said and done, be healed. But not now. Not at this late hour. One inebriated son, one hostile and angry son and one tired and frustrated wife. Not a good combination for thought-fed dialogue.

An intervening Norbert breaks his silence. "You all have a negative attitude toward one another and therefore producing only negative reactions. The notion that any of you can actually bring about anything other than further hostility goes beyond a miracle. You have all said things that you will surely regret. I recommend that we all go to bed and resolve our differences when our minds are rested."

He's staring at each one with a passive authority they recognize could quickly change to a much more aggressive style that will ultimately say, "go no further with this."

Joanie takes a deep breath, unhinged by all of this, releases it with a sigh, shaking her head. She agrees with Norbert, venting is always hurtful. Feeling fragile and defeated, Joanie resolves to remain silent for this reason. Sometimes it's better to entertain thoughts alone.

Without remorse and with a precise satisfaction, Dillon makes his way to his room, satisfied he has, once again, caused trouble for Gibby.

By the time Gibby makes his way to bed he has shrugged off any family concerns, and is once more focusing on where he is going to find a thousand dollars.

The next morning arrives as usual, announcing its presence to all the victims of the previous night. Mornings can be unforgiving, they don't change for anyone. In spite of it being a fresh, new day, those who wish to share in it must make proper adjustments. It's hitting Gibby like a wrecking ball.

All the vitamins and nutrients from the previous day have been stripped out leaving him a trembling, agitated bundle of nerves.

As usual Gibby arrives late for breakfast. Joanie has prepared him a head-clearing concoction of tomato juice, raw egg, a splash of Tabasco sauce, and only God can imagine what else. Reluctantly he sips it under Joanie's warden-ship.

Norbert and Dillon are discussing a trip to Vancouver. Dillon has arranged a meeting with a group of rabbis. Norbert is intent on providing the Jewish community there with kosher beef.

They are soon on their way and Gibby has made his way to the machine shop. His thoughts have turned back to his obsession to find the illusive $1,000. Making his way to the back door, the idea suddenly strikes him.

There before him is a row of scrapped hay balers, combines, and tractors, along with dump trucks, and other pieces of obsolete machinery. These are kept, basically, for their parts. In a matter of minutes he has calculated how much scrap iron it would take to raise the money.

Quick to get the task done before his dad and brother get back from Vancouver, he has loaded the low-boy trailer with enough metal to take into the junk yard in Powellville.

Gibby can't quite get past how underhanded and sleazy this maneuver is. He isn't ready to call it thieving, not even when they give him $1,200 for his load. "Well maybe the end justifies the means," he mutters to himself. Not wanting to think on this too long, he pages through his cell phone menu until he comes across Pete Simone's number. "Hey Pete meet me at Eddie's Pool Hall. I got some good news." Gibby has created a blind spot, at least for the time being, in going behind his father's back. He has convinced himself that as long as he intends to pay the money back, he can justify taking it. But then wrong motives rarely justify much.

Within 15 minutes they are behind Eddie's sitting in Pete's 1968 baby blue Lincoln hard-top convertible. "Dillon give you a grand?" chides Pete knowing full well the relationship between Gibby and Dillon.

"Are you nuts? Dillon wouldn't give me the time of day, much less a grand."

Gibby pauses for a moment, gazing out the passenger's side window, unconsciously not wanting eye contact with anyone. "I scrapped out some steel behind the shop."

He pauses again, his eyes are darting around trying to find a bona-fide principle that will justify his scheme. Still struggling for a just motive he further adds, "I'm going to have to replace the money." Pausing yet again, playing with the power window, "I know I'm going to catch some hell for doing what I did, but if I can come clean with the dough, I should be off the hook."

Recognizing Gibby's discomfort Pete drills him with a punch on the shoulder followed by pulling out his pistol and feigns taking a shot at Gibby. "Why Gibby, you're just a thievin' little bastard."

"Hey man quit playing with that thing before you hurt somebody," censures Gibby. "Why you carrying that thing anyway?"

Pete's gone to packing a pistol. "I'll tell you why. When people know you're carryin' they don't mess with ya man."

Pete knows he wouldn't stand a chance in an ordinary fist fight. Besides it bolsters his gangster image. Swinging the pistol away from Gibby he pretends to take a shot at a make-believe adversary.

"For God's sake, put that thing away," shouts a clearly upset Gibby.

"OK., OK. Don't wet your pants, I'm only practicing. Pow, Pow," says Pete, forming the words and bucking the pistol in a recoil action.

"That's fine, practice some other time. Right now I want to know where my $1,000's going."

Finally putting the pistol in his pocket, Pete's ready to get down to business.

"My cousin Bernie works for a law firm in Vancouver. They defended a guy on a drug charge and got him off. I got to know him during the trial. He's our age and a big shot in a Chinese gang. He's got all kinds of connections. We're going to meet him at the pool hall tonight at 8 pm."

Arriving at home later that afternoon, Gibby is quite relieved to find that his father and brother decided to remain in Vancouver for the night.

He and his mother have a quiet supper. As has become his habit of late, he proposes to leave for the evening.

"Gibby I hate to harp on you, but this going out every night until the wee hours of morning can't continue. I can't stand worrying about you night after night," pleads his mother, "besides you need your rest."

Gibby's mind is going a mile a minute. The lure of impending excitement leaves his mother's pleas as a weak and fruitless endeavor.

Trying to conceal his nervous and anxious movements, he takes in a deep breath, smiling, he assures her. "Don't worry mom. I'm only hanging out with friends havin' a few beers and shootin' a little pool."

Relieved once again to have gotten past at least one parent, he is on his way to Eddie's Pool Hall.

His big black Dodge Ram pickup cruises its way toward Powellville. It's as though he can't leave enough dust behind him to blur out the ranch and all it stands for. He's anxiously looking for a new horizon.

Entering the pool hall he is met by the familiar smell of smoke, the long necks sitting on the tables, the din of various vocal exchanges, the affable faces all giving him a sense of belonging. He feels at home.

Over in the corner, he spots Pete wearing a pair of dark glasses sitting at a table with another person. A twenty-something Chinese guy dressed in a loose, untucked black Hawaiian shirt with wildly colored flowers, a pair of sandals, a flat-billed black cap turned backwards, short in stature weighing maybe 140 pounds, tattoos of various different dragons on his arms and extending to his hands and some kind of Chinese script tattooed on his neck.

Pete motions for Gibby to join them. "Gibby I want you to meet Tommy Li, Tommy this is my partner Gibby." Pete is definitely playing the roll of a gangster to the hilt.

Gibby begins to extend his hand, then checks himself. Tommy remains sitting with one leg crossed over the other, an arm hooked over the back of the chair, a cigarette dangling from his mouth merely giving him a quick little two-fingered salute.

Reassessing this new and different fraternity, Gibby then counteracts with his hand to his forehead and returns the gesture.

"Let's get the hell out of here where we can talk," says Pete motioning toward the door. Leading the way to the rear parking lot, he gives cautious glances hoping not to be obvious. All three enter Tommy's big, black Cadillac Escalade. The driver,about their age, also Chinese, gives a quick glance toward the two new occupants as they enter the back door. Tommy takes a seat in the front leaving the two to be observed by the driver through the rear view mirror. He doesn't bother to introduce the driver, leaving the two in the back a bit uneasy.

Pete has his hand in his pocket tightly wrapped around his pistol glancing at Gibby and Gibby glancing back. The unspoken dialogue is clear in the apprehensive looks they are giving one another.

"You got the money?" This sounds more like an imperative than a question, as Tommy is gesturing he wants to see it.

"Ya, I got it right here," says Pete handing over a roll of bills bound by a heavy rubber band.

Tommy snaps the rubber band off and quietly counts the twenty 100 dollar bills. Without losing a beat he pockets the money, at the same time pulling his loose fitting Hawaiian shirt up, exposing two kilos of prime Hawaiian pot taped to his ribs.

Gibby is shaking with a mixture of fear and excitement as he quickly accepts the two kilos. They're wrapped up in what appears to be a heavy butcher paper bound tightly with a high-grade packing tape. Excitedly, he cuts a small slit in each kilo examining their contents. Satisfied, he sticks the two kilos inside his shirt and zips his jacket shut.

Looking directly at one, then the other Tommy is satisfied the deal is done.

"Happy?" he asks.

"Happy," both Gibby and Pete recite in unison.

"You got my number right?"

"Right" says both again.

"Call me when you need a refill."

Pete gives Tommy the two fingered salute indicating he understands.

Getting out of the Escalade and within minutes the two are in Pete's Lincoln high-fiving each other in uncontrollable laughter.

"Holy shit Pete, we pulled it off," says Gibby. His tension is releasing itself in still more laughter.

"Damn Gibby, I thought I was going to explode" Pete is inhaling and exhaling into his cupped hands trying to keep from passing out. "If we'd gone another minute I'd pissed my pants."

"Oh hell Pete you gotta love it. I can't remember when I had an adrenalin rush like this."

"You're frickin' nuts Gibby. I'm just glad it's over."

"Hey baby we're chartin' new waters," says an elated Gibby. "Were gonna bag this stuff and make some moolah." His grin couldn't have been bigger, broader, or brighter. "This is the kind of stuff I live on, Pete."

Over the next couple of weeks they did just that, and doubled their money. Since neither Norbert nor Dillon noticed the scrap gone, Gibby lost his celerity to bring it up and also his former compliance to pay the money back.

What Norbert and Joanie are paying most attention to is his more developed sense of arrogance.

"I thought he'd be outgrowing this 'Rock Star' stuff" laments his mother, "I think he's actually getting worse. He's out every night, until God only knows when or where."

Norbert is patiently listening to his wife.

"Don't think I haven't noticed his disrespect for you. He's definitely getting much cockier."

Gibby is spending less and less time in the machine shop. He and Pete are basking in all the attention, especially of the younger, hip crowd in Powellville. "Going Green" has taken on a whole new concept in Powellville. It means marijuana has become their drug of choice. Thanks to Pete and Gibby there is not a shortage.

"We're players Gibby," announces Pete. He's pleased with his new status. He's embraced it with eagerness. To lift themselves to even higher rankings means they have to step up their exploits.

"Gibby, see how long this has been. We've got a few bucks now but nothing like we could be doing. I've been talking to Tommy, he thinks we're ready for some big bucks."

Gibby has taken to letting his hair grow. He flips his bangs out of his eyes, takes another drag on his cigarette, and pensively looks at Pete. "What kind of big money?"

"Tommy says we can make 50 grand on a deal if we're willing to take it."

"Tommy says a lot of things."

"Ya but you gotta admit, so far he's been right on the money."

"So what's his deal?"

"I don't know yet, but when I told him you know how to fly a helicopter he got all pumped. That's when he called back with the fifty grand offer."

Gibby has been flying a helicopter since he was twelve years old. He had an eagerness to learn, so Norbert taught him. He's become a proficient asset in rounding up stray cattle. Unlike Dillon, who's focus is more on the dollars and cents condition of the ranch.

Gibby gives Pete a big grin, with two thumbs up. "When does he want to meet with us?"

"As soon as possible. He suggested this weekend."

The wheels begin to turn in Gibby's head.

CHAPTER 4

HAPPY BIRTHDAY

The next morning Gibby wakes to the sound of horns and whistles. He bolts up in his bed in a defensive position ready to take on the predator.

"Happy birthday to you, happy birthday to you, happy birthday dear Gibby, happy birthday to you." It's his mother dancing and singing around his room. She's wearing a pointed birthday hat held with a piece of elastic under her chin.

"Good grief Ma, you scared the crap out of me." Gibby is struggling to get his legs on the floor, one eye partially open.

His mother cups his cheeks between her hands and plants a kiss on his distorted lips.

"I know," she says, "but with your crazy coming and going lately, I knew this is the only time I'd see you all day."

"Geez O'Pete. Mom you're killing me," cries Gibby through his distorted, pinched lips.

Norbert is standing in the doorway. He's obviously amused watching Gibby stumble around trying to pull a sweatshirt over his head. Seeing his head come through the opening takes him back 21 years ago.

"That's the way you looked 21 years ago when I watched you come through the birth canal," laughs his father as he gives his son a hand pulling the shirt back down.

"You guys aren't funny," says Gibby. Flustered over his rude awakening, he plops back on the bed. It didn't take long for him to get over his sullenness.

The smell from the kitchen begins to override any feelings of acrimony. His mother has made a special breakfast for him. Freshly baked apple pie. His favorite.

Dillon is conspicuous by his absence. But then it's not his style to reward Gibby with any kind of celebration. After all, Gibby's behavior hasn't earned any of his brother's accolades. Furthermore, Dillon has caught wind of Gibby and Pete's throwing a lot of money around town. He remains, more than a little, suspicious of anything Gibby may be up to.

Norbert takes a special step in the direction of Dillon's office across the barnyard in back of the horse barn. Predictably, Dillon is busy in his office pouring over computer printouts.

"Missed you at breakfast this morning Dillon." Norbert's voice is soft and fatherly, the kind that shows concern.

"I had a lot of work to get out before noon. I wanted to get an early start." Dillon remains at his desk without looking up.

Norbert takes a minute to remove a stack of papers covering a chair before sitting down.

"You know Dillon I appreciate all your hard work on this ranch. You've done a great job. You've kept us in the black, and I might add, your good at what you do."

Still not giving his father his attention, Dillon remains shuffling papers around his desk.

"Dillon stop for a minute and listen to me."

Dillon gives a sigh, tosses his pen on the desk and bolts back in his chair.

"It's important for you to know what my priorities are around here. First, it's of prime importance to all of us that I love your mother, and second, that I be the best father to you boys that I can be. Gibby is your brother. Regardless of his behavior, he's still your brother."

Dillon is giving his father the respect of listening but it's obvious in his face his father's words are not penetrating the walls of his resentment.

"What I'm trying to say Dillon is that I have always held the welfare of our family unit above the welfare of the ranch. I built this ranch. But not as a legacy to myself, but to the truths our family stands for. Without that, we'd only have cows and nothing more."

Dillon finally reaches for his cast off pen, giving it a little wiggle indicating he has a thought.

"Dad, you and mom baby that little peckerwood like he's some kind of primadonna."

Norbert is giving Dillon his full attention.

"I want you to know he's not. Mark my words, he's heading for trouble. You and mom let him pull the wool over your eyes, I don't. If it were up to me, I'd have his bony ass out of here."

Norbert listens respectfully to his eldest son's frustrations. Pausing long enough to rise from his chair taking a step forward, bending over with both hands firmly on Dillon's desk forcing him to glance up.

"Do you remember last month when that herd broke through the fence how diligent you were in finding every last stray? You took particular care in searching every patch of alpines and every canyon, with the primary concern, that you would bring every single stray back into the herd". Pausing for a moment to be sure he has his elder son's full attention, he continues,"Give your brother the same concerns you do a stray cow."

Norbert raises to his full height staring at his son's reaction hoping for a spark of kindness. Dillon met his father's eyes but only for a moment. He knows he can't give him what he is hoping for. He drops his head and continued with his work.

Realizing his son is stuck in a mindset, contrary to reason, he does the next best thing, turns and leaves. "Dear Lord, please grant me the wisdom I need to hold this family together," is Norbert's heart felt plea.

"Mom I'm sorry for being such a dip shit this morning. I really do appreciate the pie." Having a second thought he adds, "And the singing. That was a nice touch. Thank you much."

A beaming Joanie holds up a large piece she had cut from the pie and set aside.

"Promise me you'll come back before lunch and eat this." Joanie has a unique way of making her boys feel singled out.

"I promise," says a much more appreciative Gibby giving his mother a hug and a kiss.

Now on his way to the machine shop his thoughts return to his forth coming meeting with the Chinese in Vancouver.

These thoughts are abruptly interrupted with the sonorous voice of April. "Happy birthday Gibby."

Turning, he spots her in the open door of the horse stable. She's grooming one of her horses.

The stable is in the opposite end of Dillon's office and on the way to the machine shop.

"Oh thanks," says Gibby. Stopping for a moment watching April, he harked back to the previous month. He had meant to see her again, but has become so involved with Pete and the Chinese, that he hadn't realized how long it had been.

"Haven't seen you around lately," says April. Her voice now has a bit of an edge that could drift over to perturbed without much effort. It's been obvious to her that their tryst was something deeper in meaning for her than for Gibby.

"Oh ya, I've been pretty busy," says Gibby. He's hoping by using his business tone she'll accept his blatant lack of attention.

Not wanting to give the impression that she cares one way or the other over his lack of attention, armed with two sets of brushes, one in each hand, she continues to brush down her horse.

Gibby can't help but notice the top she's wearing is revealing the movement of her breasts with each brush stroke.

It stirs something, not sought, but welcomed.

"I'd like to take you out for your birthday," invites April with a voice that could melt, even the coldest ice.

"When?" Is all he can manage to say as he struggles to keep some moisture in his dry open mouth.

"How about this evening after work. I'd like to take you into Powellville and buy your supper," says April, picking at a piece of nonexistent lint from Gibby's shirt.

Hormones have taken full control. His heart pounding out of his chest. The only word that can safely make it's way out of his throat, is a word with no more than one syllable, "Cool."

Not noticed by either Gibby or April, is Dillon in the back of the stable. Veiled by the darkness of the barn he watches from the shadows. He can't make out what is being said, but the mere spectacle of those two together is sufficient to bring enough envy and jealousy to cause hate and anger. The end result is stifled rage.

The grayness of this 23rd of September supper hour is barely noticed as the door bell rings at the Geiberson ranch house. Joanie, not accustomed to a guest at this hour, is surprised. Even more surprised when she finds April standing before her. "Why April, hello. What can I do for you?" says Joanie in her most nectarous voice. "I'm here to pick up Gibby," says April, surprised that Joanie is surprised to see her. Joanie's look suggests she needs an explanation.

"I'm taking him out for his birthday," says April. "I planned a dinner for him."

"Really," says Joanie with a look that accompanies this kind of non expectation. "He never said a word."

"I guess I forgot Ma," says Gibby as he bounds down from upstairs. He gives his mother a quick kiss on the cheek, bounds down the porch steps trying to put as much distance between him and any questions his mother may configure up.

April, a step behind him, announces, "I'm driving Gibby." As she jumps into her plum-colored Jeep, placing Gibby in the passenger seat.

In a matter of moments they leave a trail of dust, as April maneuvers her Jeep wagon down the dirt road leading out to the King's Highway. Without warning she suddenly turns on the two track leading out to the north pasture.

"April what the hell are you doing?" shouts Gibby, taken by surprise as he's thrown against the door.

"I've got a surprise," laughs April. She can't help but titter at his gangly body being thrown around.

"I hope to God it's better than this one," he says trying to get stabilized.

"Oh, I think you'll like it," giggles April.

The trail is much rougher by Jeep than by horse back, especially at the speed she's traveling. Her headlights are bouncing around, pointing more in the air than on the track.

Not soon enough for Gibby, she makes a hard left and stops. For the first time since leaving the ranch house, the headlights are stable enough to focus on their objective. It's the Strang cabin.

"What the heck has gotten into you April? What are we doing clear out here, I thought we were going into Powellville for dinner."

Still smirking from ear to ear, "Let's go in. I want to show you something."

Cautiously Gibby makes his way to the door of the old cabin. The first thing he notices is that the door appears to have a coat of paint. Orange paint at that.

Once inside April quickly lights a kerosene lantern, letting it cast its

yellow glow around the room. Its apparent this room has had some attention. The windows reflect the feminine touch of curtains. There is a table,
a couple chairs, and a setting for two, with candles and a bottle of wine.

"Good grief April, what have you done to this place," asks Gibby.

His approving smile is welcomed. "Not too much," says April. "I tried
to retrieve it from the critters. It looked like every raccoon in the province
has lived here at one time or another."

Continuing to look around Gibby says, "I've always wanted to do
something with this old cabin."

"I know exactly what you mean. I've always loved this place," says April.

Listening to the softness in her voice, Gibby realizes when talking
about the cabin she has as much of an attraction to this place as he does
– maybe more.

Continuing to look around the room, it's apparent, Gibby is pleased.

"Where did you get all this stuff?"

"Oh here and there. I dragged a lot of this stuff from a storage shed
of my parents.'"

The outdated 1950s Danish-style chairs and couch adorning this 19th
Century cabin, look as out of place, as an adoption gone wrong. But even
in their less than pristine condition, they appear almost brand new in
contrast to the cabin.

The last attempt to do any updating was about the time Gibby was
born. Norbert had tacked tar paper on the roof and replaced some broken
windows. His thoughts were that during branding the men could stay
out here with the herd. They may have used it once or twice, but then the
comfort of a modern bunkhouse seemed to lure them back to the ranch.

They both find themselves standing, facing the other when Gibby
bursts into laughter.

"What's so damn funny Gibby," demands April. Her voice suggest, she could be on the verge of having her feelings hurt.

Seeing where this is going he quickly goes into an explanation.

"Oh I love everything, April" says Gibby putting his arm around her. "I'm just looking at the two of us, dressed in our best, standing in the middle of this old, beat up cabin, ready to eat a gourmet meal with candles and silver ware."

As she looks around it takes April only a moment to catch the same ridiculous spectacle.

Laughing as she cups both hands around her nose and mouth, she throws herself against Gibby's chest, in a feigned attempt to appear hurt. Removing her cupped hands she forms them into little fists and playfully thumps Gibby's chest. Saying, "What do you say we eat while this stuff still has some heat." She has a free and natural way of flirting with Gibby without having to restrain herself.

He doesn't have to be asked twice. Within minutes they are sitting on old cast off straight backed chairs before a table that may have served an earlier era better.

They are enjoying a lukewarm chicken dinner, mashed potatoes, lumpy gravy, and most of all,the others company. Still laughing they take turns filling each others empty wine glass. Neither of them are making an attempt to hurry, as if the slower they go, the longer the moment lasts.

This interlude has taken on a different tenor than the previous encounter. It's as though they are digging around in the unexplored nooks and crannies of each others lives looking for new parallels of agreement. They knew each other well as children, now they want to learn of the other as adults.

"I'd like to work with young kids and their horses," says April. "How about you Gibby, you plan on staying here on the ranch?"

"Oh I don't know what I'm going to do. Maybe something with helicopters."

They find as the evening wanes on, that even without a lot of words, they both are comfortable with the other's company. But as things go with males and females they soon find the free flow of innocent conversation giving way to a tension that's demanding a more intimate expression. In a clumsy attempt to ease his ill at ease feelings, Gibby tries to kiss April. She responds with flaccid lips. Both know immediately the passion of the last time doesn't fit this occasion. Pulling back apologetically, Gibby stares at April not knowing how to respond.

"Gibby I need to apologize to you."

"For what April?"

She pauses for a moment, in an attempt to put the right words to her feelings.

"What I want to apologize for is pushing myself at you and using you. I had no right to do that."

With a grin from ear to ear Gibby responds, "The last thing I thought was that you took advantage of me or used me. But if you want to do it again go ahead. I can take it."

"Gibby, you're impossible. I want to build a relationship with you, not just to be available as a 'screw buddy'." April, more than Gibby, is hesitant to return to a "sex-lead" relationship.

"Yah, I know" says Gibby, "but it's not as though we don't have a mutual admiration connection already. We've known each other since we were babies."

"That may be true, but that was a different kind of relationship. We were more like cousins, and besides, we were just children."

"How about we be 'kissin' cousins?'" Gibby becoming snarky, "Please say yes." He's still grinning.

There is definitely a natural attraction between them. April, more than Gibby, knows that they don't have the right kind of commitment needed. At best this relationship remains fragile.

She gives him a little peck on the cheek, "OK. 'cuz' come with me. There's one more thing I want you to see."

His smile returns as she takes both his hands in hers and gives him a little tug.

"And just what may that be?" Gibby pretends a little stumble as she continues to tug on him.

"Put your jacket on and come with me."

Closing the door behind them, they step out into the coolness of a September evening.

With April leading the way, Gibby stumbles over something in the dark. Now only half laughing, Gibby says "Where in the heck are you taking me?"

"Take my hand, and you'll soon see." She leads him under over grown alpine branches on what may have been a path at one time.

"Good grief April, it'd take an Indian tracker to get us through this," says Gibby still good naturedly.

Without warning, they suddenly break out into what appears to be a clearing, but soon discover April has led him to the lake.

Gripping his hand even tighter April exclaims, " Oh Gibby, look at that. Isn't it just beautiful?"

The moon is a huge orange ball of glowing wonderment. All the surrounding trees seem to have passively fallen into paying homage as they cast their obsequious shadows.

As it has always been with the young, many of the impressions forcing their way into their young lives come from agencies outside of themselves, such as,demands from educators, parents, employers, religion. This spectacle designed by The Creator alone, is a welcomed imposition.

"My God April, this is absolutely awesome," says an awestruck Gibby. "How did you know about this?"

"Gibby Geiberson. How long have you lived here?" Not waiting for an answer, "Your problem is if you can't drive to it, you don't go to it."

Still awestruck by the silent beauty, he admits, "You're probably right." There's a bit of a flair in his voice as one who takes pride in driving mechanical things. "Well i*t is* the biggest moon *I've* ever seen."

"I don't think it's the biggest you've ever seen Gibby, but it may be the biggest you ever noticed," corrected April, with a slight sigh of impatience.

Continuing to marvel, he says, "I can't believe the brightness, look how it reflects off the lake."

"It's called a harvest moon you dough head. It's like this every year at this time. The farmers of past times depended on its light to finish their harvesting." April reports with a slight air of authority, she takes pleasure in the edge of knowledge she has on Gibby.

As is usual with Gibby, the way he enjoys things is more than just the single dimension of sight. Wanting to immerse himself into this phenomena he answers his impulse by skipping a stone across the sleeping lake, making the moon begin to play in harmony with the water, bending its' light into ripples bouncing along as a shimmering luminary extravaganza. With fingers interlocked, they stand facing each other.

The air is cold against any bare skin. It makes it a natural reaction to pull one another in a bit closer. They both find themselves enjoying the moment. Aware of the transitiveness of times, Gibby falls in with his feelings. It's as though his brain and hands are separate. Finding he has grasped Aprils face in both hands, he draws her lips to his. The moonlight has given a particular sensuous tone to her features. Continuing to stare into each others eyes for this minute, their souls seem to open to the other.

They feel each others hot breath against their cold faces. Pulling one another in even closer, the wonderment of this moment can only be expressed in passion. Their lips meet. Neither have been kissed, or kissed, as they are kissing the other in this moment.

The wetness of their mouths only serves to solicit more passion. They kiss until their lips are numb. Once again Gibby's hands have found their way to April's breasts. They feel warm and inviting against the cool night. Their caresses have made them both impervious to the cooling September evening. As if on cue, they have removed enough of the others clothing to realize,and in spite of their misgivings, that the wine, the moonlight, an attraction to one another, are going to have their way.

With Gibby sitting on a stump, April straddles him, guiding him into what she had hoped was going to be a forbidden area. Having once again satiated their passion, it begins to snow lightly. They're big, white, wet snowflakes that come in the fall in this part of the country. April can't help but contrast herself against this pureness. They both are quieter as they struggle to get clothing back on before it becomes wet. It's darker now as this passing snow cloud obscures the moon's light, making their way back to the cabin more difficult. They burst into only a waning warmth, as the fire in the stove has given way to an encroaching coldness.

Neither one has spoken. Gibby finally lights a cigarette, takes a drag, and passes it to April. She, in turn, takes a drag and hands it back.

"Jesus, Gibby, where are we going with this?" as if including The Divinity in her question it would be answered more clearly. He already senses April would prefer more of a commitment than he's able to make.

Gibby sits quietly, pensively inhaling another drag, hoping that action will free him from the darkness this question poses, and mystically bequeath him with a clear answer.

"Let's just take it one day at a time and not get all wrapped up in trying to own one another." It's the best he can come up with.

This is not the answer April wants to hear. Sensing the apology she really owes, is one to herself. She is not a particularly religious person, but she also has a strong sense that the relationship she and Gibby are developing, doesn't set will with her natural concept of the will of a Higher Power.

"Gibby, I just don't think what we are doing is right. It's almost as though we're sex buddies. You go your way and I go mine until we want sex again."

It's becoming obvious to April that Gibby's sense of commitment on a scale of one to ten is about a one.

"Geez April it's only sex, you act like it's on the same level as murder," says Gibby.

"Maybe in a way it is Gibby. It's like we're murdering something barely developing between us that goes deeper than a climax," she says.

"Well it's not like I don't care for you April, it's just I can't do it 24-7."

Making their way back to the ranch compound Gibby has taken the wheel. April is sitting as close to him as the console will allow. Her left arm is through his and his hand is resting on her knee.

Her thoughts are, "Please God, make this real."

Gibby on the other hand feels pressure to commit to a relationship he knows he can't maintain. Bringing the Jeep to a halt in front of the ranch house, he leans over and kisses April one more time. Trying to make light of what has become a tense situation he jokes, "I think I'm getting some feeling back in my lips."

She answers a little more affectionately as she wipes her fingers across his swollen red mouth, "I'm sorry I made them numb, but your lips are kissable."

With that he hops out of April's Jeep, and heads for the house. Something catches his eye in the second floor window. It's Dillon just pulling back hoping not to be seen. It's too late. Not knowing what to make of it, except that it's making him uneasy. Trying to enter the house as light-hearted as he can, he sings out, "I'm back."

"I don't believe it," says his mother sarcastically looking at her watch, "this is the earliest you've been home since I can remember."

"Oh Ma, it's not either." He knows it's probably true, but something tells him to challenge it anyway.

"So, what did you and April do?" asks Joanie, in only what can be described as a mixture of a prying mother faking a legitimate concern, with an impulsive imperative. She gives Gibby an intense study while waiting for his reply. Before he can construct a generic answer, his mother's out of her chair with a squinted, sideways look, taking him by one ear and turning his head from side to side.

"What in the name of all that's holy did you do to your face? Your mouth is all red and swollen."

"Oh I ate some shell fish. You know what they do to me," lies Gibby, knowing even he, wouldn't accept such B.S. If told to him.

"Yes, but you were five and you had a rash on your chest. This looks like they jumped out of their shells and hit you in the mouth."

Knowing his mother wasn't born yesterday, he knew better than to go head to head with his lie.

She gave him her "hum" which silently says "I know, that you know, that I know, you're giving me a line of crap."

Gibby, happy that his mother isn't pursuing this further, shrugged his shoulders giving his head and mouth a little twist and headed upstairs to his room.

His walk is suddenly blocked as Dillon steps from his open door.

"What the hell you doin' Dillon," says Gibby, unable to get by.

Rather than confront Gibby with April, his anger comes out sideways, "What you doin' hanging around that loser Pete?"

Gibby attempts to walk around Dillon without answering.

"Hey I'm talking to you," says Dillon, grabbing Gibby by the arm.

Jerking away, he looks at Dillon without a word and continues to his room.

"People are talking Gibby. Their saying you and Pete are blowin' a lot of money. Where you getting that kind of dough anyway?"

Closing his door behind him he began to wonder, *"Does Dillon know more than he's letting on on?"* Thinking about it for a second, *"nah"* he concludes.

The next morning Joanie makes a deliberate visit to the barn.

"Norbert I'll be back in a few minutes I have to check on a saddle I left out in the stable."

Norbert looks up from his work and gives her a knowing "right."

Some of last night's snow fall remains here and there as a reminder of things yet coming. The ground feels damp and cold as Joanie makes her way. April is busy filling feeders and measuring oats for each horse.

"Did you and Gibby have a good time last night?" asks Joanie, still feigning an attempt to locate her saddle.

April thinks she detects a bit of animosity in the, too-innocent question, and cautiously but also politely answers .

"Yes we did." April's answer is a bit grounded.

"Too bad Gibby had such a bad reaction to the cod," says Joanie. It's her nature to pry a little more.

Not knowing what Joanie is talking about, but afraid to let on, April agrees.

"Yes it is. How's he doing this morning?"

"Oh he's doing fine" says Joanie. "He said he had a clam jump out, and hit him in the mouth, but he's OK. Now."

April, puzzled at this last remark, but more than delighted to see Joanie turn and leave. Joanie is satisfied through her motherly trickery that there is much more to this story than either of them are telling. Meanwhile Norbert and Gibby are sharing a task at the machine shop, giving Norbert an opportunity to engage in a father-son moment.

"Gibby do you think I love your mother?"

Taken back a bit by the forthrightness of his father's question, Gibby hesitates for a moment, hoping to blink his way to the right answer, "I hope you do Dad."

"Do you know how I demonstrate that love?" inquires his father.

Gibby is beginning to show his uneasiness with the bluntness Norbert is demonstrating with his question.

"By making love to Mom?"

"No."

Gibby's embarrassment can no longer be hidden, as his face has turned a beet red.

This is already more information than he desires to know about his father and mother's private life.

Norbert continues, "That's only the celebration of our love for one another. The real love making is when I clean the ring out of the bathtub."

"What the hell are talking about dad?"

"Give it some thought son." With that Norbert made his way to the door.

5

A TALIBAN EXPERIENCE

Darkness comes early this time of year in British Columbia. People remark how they go to work in the dark and come home in the dark. The daylight hours are shortening. It's almost November. The nights produce frost on the ground by morning but the days are still above freezing. The weekend is here. It's Friday night and Gibby is all excited. He's going through the motions of gathering his fishing equipment and packing up his truck.

"Where you goin' with all that stuff" asks Norbert.

"Fishing' dad. I'm goin' with a bunch of guys from town."

"You and your buddies have a good time and bring home a couple big ones," says Norbert, waving to his son, as he makes his way down the long driveway to the King's Highway.

Pete's urban life style is so different from Gibby's that Gibby's arrival in his driveway with a pick up loaded with fishing gear is ignored or at least not questioned.

"I talked to Tommy. I told him we'd be in Vancouver in a couple hours so we better get movin'."

They agreed to leave Gibby's pick up. Pete thinks to better impress the Chinese, his vintage Lincoln would be better suited.

They are within an hour of Vancouver when Pete's cell phone goes off.

"Ya, OK Tommy. OK I got ya," says Pete to the faceless voice on the other end of the conversation.

Gibby, not used to being on the outside of anything, peers intently at Pete.

"Wha'd he say, wha'd he say?"

"We're supposed to meet him in the parking lot behind St. Agatha Catholic Church," reports Pete.

"How in the hell are we supposed to know who we're supposed to meet?" questions a visibly impatient Gibby.

Slapping both hands deliberately on the top of his steering wheel bending slightly forward gazing sarcastically at Gibby. "How many frickin' Chinese you know go to St. Agatha's?"

Answering Pete's question with a gesture, Gibby raises his middle finger.

"Well, don't be such a dumb ass," says Pete.

The hour whizzes by. No sooner have they entered the church parking lot when a black Escalade pulls in behind them. A tinted window on the Escalade runs down exposing the familiar face of Tommy Li.

"Get in." A thumb gesture over the shoulder indicates he means the back seat.

Looking at each other with that, *"What in the hell are we getting ourselves into" look, still trying as best they can to remain composed, they nevertheless comply.*

The only other occupants are Tommy and another Chinese male driver. Tommy is wearing his signature Hawaiian shirt with huge floral patterns and a black leather waist high jacket. The driver is the same scrunchy-looking guy they saw earlier in Powellville. His eyes remain fixed with the same expressionless, straight-a-head stare.

"Put these on," orders Tommy handing each a dark- colored hood with no eye holes.

This strikes both of them as an odd request that is, as the moments fly by, quickly turning into a scary behest. Trying to think of a convincing reason to put this imperative off, Pete runs the fabric around his fingers. "I can't quite believe what your asking us to do. Do you really think this is necessary."

Tommy dead panned Pete giving him a 'no vacancy' of mind answer. "Really!"

After complying, they can't help but wonder if they should have made a better decision. The ride is silent, other than Tommy saying single words in Chinese. The driver responded by turning right or left, speeding up, slowing down or stopping and starting again.

Gibby wonders to himself, "What the hell are they doin' driven' us in circles?" as he strains his eyes to catch any change in light.

Not being able to see, they soon find their other sense are becoming keener to sensations of going up or down. Suddenly their stomach drops, telegraphing a sudden, and rapid decline. The street noise has ceased. There is a strange empty echoing, as the S.U.V.'s knobby tires compete against a hard surface for attention. With the vehicle coming to a halt, Tommy orders its two extra occupants, still hooded, to be led out into what is an underground garage, then to an elevator. Pete has been in a similar sounding elevator in an uncle's warehouse. He suspects it to be a freight elevator. For the moment, only the sensation of moving is the single thing either of them can detect. Whether up or down remains undetectable. The hushed tones of Chinese words is all they can hear.

Before long they find themselves enduring a backward push into a seated position. Their hoods are finally removed. The only other person in the room is Tommy. Soon, a old Chinese man, assisted by a younger man, enters the room. The older man seats himself behind a large wooden, rather ornate desk carved in high relief with mountain scenes, water falls, and a variety of birds and mammals. The whole room appears to be windowless, on the other hand there are heavy embroidered drapes where windows would be expected.

Tommy immediately assumes an obsequious posture bowing his head until the older man is seated. The older man spends the next several moments staring directly at the two unhooded strangers. The old man motions for Tommy to come closer. It's obvious he prefers to speak in Chinese using Tommy as the interpreter. Gesturing toward Gibby Tommy says, "He wants to know which of you can fly a helicopter."

Gibby not sure what the proper gesture should be timidly raises his hand.

The old man spends another minute studying Gibby. Even though they have, at most, been in this room for five minutes, to Pete and Gibby it seems like, at least, an hour. The old man makes a head gesture to Tommy in the form of an approving nod as he slides out of his position behind the large desk, the assistant returns to aid the aging crime boss. Tommy remains in a head down position until the old man has left the room.

After the room empties Pete asks, "So what's going on Tommy."

"The boss approved you," says Tommy with a half smile.

"Just like that? We didn't talk to anybody," says Pete.

"You didn't need to, I did all your talking," says Tommy still with a half grin.

Gibby and Pete shrug their shoulders and give each other a look that says, "Oh what the hell."

"Come on we've got work to do," says Tommy using a hand motion indicating he wants them to put their hoods back on.

"Come on Tommy, what's with these hoods?" says Pete.

Tommy gives Pete a hard stare that says they aren't going anywhere with out the hoods.

Along with Pete, Gibby has his reservations, but nonetheless follows suit. Soon they are traveling again. From the leather smell they presume it's the same Escalade. The ride soon leaves the smoothness of asphalt to the roughness of a gravel track. When the S.U.V. finally comes to a stop, the hoods come off and they find themselves in the middle of a woods. There is a pole barn at the end of this two-track road but it's hard to determine any other buildings in the darkness.

"Follow me," says Tommy motioning toward the pole barn.

The front of the building reveals, what can only be described as a huge garage door, and off to the side, is a smaller commonplace door designed for regular human use. Tommy quickly unlocks the small door, leading them into a cavernous, black, windowless void. In short order, he flips the lights on. It proved to be everything but. There before them is a new state-of-the-art, two-seat, Robinson helicopter.

"We want to see you fly this thing,"says Tommy, still sporting a half grin. He's enjoying what's going down so far.

After looking it over, Gibby concludes, "It's a newer version of my dad's, but it's not much different."

With the aid of Pete and Tommy, the three of them power up an aging Toyota truck that's used to tow the helicopter out of its hanger. The Teflon-like padding on each of the two bottom rails keeps the dragging noise down as they slide the big dragon out of its cave.

Once out, it takes Gibby only a few minutes to begin to flip a few switches, examine the blades, and start the engine. The engine roars to life, as he continues his check list. Essentially satisfied, it's now time to get this machine airborne. With one motion of his hand this behemoth roars itself into action, easily lifting itself from the ground. After taking itself straight up several hundred feet, and then with another simple hand motion the flying dragon begins traveling in a horizontal direction. Taking this as an opportunity to get a fix on his location, he surmises he's on the south-east outskirts of Vancouver. Satisfied, he then maneuvers around in a big circle, well aware of those monitoring him. Fifteen minutes later he returns without a hitch.

"You flew that thing like a pro. I think we got some work for you," says Tommy, still grinning and with two thumbs up.

"Thanks. It's a nice piece of equipment," says Gibby, still focusing on his task to leave the chopper in good order.

"I think my grandfather and uncles will be pleased when I tell how well you handled it."

There hadn't been an opening to discuss the meeting with the old Chinese man until now. Gibby seizes the opportunity.

"That old man is your grandfather?" Gibby's voice nearly explodes from left over adrenalin. His head is always much clearer after and his thoughts seem to be going somewhere after experiencing an epinephrine rush.

Tommy nods adding, "The guy taking care of him is also my uncle. He's the family boss. Grandpa used to be but Uncle Marty is now. Grandpa has a lot of connections around the world so he's still an important part of the family business." It happens that Tommy's family is a powerful smuggling family in China as well as the United States.

With Gibby satisfied the big bird is bedded down, they head back to the Escalade. Pete has taken to wearing a fedora and sunglasses, because he says, "It makes me feel like a 1930's gangster." Right now he has the fedora in one hand and the hood in the other with that intent look that says "which one Tommy?"

"Oh I think we can let the hood go," Tommy says.

"Good, I was beginning to empathize with those guys held by the Taliban."

Tommy laughed, but quickly added, "You guys need to know only on a need to know basis. Believe me, it's a lot safer for all of us that way."

"I'm good with, or without the hood Tommy, what ever way you want," says Gibby with a shrug.

"You guys are being given a peek, and only a peek, into what my family has been doing for generations." Tommy says this with an air that silently says *"you know all you need to know for the present."*

Gibby gets this. His response is to wait. Pete on the other hand has never been one to wait, and pushes beyond the comfortable place Tommy wants to leave things.

"So what all does your family do?" questions Pete.

Tommy gives Pete a deadpan look that can only be described as something that's setting him up. "We're in the iron and steel business," says Tommy still dead panning Pete.

"The iron and steel business?" says Pete quizzically.

"Ya. My ma irons and my dad steals," says Tommy with the same serious, bland gaze.

Gibby gives Tommy a wink and a knowing grin. Pete on the other hand replies,"Oh", remaining just as puzzled.

With that Tommy says, "OK, let's load up. I'm running you guys back to your car. I have some other business to finish before I get back to you with the next step."

Back behind St. Agatha church, out of harms way, safely in Pete's Lincoln, fosters a moment for discussion. "What do you suppose we have to do for fifty grand," says Gibby thinking out loud.

"Well you can bet it's got something' to do with you flying' that helicopter," says Pete.

Stroking the side of his face until the silence becomes awkward Gibby is strangely drawn to the whole idea of flying. "Ya, I don't think it'll be the same as rounding' up cattle."

Pete, not quite able to absorb the full connection Gibby has with this edgy living, says, "By the way, I've never seen you do that. I almost crapped my pants when I saw you take off in that thing. Hell dude you looked like a real pilot."

Lost for the moment in his own world, Gibby leans back in the seat with his eyes closed content to wait for Tommy. St. Agatha's is an ominous cut stone church that seems to consume the street noise. When it is quiet, it is quiet. Exhausted, Pete's joining Gibby's quietness. He's pulled his fedora down over his sunglasses-covered eyes, when a tap-tap-tap came from the driver's side window. Pete's head snaps around as he gasped. It has become clear that two uniformed policemen, one on each side of the car, are producing the tapping noise with the end of a large flashlight.

Pete's head jerks back to the passengers side, as a beam of light streams across his face. Completely disconcerted, the only words forming are, "what the hell", as he sits up to run his window down.

"Good evening gentleman," says the patrolman. His voice leaves no question, he is definitely in charge.

"Good evening," echos Pete, clearing his throat with a voice taking on a slight quiver.

"Could I see some identification?" comes back the, much in charge policeman. With tension mounting, Pete's shaking hand gives his driver's license to the steady hand of the patrolman.

As Gibby turns over his license in a matter of fact way to the waiting officer, he can't help but notice Pete having a difficult time. It seems Pete's fears are rising up to greet him. If this is not enough, he spots Tommy's Escalade leaving the parking lot.

With the police officers out of earshot, Pete tries to make sense of what's occurring.

"What the hell is going on Gibby, are we going to jail?"

To Gibby this appears to be a routine investigation on the part of the police. "What the hell's the matter with you Pete? You're fallen apart on me."

"I know, I can't help it. Cops make me nervous," confesses Pete.

"Are you serious, Pete" says Gibby shaking his head.

Within a couple minutes the patrolman returns handing back their identifications. "Give me a good reason you two are back here," says the officer.

The imperative is directed to Pete. He's too nervous and scared to respond, leaving Gibby an opportunity to practice asserting a cooler head under fire.

"We're from Powellville up north. We don't know our way around Vancouver so we were told by our friend to wait here until they came to pick us up," says Gibby not elaborating any further than necessary. "Why is there a problem?"

"The problem is, you made the church sexton nervous. They've been having a lot of break-ins in this neighborhood. And since this is a private parking lot, he wants you moved," states the constable.

"That's not a problem," assures Gibby talking from the passenger side, over and past an unblinking Pete who's hands appear to be frozen at a 10:00 and 2:00 o'clock position on the steering wheel, "Where would you suggest?"

"There is a public parking facility around the corner. It's only a few dollars an hour and legal to park all night."

"Thanks officer we appreciate your help."

Pete finally releases his steering wheel long enough to extend his hand to the policeman as if to shake hands. The patrolman declines and returns to his patrol car.

Pete is finally returning to his old self. "Dude I didn't think we were going to pull this one off," says Pete retrieving his 9mm from under his seat.

"What the hell you doin' man. I didn't know you had that here," says Gibby with a definite air of dissatisfaction.

"I didn't tell you cause I knew you wouldn't go for it, but I don't trust any of these chinese bastards," says Pete definitively.

"Calm down Pete, your actin' crazy," says Gibby. He's definitely having second thoughts about this partnership.

"I'd rather be judged by a few than carried by six," says Pete, patting his pistol, having heard that saying somewhere in a U.S. movie, simultaneously reaching for his ringing phone.

"What the hell is going on," demands the voice of Tommy Li on the other end.

"Nothin' really" assures Pete, "They only wanted to know who we are, and what we're doing. Don't worry, everything's cool. All we have to do is move to the public parking lot around the corner."

"Good," says Tommy, not sure what trouble these country bumpkins will conjure up. "We'll meet you there."

Not sure what to expect, Pete follows orders, nervously driving his Lincoln to the parking lot. It's a well-lighted space with several dozen parking meters designed to accept "loonies". It's available parking designed to service the apartments around the area.

Living on the edge of fear is exhilarating to Gibby. The routine drive from the ranch to Vancouver had been routine, but that's where "routine" ended, and the adventure began. There's twists, and turns, and corners that can't be seen around yet. Gibby thrives on this kind of stuff. Adrenaline is addictive, it has always been Gibby's drug of choice.

Pete, on the other hand, finds this life style disconcerting. He likes life predictable.

Having pulled into a parking slot, Pete is toying with his pistol again seemingly checking the clip and sliding the mechanism back to assure himself there is a load in the chamber.

"What the hell you gonna do with that gun Pete?" lampoons Gibby. His sarcasm can't be missed.

Sticking it in his belt under his coat he says "I'm keeping it close to me. I don't trust any of these slant eyes." It's all the bravado he can muster.

It's not that Gibby is opposed to guns, it's that he's having many second thoughts about Pete carrying one. This thought is quickly verified.

"These guys start screwing' around with me, I'll take em all out," says Pete. He's clearly falling apart. Paranoia never comes on slow, it's either full bore, or not at all. The quick deal he had envisioned, has quickly become his nightmare.

Trying to salvage what's left of his partner, Gibby begins to see clearly Pete's Achilles heel.

"Pete, we haven't met anything we can't handle. You,re falling' apart before we barely get started."

Before Pete can respond, his phone rings. It's Tommy.

"Ya, OK, ya I understand. OK no problem?" says Pete, flipping his phone shut.

"So what did he say?" asks Gibby. It's becoming hard for him to hide his disdain in letting Pete handle these details.

"We have to walk down two blocks to a restaurant called the 'Good Fortune Pizzeria'. Tommy says he'll meet us there. This is getting too god-damn bizarre," grumbles Pete.

The night is cold. Temperatures are dipping down to just above freezing. In spite of its chill the night is bringing out something wild and free in Gibby. In spite of the dangers, there is something not readily seen pulling on him. For those who live in this dimension, there is no need for explanation. And for those who do not share this adventurous narrative, no amount of commentary brings sufficient understanding. For the next two blocks nothing is said. Each is lost in his own thoughts.

Pete reluctantly and even fearfully takes the next step. He's on the outer parameters of his stress management capabilities. Gibby, on the other hand, is at an almost full-court press. He has made a mental, physical, and for him, a "spiritual" commitment to this endeavor.

"All I want to do is get another kilo, and get back to Powellville," frets Pete.

Gibby is paying less and less attention to Pete's prattling. He's fixated on all the city lights, the traffic whizzing by, the lure of every flashing neon sign. His thoughts seem to chase themselves as something more catches his attention.

"There it is, right there" points out Gibby. The colors are yellow and red with embossed dragon on the half curtains covering the bottom portion of each window.

"What the hell kind of Chinese owns a pizzeria," mutters Pete.

Disregarding Pete's querulousness, the restaurant is warm, dimly lit with traditional Italian checkered table cloths accented with a Chinese embroidering.

"Where else, but in Vancouver," thinks Pete. His misgivings are swelling when he takes notice that he and Gibby are the only occidentals in the entire restaurant. The clientele is definitely Asian, all under thirty five. Some with young children, others, seemingly, on dates, but all at home in this eclectic mixture of Americana, Italian and Chinese traditions.

Tommy and the young mystery man, the ever-silent chauffeur, are sitting in a back booth against the wall, next to the back entrance that empties into the rear parking lot.

"Sit down," motions Tommy with a tattooed hand.

Both slide into the booth opposite their hosts. "This is Mooch, or sometimes Moochor, or even Moochie, whatever the state of mind brings to the forefront." Tommy's pointing with the same tattooed hand toward his companion.

Mooch is wearing a wide-billed cap turned sideways and pulled down over his forehead giving his face a mushed look. They immediately recognize him as Tommy's clandestine driver.

Mooch gives them the two-fingered salute, which they both return.

Tommy swings a plastic shopping bag across the table toward Pete. "This what your lookin', for?"

Pete's head swings from side to side concerned about who may be watching.

"Don't worry about it Pete, my cousin owns the joint," chuckles Tommy.

Pete stares at the bag for a moment, peeks in only to be met by the familiar packing.

"I double bagged it for you," laughs Tommy, watching a frantic Pete try to get inside.

Satisfied, Pete slides the cash-filled envelope across the table.

Satisfied that he's fully compensated,Tommy thumbs its contents, pocketing it just in time to have the pretty Chinese waitress set down a steamy hot pizza with a squid topping.

"You guys may as well stay and help us eat this thing," says Tommy with his usual knowing grin. It's not even close to a reasonable assumption that these two occidentals would ever consider taking him up on the offer.

Gibby and Pete, both in agreement on this offer. "No thanks I think we'll pass," says Gibby, hardly able to take a second look, as the pungent aroma strikes his nostrils.

Pete has seen, heard and had enough. "Yah, we have to get back to Powellville, I got a lotta business to take care of." The word 'nervousness' comes to mind.

"That's too bad," says Tommy, "I had planned on taking you guys out on the town."

"Hey that sounds great to me," says an excited Gibby. He came forward from being slouched down in the booth. This is the kind of stuff that clicks with him.

"And there's plenty of poontang," adds a still grinning Tommy.

At best, Pete's look is one of diffidence, moving quickly toward fear. He's standing by, but barely able to keep from bolting for the door.

"Come on Pete, quit acting like a jackass, and relax," chides Gibby once again trying to resist the urge to snap at him.

"Relax! Relax!" bellows Pete, "What the hell am I supposed to do with the kilo of pot, stuff it up my ass?"

The silent consensus of those around the table is that this may be a good idea. Gibby took one last, long, contemplative drag on his cigarette before butting it. It's an effort to allow a second thought that does not involve butting it out on Pete's forehead.

"Why don't we just take it to your car and lock it in the trunk?" Gibby's voice is fricative and painted with contempt as he sighs. Counter acting, he settles on butting his cigarette in Pete's coffee cup.

Pete's always been a smooth talker when things are predictable. For all his magniloquence, he's always been persuasive enough to have Gibby side with him, but now he's isolating himself. He's standing alone. Gibby is not falling in line behind him. Pete actually looks like he could start to cry.

"OK, OK I'll go." Pete's voice is clearly stressed.

After securing the weed in the secret compartment he has designed under the spare tire, Pete climbs back into Tommy's Escalade. With that accomplished, Tommy begins to pass a small, lacquered box along with a small spoon. Predictably the air lifts, as its white, powdery, addictive contents begin to loosen the mood.

"OK kids, it's show time," says Tommy signaling Mooch to hit the accelerator. The roar of the engine reverberating against tall buildings causes Tommy to shout. "Hang on boys and girls, tonight is gonna be a helluva ride." Throwing caution to the wind, they're moving fast, hoping as the young do, that they are drawing attention and are envied for their cavalier ways.

This is a cocaine first for Gibby and Pete. Up until now their focus has been to get a quality weed for themselves and their clientele. This experience is opening up a whole new dimension. Gibby wants badly to envisage this as an opportunity to begin to redefine himself. The life on the ranch is quickly being replaced by the lure of the city's night life.

Mooch pulls in front of an arcade of flashing neon lights. It's Tommy's favorite dance club. It's the Club Nitro, a high-energy club swarming with young bodies sweating out raw hormones. Tiered seating of tables and chairs surrounds a sunken dance floor, strobe lights flash with the music, accented by the piston like movements of those on the floor. It's pure synergistic energy.

This is the zenith of a visceral experience. To Gibby, it"s welcoming. To Pete, it's paranoia at every turn. Catching a glimpse of himself in one of the many mirrors surrounding the exterior walls, further heightens his anxiety. The pancake makeup he uses to cover his wine-colored birthmark has totally disintegrated, leaving him even more vulnerable and exposed.

"What the hell am I doing here!" remonstrates Pete as his thoughts race. The unpredictable nature of this misadventure is blowing straight through the roof of his discontent. In Powellville, Pete has painted himself as young, cool and hip. In Vancouver, he's a pathetic impersonator. His narrow shoulders and slightly stooped posture give him a diminutive appearance. Paranoiac fear is pulling him into an unpredictable insanity. He grips his pocketed pistol tighter, as he's bumped and pushed. His breaking point is not too far away.

Tommy's idea is not to stay too long in any one place. To him, being seen is what a club experience is all about. Soon tiring of this place, he's on his phone to have Mooch bring the Escalade back to the entrance. Having a driver and being chauffeured is exactly the grandiloquent impression Tommy wishes to convey.

For Pete, it's just in time. He's exhausted from tension. Between the drugs, the flashing lights, the jammed-packed floor, he's terrified. Feeling safe once again in the bosom of the S.U.V.'s back seat, his relief is equal to that of a fighter who is in an unwinnable bout stopped in the third round of a ten round fight. He's damn glad it's over. It's only midnight but for the remainder of this verdant crew, the night is still young.

"I know a high-classed whore house," reveals Tommy. "They get a couple hundred 'loonies' an hour, but these 'Hoe's is high class.' They're worth every penny."

"I'm up for that," says Gibby grinning from ear to ear, taking another nose hit from Tommy's lacquered box.

Tommy smiles a little bit at Gibby's look of surprise. Tommy has shifted his patronizing flounce into high gear with these country boys.

Mooch pulls the Escalade in front of a huge white-pillared porch, attached to an even bigger white, wooded-framed, three-story, late 19th Century house. It could easily be mistaken for some sort of a sorority house . The steps are wide, and seem to offer an invitation to come up to an equally summoning porch that wraps itself around the house. Each brightly, lighted window contrasts itself against the darkness, piercing its brilliance out into the cold night. The top floor is equipped with several dormers acting as sentinels against the surrounding neighbors. It's a grand, old house.

"Wait here, I'll be right back," says Tommy with a remonstration between official and determined.

Gibby can make out, through the huge front door, Tommy talking with a strikingly beautiful blonde woman, well-coiffed, wearing what appears to be a snow white slack suit, with black, shiny, and very high heeled shoes.

Within a few minutes Tommy is back with a triumphant expression.

"Everything's all set to go." This is part of Tommy's work he thoroughly enjoys.

Mooch is not only Tommy's driver he is also his cousin. He's well aware of the turnpike he courses his clients through. His job is to facilitate the action, drive and be a personal bodyguard for Tommy. Entering the bordello through custom doors paneled with beveled glass panels etched with parallel swans facing the other, they are met with the accommodating expression of compliance by one Peaches O'Shay. Getting a closer look, Gibby realizes she is much older than she looked from a distance.

"Hello boys." They are greeted by the sultry sound of one whose voice has been pampered by years of cigarette smoke and good whiskey. She also has had the benefits of a face lift, leaving her eye sockets slightly egg-shaped, augmented breasts that expose at least six inches of cleavage, and botoxed lips that look swollen and misshapen. At first glance, they give her the appearance of having been recently slapped in the mouth. It's as though they've been lifted from someone else, and trying as they may, can't join the rest of her face.

"What can we do for you?" The same sultry voice is now speaking through these bright-red,puffed-out lips that don't seem to move. Slightly amused at the "doe in the head light" look on Gibby's face, she takes control over the situation.

A slight gesture of Miss Peaches' hand, and one by one, a parade of women single file into the room. All are in various stages of dress or undress. Some expose warm looking silk- covered breasts beneath loose-flowing, see-through garments. Others are in thong bikini attire with tops that barely cover nipples and bottoms that look like the cheeks of their butt ate the entire thing, leaving only a string bifurcating their heinie. Still others are in cheerleader outfits. There seems to be one of every type for each particular fantasy of every male.

Gibby has involuntarily stopped breathing. He's suddenly surprised to find himself pleasantly horny. This bevy of babes all seem to be looking directly at him. At this point his body demands air. He gasps and along with the air comes, what can best be described as drool. His drool-catching bronchials protest causing him to cough uncontrollably.

Sitting down in the nearest chair, Miss Peaches alternates slapping his back and massaging it.

"There, there big boy, take a deep breath. You'll be OK."

As Gibby slowly makes his recovery, the line of giggling girls assume the same patient, flirtatious poses. Each girl gives Gibby the impression that the whole purpose of her creation is to please him. He is becoming self-conscious and embarrassed at another involuntary reaction. The bulge in his pants.

Far from being fully recovered, and in control of himself, he sits back and enjoys the task of having to choose anyone of these beautiful and willing sex partners, for a price of course. In this case, it's a Triad-owned business, the girls are expected to be extra attentive to whatever and to whoever Tommy should ask of them.

Gibby finally zeros in on a freckled, red-haired girl that, who not surprisingly, looks a lot like April. Grabbing his hand, as though she had been waiting for him her entire life, she walks him down the hall before disappearing behind a closed door.

An hour later Gibby emerges. He's met by Tommy's, ever-toothy, smirk. Tommy and Gibby are developing more than a just a working agreement. They have taken a genuine liking for one another. Tommy's idea for a budding partnership is that as they are developing a trust between them. From this foundation they can look for business opportunities beyond the Triad's plans to merely use his flying talents.

The young, freckled-face girl is still hanging on to Gibby as though they are now sufficiently acquainted to move their relationship to meeting this way on a regular bases. She gives Gibby a kiss. When walking away, she turns long enough to give him that little girly wave with her fingers.

"You look like you've been struck with a golden ray of sunshine," laughs Tommy holding the door ajar for Gibby's obvious rubber-legged exit. Gibby can't believe how this experience has left him feeling. It's way too good to be true. He's just waiting for the next shoe to drop. Neither of them has to wait long.

What they meet at the Escalade is completely unexpected. Mooch is leaning against the driver's door, smoking a cigarette. He trades a quick nod with his cousin motioning him to look in the back seat.

Tommy's smile totally disappears at the sight in the back seat. There is Pete, on his stomach with duct tape around his neck to his hands, behind his back, then taped around ankles bent toward the back of his head in such a way that if he struggled he would strangle himself. He also had a piece taped across his mouth. In simple words -- he's hog tied Chinese style.

Tommy, looking back and forth from captive to sentry, hoping for, at least, a few more forthcoming details.

The look on Tommy's face tells Mooch, that now is time for those details. "He asked for, and I gave him a hit'. The next thing, he's shouting about someone trying to kill him, when I asked who 'they' were, is when he pulled a gun. I was afraid he was gonna shoot the car up so I cold-cocked him, and duct taped him before he came to."

For a moment Tommy's grin had turned to a frown, but since no one is hurt, he's beginning to see some ironic humor in the pathetic, back-seat prisoner.

"You done good," says Tommy, with a good-natured grin pulling Mooch's hat down over his eyes.

Turning to Gibby he says "Get rid of this turd, he's like a fart in the wind, never knowing where he gonna blow and stink up the place."

"You're right, absolutely right," says Gibby, not at all happy with what he sees.

Looking with disdain at this duct-taped mess, he begins to untape

Pete, shaking his head, and in a condescending voice, "What in the hell are you thinking. You're acting like a moron."

Pete is blubbering like a baby girl, saying nothing. Just hours earlier he was in charge of this whole liaison, now he's reduced to a whimpering, gasping, sycophantic heap.

Dropping Gibby and Pete off at the parking lot, Tommy promises Gibby to be in touch soon.

Mooch hands Gibby Pete's pistol. "If I were you, I'd keep this, that peckerhead's gonna kill somebody," he says in a less-than-amused stillness.

Gibby nods in agreement, as he also takes Pete's keys. Stopping only for red lights, they head north starting the long trip back to the ranch. He grips the steering wheel so hard that it's cramping his shoulder muscles. Remembering the two Percodan Tommy had given him for the long ride home, he tosses them to the back of his dry throat, then with all the saliva he can muster, he swallows.

The return trip is silent as Pete is sleeping off the remaining residue of the night's drugs. Pulling into Powellville three hours later, Gibby leaves Pete sleeping in his driveway. He then heads home to await Tommy's call. At this point, he can only imagine the next adventure.

CHAPTER 6

EMERGENCY ON THE HIGH PLATEAU

An emergency has developed over night for the cowboys up on the high pasture. Along with 13,000 head of cattle, they have been caught in an early snowstorm. In some places the drifts measure three-to-five feet deep, preventing the buckaroos from moving the cattle to a lower pasture. If this crises is not addressed soon, these cows will begin to stress from a lack of nutrition. Cows losing weight is the last thing a rancher wants to see happen.

Norbert has faced these types of crises many times before. He has never had a problem taking care of what needs taking care of and the wherewithal to manage the problem. He plans his work, then methodically, works his plan.

For the most part, work done with cows is done on a horse back, although in times like these special equipment has to be kept on hand. In this case, the job is going to require a Caterpillar tractor with a snow blade capable of busting though even the most stubborn snow drifts. Since there are only dirt trails leading to these high pastures, the Caterpillar tractor is going to have to be hauled by truck and trailer only as far as the road permits. When finally unloaded, it then must make its way to the troubled area under its own power.

Back at the ranch Gibby and Dillon are awakened by the same procedure his father uses with them every morning.

"Wake up and piss, the worlds on fire." At the same time pounding on their bedroom door.

For Norbert, eating breakfast is never missed, nor is a quiet time with his Creator before breakfast. Because of the risk that his day may get away from him, he spends a few minutes in prayer and meditation seeking divine guidance. For this exercise, he neither explains, nor apologizes. Norbert has eliminated many a problem in life by remembering what caused them and winnowing their causes off to the side.

At breakfast Norbert lays out his starting plan. "Dillon, I'd like to ride with you hauling the 'Cat'. Gibby I want you to fly the helicopter over any alpines. Those cows usually head for cover when a storm blows in. We need to recover any strays before the cougars find them."

As soon as breakfast is finished, a meeting is hurriedly called in the horse barn. Each buckaroo is given a designated task. There is no question who's in charge. Norbert's orders are clear and concise. He is unquestionably, the "God Father" of the Circle G Ranch.

Within the hour everything is rolling. Dillon and Norbert have the 'Cat' loaded and are heading off on the two-hour, twenty-five mile ride across, what is best described as, cow trails. Norbert purposely chooses to ride with Dillon. He has wanted time alone with his first born, this drive is making it happen.

"You're a good man Dillon, you've developed into an excellent supervisor. I don't know what the ranch would be without you."

Dillon has heard his father say similar things to Gibby for less, so he has some reservation as to how sincere his father is in these accolades toward him. Dillon's first thought is always his worst, at least, in regards to his socialization skills. Guardedly, and certainly less than sincere, he manages a "thanks."

Instinctively his hands meet e gear. He slams them a little harder, as he reminds himself how his parents coddle Gibby. Dillon's anger toward his younger brother does not allow him to be silent. Turning toward his father, he begins to unleash.

"Dad you know Gibby didn't go fishing this past weekend," he blurts out. Not waiting for his father to respond, he further adds, "His truck sat in Pete Simon's driveway with all his gear the entire weekend. He's up to something, and knowing Pete, it's probably no good."

"I already know that Dillon," says his father calmly.

"You think I'm overreacting about Gibby, don't you Dad?"

"What do you think?" asks his dad in the same calm voice.

Dillon pauses for only a moment, yet keeping his eyes on the rough, dirt trail.

"I think you and mom are naive when it comes to the crap Gibby pulls."

Norbert is still silent for the moment pulling his thoughts together. "I've heard this concern from you before."

Pause.

"Let me ask you something, Dillon, what is your real concern regarding Gibby?"

Dillon does not like being put on the spot by anyone, including his father.

Norbert doesn't wait for an answer that he knows it's not going to be forthright.

"I get the feeling your resentment toward your brother has little to do with his crazy night life with Pete Simon."

Dillon knows exactly why he has resentment toward his younger brother. It has everything to do with April Landers. His obvious problem is an ego complicated by an inferiority complex. It will not allow him to bring these feelings to the surface, much less discuss it openly with his father.

Instead, he continues to mask his resentment by saying, "You keep rewarding him for his bad behavior, and I think that's just, plain wrong."

Norbert thinks to himself, "*This boy points his finger toward his brother, but fails to see the three pointing back on himself.*" As a good father he has made it his business to know his sons, both their strengths and weaknesses. He presses on.

"You've known Gibby his entire life, he's always been on the edge of trouble, but it seems to me that lately, *your* resentments have intensified."

Dillon remains silent. He does not have the will nor the skill to discuss his romantic sensibilities, consequently, his romantic feelings toward April are displaced with anger, frustration, and rage. Then, as is usual with this sort, he bellows, "I don't know what you're talking about, he's always been a pain in the ass." He feels trapped in hurt, embarrassment, and now entering a mode of borderline panic.

Norbert is wise enough to know when to let up. He would like nothing better than to have his family's strife settled. Unfortunately, it's not for today. Dillon is determined to shut everyone, including his father, out of his life. There is no cure under these conditions.

Dillon's prayer is that his father get off this subject. His prayer is seemingly answered, as a big buck jumps out in front of the truck, causing a mild panic of a different sort. It is enough to change the subject.

Back at the ranch Gibby is preparing to launch the helicopter just as he spots the familiar female form crouched under the rotating propeller blades. Making her way forward, she's holding one hand on the top of her cowboy hat , preventing it from blowing off, while the other reaches for the chopper door.

In a definite and flirtatious pantomime, she mouths the words through door window, "I want to go with you." Throwing it open, she climbs in.

Gibby's surprised eyes dart from side to side, as though some other surprises may be lurking. Just as he again begins his ascent, his eyes dart around once more, just in time to see another human form appear. This time it's his mother, frantically waving her arms.

Setting the helicopter back down, he throws the cock pit door open, expecting she had some important instructions from his father.

"You forgot your lunch." She shouts over the noise of the engine.

"Geez mom thanks but I gotta get this thing in the air," says an impatient son.

His mother hesitates for a moment as she stares at April. *And she's sitting next to her son.*

"Ma, I gotta go." Gibby knows his mother well enough to know that an unspoken pause speaks volumes. He knows April is the focus of her attention. Finally she lets go of the door, but not of the situation as she backs out of the way. She stands powerless, as Gibby lifts the craft off the ground, and heads off. Before long they're cruising at 100 mph. The noise of the blades prevents normal conversation. Nonetheless, April is mesmerized. She has never been in the air.

"Gibby, this is absolutely beautiful," she shouts over the noise of the engine. "I can't believe I've never done this before. Oh look there's 'our cabin'." Her words fade off as she caught what she had just said, but once a word has been said, it cannot be unsaid.

Gibby pretends he didn't hear exactly what she said, especially the part about "our cabin." Still not sure what to make of this sudden change in his and April's relationship, he can't help but think they have been haphazardly flung together. He feels much out of control when ever April is around, but then he feels he has no power to merely walk away from the strong attraction that's growing between them. When she isn't with him and he's busy with Tommy, he regards her as a distraction. Now, with her next to him, things change. Under these conditions he finds it not so easy to ignore her feminine enchantment. The expression on her face is one he has never seen nor could ever imagine. He only knows he has never seen her this radiant. Her red hair is ablaze with the sun bouncing from it and her eyes are alive with excitement.

"Yup you're right, that's Ol' Bill's cabin," says Gibby, nervously leaving out the "our cabin" part.

From the air its impossible to discern a twenty-foot snow drift from a one footer. The distance in the air makes calculating depth an impractical exercise. Nonetheless, Gibby begins his task. He's flying low enough to spook strays back to the main herd. Cows hate being alone and they always look to a leader. It usually takes a couple of low passes to spook them into figuring who that leader will be. It's not going to be a strong independent leader but more often than not, it'll be the cow that becomes frightened the quickest.

In spite of these horses being a tough breed, the buckaroos on the ground could never search as many wooded areas as fast as the helicopter. Gibby can see where these horsemen are attempting to keep the herd settled. This is also a tough breed of cows. They wade through a foot of snow without hesitation, but when they reach a wall of three-to-five feet of snow everything comes to a standstill. It takes precious calories for each cow to have to crawl through a foot of snow. It's almost as bad for them to have to break through packed snow to get enough grass to eat.

It's proving to be quite an experience for April. She's never seen a herd from the air. The cows cover a good square mile. April's face is bright with delight, her eyes dancing. She looks alive and animated. Gibby finds he is strangely comfortable with her in ways that he can't quite put words to. He realizes he still delights in harking back to earlier days by just being happy to show off in this new chapter of life, instead of a motorcycle, it's now his piloting skills.

"Oh my gosh Gibby, they look like ants all crawling in unison," shrieks an enthralled April.

Turning to him, genuinely breathless, "Gibby, why have you never taken me up here before?"

"Because you have never jumped into my helicopter before," says Gibby with a boyish grin.

They're clearly able to see the low boy. It's finally reached the end of its usefulness. Now Dillon is unloading the 'Cat' and preparing to run it up the pass. A two-mile jaunt at best, through drifted snow, and at least, a twenty percent grade. In order to bring the herd down, he's going to have to widen the blocked pass, at least, 300 feet. A breach that wide, in these conditions, is going to take the rest of the morning and early afternoon. The temperature is beginning to rise, making the snow wet and heavy. The ground is far from being frozen, and if Dillon doesn't get as much melting snow off as possible, the trail will become a muddy mess.

Meanwhile Norbert is busy giving orders to the dozen buckaroos who trailered their horses in a convoy behind the lowboy. Jed, also knows what has to be done. He's busy saddling his horse, along with trying to organize the half dozen hyper, yelping, cow dogs. These cow dogs are a mixed breed, and just as Jed attests, 'their smart as the devil and can out work any three horse and riders.'

The strategy is being worked out. Horses, riders, and dogs are following the trail Dillon has, in short order, broken through. They're spreading back about a half mile. Most men and dogs are taking the lead behind Dillon's Caterpillar, but a couple stragglers remain, struggling to bring up the rear. All is working well until the all too familiar 'whinny' of a spooked horse. It has thrown its rider, and is now running off leaving the hapless man injured on the ground.

"Damn that horse," says the downed horseman. It's obvious he's injured. While struggling to get to his feet the cause of the spooked horse has quickly made itself known. The horse had caught the scent and immediately the sight of its mortal enemy, a mountain lion. The big, 250-pound cat has turned his attention to the seeming helpless man thrashing around and unable to get to his feet. In a single pounce the monster is on the defenseless buckaroo. His blood curdling screams can be heard well up the trail. The giant cat has his jaws locked firmly around the cowboy's head, dragging him toward some bush.

By this time, his tortuous screams have gained the attention of, at least, a couple of the other horsemen. Their horses are just as disinclined as the first to move toward the enemy, thus forcing their riders to dismount and run on foot toward the struggle. They arrive with an arsenal of hand guns and rifles, which have already become too risky to use for fear of striking, the already, helpless victim.

Hugh Hodges is the first to arrive, on a full-court press, he pounds the puma with the stock of his rifle. By this time, the cowboy has been mercilessly dragged some 30 feet toward the underbrush. He continues his assault, now joined by several other men who are also swinging their weapons as the big cat twists and turns successfully avoiding their blows, all this time managing to keep a firm grip on his ill-fated prey. What seems like a never-ending endurance test, the lion finally relinquishes his grip on the torn scalp of this brutalized buckaroo. The animal begins an immediate retreat. The retreat did not last long, as the crack of a rifle shot sent the menacing predator to its happy hunting grounds.

The shot came from Norbert's .306 rifle. The one thing to which Norbert remains unforgiving is any injurious threat to his family, his men and his herd. The downed man is Sid Fiek, a twelve-year veteran of the Circle G Ranch. Norbert is by Sid's side in a heartbeat. His scalp is half torn off with one eye hanging on his cheek. It's a gruesome sight for anyone to have to deal with, but Norbert has dealt with worse. Carefully folding the torn flap of scalp back into its place, and resting the dangling eye back on its socket, he quickly contacts the helicopter overhead.

"Gibby bring that chopper down. Sid's been attacked by a mountain lion. We have to get him to the hospital in Vancouver pronto!"

Gibby responds immediately. Within minutes of landing, Sid has been deposited in a small cargo hold behind the seats. His head has been bandaged as best these men can do with what they have with them, and it's obvious his leg is broken. Gibby's fuel is low so it's decided Sid is replacing April. It's going to be a tight ride. He's two hours from the hospital. Not only is Gibby watching Sid go in and out of consciousness, but also his depleting fuel gauge. He has no time to stop at the ranch and refuel with his passenger near death from loss of blood.

Norbert suggest they all say a prayer for Sid. That being done, he turns to the displaced passenger looking somewhat forlorn.

"April I don't have a clue why you're here, but you're going to have to mount up and take Sid's place," says a perplexed Norbert.

"That's fine. I can do that," says an agreeable April. She is always ready for this kind of action.

Since she entered her teen years, her father has kept a close eye on those who would keep a close eye on her. She hasn't mixed much with the cow hands, not because she isn't capable, rather her father sees it as throwing his daughter into a field of unfettered and uncontrolled testosterone. Jed is as surprised as Norbert to see his young daughter appear on the scene. Straightway they both readily agree, she's going to have to take Sid's place. Norbert, Jed and each man on this team know it's going to take every man, horse, dog, and in this case, woman, to reinstate a sense of order and control over this mindless wandering of 13,000 cows.

"Lets get you mounted, kid," says Jed good naturedly to his daughter as Sid's retrieved horse is brought to her. She can't conceal her excitement over being drafted into this adventure, bringing a big, broad smile over her freckled face.

"Stay alert and be careful, darling," implores her father,handing her his extra pistol.

"Don't worry daddy," assures April, cramming the gun into her belt.

Grabbing the reins, she turns Sid's horse, digging her heels ever so firmly into the sides of the big mare, pushing forward to join the rest of the gang. The horse knew immediately who is the master and is ready to work.

There is no more to it than this, a horse and a rider and some recalcitrant cows actualize a purpose for their way of life. This synergistic blend of horse, rider and cow can only make sense in the context of all of these participants and their mutual dependence. Many of the ranchers in this area use snow machines or quads, but still depend primarily on the horse. Both the riders and the cows have a special relationship to these beasts of burden. Machines can't bridge this gap.

The sun has broken through the clouds, giving the black and white landscape a new brightness. In the path where Dillon has plowed can be seen the green meadow grass, declaring its deep color to be the reigning duchess of this vista.

The cowboys have fallen in behind Dillon. The track is much easier on the horses than trying to buck deep snow. A buckaroo knows what his horse can do, always pushing for excellence, yet at the same time, respecting their individual abilities. It's a matter of status how well a buckaroo cares for his horse, so it's also well judged to realize the beast has some limitations. The sound cattle make is a sound the buckaroos never grow tired of. It's part of the lure that keeps bringing them back year after year. On the other hand, any one of these boys can tell you, "They are the dumbest critters 'at God ever made."

As usual Dillon is all business. The roar of the diesel engine is making it impossible to hear anything else. His attention is on the task at hand, paying little or no attention to the string of cowboys passing by. That is until he notices the recognizable form, the arched back of one April Landers. "How in the hell did she get here," he mutters to himself.

Her alluring posture is not something that most red-blooded men can easily ignore. She has not given Dillon even a glance as her thoughts are only on the excitement ahead.

The buckaroos know better than to be overheard making jokes or unsavory remarks about Jed's daughter. He can fire them as quick as he hired them, maybe give them an ass whoopin' to boot. The unwritten rule is to mind one's manners around females. Young, beautiful and red haired, she's only to be glanced at, keeping one's thoughts to one's self

It's four o'clock in the afternoon. There's only an hour of day light left on this early December day. Things are coming together. Dillon has managed to widen the pass allowing more cows to filter down into the valley. As the sound of the Caterpillar distances itself, the ensuing quietness of the late afternoon is only interrupted by the "mooing" of 13,000 head of cattle and the occasional "whoops" used by these boys to bring the herd together.

All in all,Norbert is satisfied with the way his buckaroos perform. Admittedly, these boys do a lot of crazy things when they go into town, but on the ranch, they're all business.

At the moment he's managing a call to Gibby. "You got Sid there OK?" asks Norbert.

"Ya, I got him there just fine. I was worried about running out of fuel, but we made it. The hospital has a fuel station and they agreed to sell me enough to get back to the ranch."

"How's he doin'?" asks Norbert. Gibby is not surprised at the concern he hears in his father's voice.

"They had to induce a coma to keep him from thrashing around so much. They managed to set his leg, got at least 300 stitches in his head and they managed to save his eye," reports Gibby. "How things going with the herd?"

"Dillon's just finishing loading the Caterpillar. We'll be back at the ranch in a few hours."

As Dillon rounds the back of the lowboy, he spots April. She's preparing to put Sid's horse back in the trailer.

"April how in the hell did you end up out here?" Dillon has been busy and missed the whole episode with Sid and the mountain lion. Until now he knew nothing about Gibby landing the helicopter and having to fly Sid into Vancouver.

"I flew out with Gibby," she says in a matter of fact way.

All who have met Dillon would agree that he is a handsome, well built, responsible man, however, there is something in his personality she finds unattractive. It hasn't helped his case when she has caught him, at various times, staring at her with no explanation. He makes her uncomfortable.

Dillon would like nothing better than to have April replace his father, to have her ride back to the ranch with him. Before he can form the words to ask, she spots her father.

"Daddy, can I ride back with you?"

"You sure can, darlin'," assures her father.

"Thank you, daddy," she say pecking a kiss on his cheek.

"I want to tell you, you did one heck of a job today. You're as good with a horse as any of these boys."

"Oh, daddy you're just saying that to make me feel good."

"Maybe so, but it's more truth than fiction." Jed is seeing a depth in his baby girl he has not seen until today. Lately she has seemed quieter, more introspective. He can't determine yet whether this is a good thing or a bad thing. He merely recognizes their relationship changing.

As usual Dillon senses a rejection without it ever being verbalized. Either way, to him it feels the same. He's quiet on the way back. Norbert is willing to let it slide in the hopes that it's nothing more than fatigue.

His thoughts frustrate him. *"After all, don't I have the kind of qualities a woman would be happy to have in a man? Why in the hell does she prefer that irresponsible fool of a brother?"* His contempt for Gibby is reaching new depths. On April's return home she is forced by fatigue to go directly to bed. She can't remember when she has been this tired.

"She worked damn hard today, Karen. I was proud and surprised to see her making good decisions with those stupid, unpredictable cows. She more than held her own," says a delighted father.

"That may be so, but now I think she's coming down with something. I was in town today and half of Powellville is down with the flu," says Karen. Karen believes she possess an extra sense when it comes to the well being of her family. She believes herself proven right the next morning.

"Oh my God mom, I feel so sick." April gags over the toilet.

"I wouldn't be a bit surprised if you haven't gotten yourself all run down and caught a bug. You need to stay inside today and rest," says her mother, holding her hand to April's forehead checking for a fever.

April is indulgent with her mother's pampering, "B*ut this doesn't quite feel like the flu*," she thinks to herself.

It's a few weeks before Christmas. Norbert particularly loves this season. By in large he's a peaceful man, finding the "Peace on Earth" theme of Christmas a good fit. Christmas lights are strung around each pillar, roof line, and window of the huge two-story ranch house, transforming it into an luminous wonderment of colored brilliance. To emphasis this locus and not misunderstand the nucleus of Christmas, Norbert has imported a life-size Nativity scene from the Christmas themed-store Bronners in Frankenmuth, Michigan. It's the time of year when Norbert expresses his simple faith in the Babe of Bethlehem in a dramatic way. His hope is that he will inspire others, and especially his family, to also discover Peace on Earth through this Babe.

In contrast, and in spite of Dillon's election to "Warden" in their parish, Dillon is less concerned with the religious sentiments of his father and more concerned with the practical details of finance and ranch management. It has also come to his attention that some of the obsolete equipment behind the machine shop is missing.

"I don't know why or how, but I know that 'dough-headed' brother of mine is behind it," thinks Dillon.

Making the short walk from his office to Gibby's machine shop domain, he confronts his brother. "Gibby, what happened to that old combine out back? It's gone and no one has taken it out of inventory."

He's suddenly overcome with a forgotten, belated guilt. "Ya, I took it to the scrap yard. I thought we should start getting rid of some of the junk back here. I just haven't had time to get with you," says Gibby, trying to stay within his usual nonchalant tone.

Unable and unwilling to conceal his irritation Dillon continues his inquisition. "So what did you do with the money?"

"I put it in the safe for petty cash. When the shop needs something, we buy it."

"Damn it, Gibby, you know damn well that's not the way this ranch is run. You don't just take it upon yourself to make these decisions without letting me know."

Dillon's tactless approach brings about Gibby's predictable smirk, which further infuriates his brother. Justifiably so, and firmly set on his high horse, Dillon storms out slamming the door. Dillon is meeting each of these confrontations with a strengthening resolve to get Gibby off the ranch. Just how and when, he doesn't know but *"He's got to go"* has become his obsession.

CHAPTER 7

QUICK AND CLEAN

A week has passed since Gibby left Pete in his driveway. He has tried on a number of occasions to contact him by phone and gotten no response.

It's the following Friday evening when Gibby finally catches up with him at Eddie's Pool Hall.

"Hey Pete."

"Hey Gibby."

There's a noticeable amount of tension.

"I've been tryin' to reach you all week. How come you haven't returned my calls, and what about that kilo we bought from Tommy?"

"You weren't around so I've been selling it," says Pete rather timidly handing Gibby a roll of bills.

Gibby quietly accepted the payment, but at the same time he knew that Pete knew that he knew that things have drastically change.

Sensing that Gibby was going to say things that he may not want to hear, especially, concerning the fiasco the previous week in Vancouver, Pete gets a jump on the conversation.

"I've been thinking, maybe I don't want to get involved with the deal that Tommy's buddies are cookin' up. You know me, Gibby. I like easy deals, a kilo here, a kilo there. Somethin' not too nerve wracking."

"Ya, that's fine Pete. No sense in pushin' yourself over the edge," says Gibby. This conversation has saved him from having to tell Pete he's out anyway.

Within a few days, the much anticipated call comes. "Gibby, Tommy here. The deal is on."

"Good. When?" comes back a voice truly marked with anticipated excitement.

"Can you meet me at the same parking lot in Vancouver on Saturday afternoon? We can talk about it then."

"I don't see a problem with that."

The weekend soon arrives. As usual, he makes up a lie as to where he is going. Neither Norbert nor Joanie are convinced he is being forthright.

Nonetheless, at 21 years old they find monitoring their son's behavior futile. Dillon,on the other hand, is not bound by his parents seeming nonchalance, and, as usual, feels compelled to confront his brother. Gibby is packing as he looks up to find his brother standing in the door of his room as though he's ready for bear.

"I don't know exactly what you're up to," says Dillon, "but from what the talk in town says, is that you're setting yourself up for a hell of a lot of trouble."

Gibby keeps packing, ignoring his brother. Dillon presses on.

"Just whose pocket do you think the money is coming out of to pay for your bullshit when it turns south?"

Gibby continues his silence allowing Dillon another barrage.

"Why don't you just ask dad to cash you out of the ranch and get the hell out of here and pay for your own stupid life?"

Gibby slams his suitcase shut and heads for the door. Breaking his silence and looking directly at Dillon, "Ya know Dillon, because your such a prick, I'm going to give that some extra thought. I don't think that, with or without Dad here, I could stand to be around your sorry ass much longer anyway."

With that, he climbs into his truck and leaves. His mind soon leaves the ranch behind in anticipation of the next escapade. The miles fly by and he soon finds himself in Vancouver at the now familiar public parking lot. The familiar black Escalade is there waiting for him. He pulls in along side and parks. He runs his passenger window down as the Escalade runs its driver side window down.

"Hey Tommy, sup?," says Gibby, talking across Mooch who's in his usual place behind the wheel.

"Good news, we got some business for you."

"Great! " answers an excited Gibby.

Always being conscious of being watched, Tommy directs, "I want

you to wait five minutes, then drive down the street to my cousin's pizzeria. Park in the back, go in through the kitchen entrance, and wait for
me there. With that, he pulls out of the parking space with a wary eye for
anything that looks suspicious.

Gibby does as he's told, waiting the full five minutes before making
his way to the restaurant. Following Tommy's directions, he parks in the
back, then makes his way to the kitchen entrance. A pretty Chinese waitress meets him, escorting him to a small office off the kitchen inviting
him to take a seat. Again, Gibby follows instructions and sits down. The
young girl leaves, closing the door behind her.

The room is small and cramped with a couple of armless, straight-backed
table chairs against the walls, each stacked with boxes. The desk is barely
visible beneath piles of papers. There is a small computer table behind the
only empty chair in the room. Obviously, with only a simple turn, it serves its
occupant access to both computer and desk. The screen saver is flowing the
same types of gobs Gibby remembers being mesmerized by as a child with
his mother's lava lamp. Watching it is making him a little sick to his stomach.

The smell of fish seems to permeate the whole room. It isn't long before it's source draws attention to his eye. It's from an open container on
the desk with what looks like dried strips of octopus. The sound from the
kitchen can be heard through the closed door. The clunk, clunk sound
of the big pizza knife used to segment the round disks into pie- shaped
pieces. He detects a male voice speaking Chinese, then another seemingly
answering the first.

The door suddenly opens. It's Tommy. He's carrying a pizza box. With
just a couple of steps in the cramped quarters, he sits down behind the
desk placing the pizza box on top of the cluttered surface. In a dramatic
way, he sits back with his elbows resting on the arms of his chair with his
fingers locked, making the shape of a pistol and pointing to the pizza box.

"Open it." His voice is all business. He's giving Gibby a deadpan look waiting for him to respond.

Gibby pauses as he surveys the situation. He finally succumbs and reaches for the box. Opening it he finds two envelopes.

"Open that one first," points Tommy, still with fingers locked and still pointing in the pistol position.

Opening the envelope, he finds what looks like a flight plan and a key ring with several keys.

Gibby looks at Tommy as though waiting for the next step.

"Now open the other," points Tommy to the second envelope.

Without comment Gibby opens the second envelope. It's full of cash. Gibby remains silent, first looking in the one hand at the flight plan along with the keys, and in the other, a wad of cash.

Tommy broke the silence. "There's $25,000. Finish the job without a hitch, and another 25K will be waiting."

The adrenalin is pouring into Gibby as he begins to quiver slightly. This is exactly what he has been waiting for.

"Now listen to me carefully," continues Tommy. This is the most stern voice Gibby has heard from him. "You don't need to know what your cargo consists of but in the event you need to abort, I want you to follow this procedure. You will find your cargo on the passenger seat of the chopper. You will notice there is a cord attached to the package. The other end is secured to the helicopter rail. All you will need to do is, open the passenger side door and push the package out. When it reaches the full length of the cord, it will break the package open and the contents will be lost to the wind."

"How will I know if I need to abort," asks Gibby apprehensively.

"You'll know," says Tommy with a strained chuckle.

"That doesn't sound so good," mutters Gibby with that same nervous chuckle.

Seeing the apprehension growing in Gibby, Tommy readily adds, "If you follow the flight plan you should have no problems." Then adding a grin and reassuring wink. "Unlike last time you won't be blindfolded, you'll find directions to the hanger along with your flight plan."

Gibby is listening while at the same time sorts through the papers.

"It says here in the first paragraph to 'dump the sign'. What sign?"

When you leave here you will notice a pizza deli sign stuck on top of your truck. You're going to get an address and a pizza to deliver. If you're being tailed by anyone this should be enough to make 'em forget it. Then follow the instructions on how to get out to the hanger.

The first part of the instructions leave Gibby with a sense of accomplishment. The pizza has been delivered. Now for the trip to the hanger. It involves about a seven-mile ride out in the boonies. He soon finds himself turning down a long, private driveway where he meets a locked gate. Sorting through the keys, he unlocks the barrier, re-locking it behind him, then proceeds down the two-track trail. Another mile through a twisting narrow road, with alpines skirting both' sides, leads him to the clearing he had previously been to once before but then only under the cloak of darkness.

The only structure present is the hanger. Sorting again through keys, he unlocks the door and snaps on the light. Setting majestically in the middle of the floor is, the now familiar, Robinson R22 helicopter. An aging Toyota pickup is parked in its front. Its plain purpose is to haul this big dragon out of its lair.

It takes him about ten minutes to quickly pull the chopper out, lock his truck, and place the Toyota back in the hanger. He then climbs into the cockpit and starts the engine.

In the accompanying front, bucket seat, is a large, but tightly-wrapped package. Gibby gives it a curious little push. Whatever it is, it weighs about

100 pounds. As previously informed it has a twenty-foot cord attached to it. The other end is secured to the outside frame. In the case he needs to rid himself of this cargo, all he needs to do is open the door and push it out. Taking a moment, he inspects the setup, assuring himself it will do the job it;s designed to do.

Once in the air, he flies over the Cascade Mountains. These precipices were formed eons ago by the Earth's plates slamming into one under the other, and then being attacked by a couple ice ages leaving thousands of mountain lakes sprinkled among these alpines like so many cast off blue diamonds. His adrenaline begins to rise as he reaches 1,000 feet. His mind is focused on the next land mark. At this point, he's merely flying over, and then around some of these foot hills. The familiar sound of the rotating blades gives him a welcomed sense of community with his craft. It's only when he's in the air like this, unreachable and free, that he experiences this high level of contentment. The smooth sound of this high-tech engine and the familiar THUP THUP, of the rotators, is to him, the living heart beat, giving life to a normally, inanimate machine.

He is also professionally aware of the task at hand. He has work to do. Being aware that he has a fuel range of 250 miles. This flight is ninety to its objective, and ninety miles back, leaving little room for getting lost.

Reviewing his flight plan, he spots the Thompson River. This is obviously, a rough and remote area, devoid of any roadways, save an occasional two-track logging trail. He is to follow it until he comes to a cabin with the Canadian maple leaf designed into its roof. Spotting it after an hour in the air , he checks his watch. It places him right on time.

Making a landing in an open field next to the cabin on a landing pad well marked with the traditional white cross. A bearded man in a red flannel shirt and red suspenders appears carrying a gym bag. Behind him is a younger man, also somewhat disheveled, carrying a rifle slung over his shoulder, and pushing a wheel barrow. The bearded man has a noticeable limp as though something in life struck him hard. For all intents and purposes they have the appearance of being the average Canadian mountain men, or possibly again, run of the mill hunting and fishing guides.

Gibby's instructions are not to shut the engine down, but only to exchange the package for the gym bag. The switch is made with no fanfare or conversation, only a few hand gestures are made.

As Gibby lifts off, he sees the wheel barrow making its way to, what appears to be, an old-style, wooden inboard Chriscraft boat setting on the river's edge.

Swinging around for the return trip, he feels relief to be rid of his cargo. The hour it takes gives him the time to think. Dillon's idea for him to ask their father for his inheritance has again captured his thoughts.

Like many of the ranch horses that run free when the tight bit is taken out of their mouths, Gibby too has a yearning to run free, to rid himself of some of the seeming oppressive discipline forced on him by his family.

His thoughts have forced the time to fly by, soon seeing the familiar land marks of Vancouver. Still in the air over the hanger, he spots the familiar black Escalade parked near the entrance. Before he can exit the landed craft, Tommy is already making his way to meet him. Grabbing the duffel bag, he tosses it to Tommy, figuring that's what's on his mind. He catches it, unzips it exposing its contents. Gibby has suspected it to be cash. His suspicion holds true. It's more cash than he has ever seen in one place, $100 bills all neatly wrapped and stacked. It's a beautiful sight to Tommy, he begins to grin, handing Gibby another envelope.

"Any problems," asks Tommy.

"Nope. Quick and clean," assures Gibby.

"Good," says Tommy.

"Got any more work for me," laughs Gibby examining the envelope. It contains the other $25,000. His appetite for this kind of action is truly whetted.

"Oh ya, don't worry we'll have more work. Just give me back all those keys and I'll lock up."

Gibby removes his truck from the hanger, placing the helicopter back, and leaves $50,000 richer.

CHAPTER 8

THE NIGHTS ARE DARK

"The younger son said to his father 'give me my share of the property.' So he divided his property between them." Luke 15:11

Sunday morning arrives with some fanfare. It's the beginning of the Advent season. As is the Geiberson tradition, they are preparing to attend a small country Anglican church some fifteen miles north.

Gibby and Dillon probably would not bother with this tradition if it were left to them. Knowing how important this is to their parents, they individually ready themselves in bedrooms adjacent to one another. They do not speak.

"I don't know what's getting into these boys. They've always had some rivalry, but it's getting worse these days," says Norbert shaking his head.

"I've noticed the same thing. They don't have a kind word for one another," says Joanie running a brush through her hair.

Norbert has chosen to love his family unconditionally, in spite of its short comings. The last thing he doesn't want to happen, is that he stop loving them because of their behavior. This morning in particular, he prays for even a stronger commitment to continue to have patience with his family. Watching his wife of twenty five years fuss with what dress she's going to wear, he realizes yet again, she is still the love of his life. She possess a demeanor of which he has never tired. Both sons are now stuffed into suits, looking like some kind of captured prey. He can only smile to himself, satisfied that a life worth living, is one that is met right where it is.

The service soon ends and the Geibersons head back home for Joanie's favorite part of the day. It's where her family sets down for a meal together.

She soon she is busy in her kitchen. Like many mothers, she is of the opinion that a good meal can be therapeutic. A pot roast with potatoes, carrots, gravy and the last of a bushel of apples that's been transformed into a strudel. The food is thoroughly enjoyed and proves to be the glue that keeps the boys in their chair. They are readily communicative with both their parents, but it does not go unnoticed that they are yet ignoring one another. As fathers and mothers do, they ponder over things like this. Not having a solution for this problem, both decide to let it pass for the moment.

Just as dinner ends, the door bell rings. Dillon is nearest. Opening the door, he is startled to find April standing directly in front of him. His attention to her cannot be ignored as an involuntary rush of excitement overtakes his mind and body.

An uncomfortable moment passes as he stands speechless staring at everything about her that he finds attractive. Her shapeliness, her statuesque posture, her red hair twisted into braids reaching her shoulders. She quietly breaks the silence.

"Hi Dillon, is Gibby home," asks April in her soulful voice.

Moving past Dillon as he does, Gibby answers with a, "Ya I'm here."

"Can I talk to you," she asks. Her eyes reveal something is wrong.

Trying not to notice his mother's glance he quickly moves April back through the door closing it behind him.

"Whats sup April" Gibby questions her with a grin. She seems a bit more anxious than he is used to seeing her.

"Let's go for a ride" she says turning towards her Jeep.

Not sure what her strange behavior is indicating, he follows her.

She drives them down the lane toward the cabin, not sure what she is going to say or do. Arriving, she pulls in and stops, leaving the motor running. She slowly and purposely turns toward a still wondering Gibby.

"I'm pregnant," she announces letting the words shoot out like they were pent up projectiles. These words hit Gibby like a brick bat.

"You're what? Did you say pregnant?"

April is nodding her head as the tears are now flowing like torrents down her face giving her a disconsolate and forlorn expression. The green light from her instrument panel is refracting a sickly glow off her wet face, further adding to her loss of dignity.

"Are you sure?" Gibby's face and voice contain a hopeful uncertainty.

Still sobbing she responds only with a little nod. She is hopefully looking to Gibby for some kind of answer or support or, as yet, some unknown relief, as she continues to wipe her tear-stained cheeks.

What started out to be a full dry handkerchief has turned into a small wet ball as she continues to roll it between her eyes and nose. Trying as she may, she can't find a dry spot.

Both of them share a moment of contrition. What had originally been thought of as the moment "destiny" had brought them together, now is seen as a stupid lapse in judgment. It is the same lapse in judgment that has brought kingdoms, throughout history, to their knees.

Gibby's thoughts quickly perceive himself to be the victim. His thoughts are *"If she hadn't purposely stalked me, I wouldn't be in this mess. I now I'm screwed."*

April knows she has played an active role in her pursuit of Gibby. Inasmuch as she once was able to bring to surface his romantic inclination, now she hoping that she can do the same with his inclinations to become a responsible, adult male.

From Gibby's body language, this latter inclination is quickly dissolving.

"Please Gibby, please don't hate me," pleads April. Her guilt is obvious, and at least for now, she is seemingly giving Gibby a pass in this whole fiasco.

Gibby isn't ready to answer. He sits motionless, looking out the passenger's side window. Willing to accept the "blame" pass he's getting, he's more than willing to let April bear the responsibility. Finally opening his mouth long enough to say, "I don't have a clue about this. I don't know what you want me to do."

Without waiting for her to answer, "I could drive you into Vancouver if you want to have an abortion."

This is not the compassion April is hoping for. What she remembered of Gibby was when he met dicey situations where most would run, he would stand and fight. This is the strength she hoped to see form her childhood friend. Now he's giving every indication that he's choosing not to stand and fight. In this emotional upheaval, both of them seem to be at the total command of whatever dominate emotion makes its way into their thinking. The distance between what she had hoped from Gibby, and the reality he is giving her, is proportionately and exactly the degree of her resentment for him. She has gone from fear, to resentment, to anger in a flash.

Recognizing she is getting no support from him, she gives one last pernicious smile and starts her engine. She doesn't look, or speak to him all the way back to the main house. With unyielding emotions draining her, April feels nothing now, just emptiness. By the minute, she is taking on a hardened and self-devoted front that does not include Gibby.

She drops him at the door of the main house. She continues her silence looking straight ahead as Gibby, also laconically, dispatches the vehicle.

Standing alone in the driveway, not wanting to answer any questions his family may impose, he turns makes his way to the machine shop. After unlocking the door, he heads for a small tool box which he unlocks. Taking out a bag of marijuana along with rolling papers and a half-full fifth of Canadian Club. In quiet desperation, he takes a pull on the fifth and begins to roll a joint. Before long, he is leaving the world, with all its tensions and problems. He slowly drifts into a self-induced euphoria. Soon, he's passing out on a pile of old discarded horse blankets. For someone trying to escape the world through drugs and alcohol, the grim certainty is that the fantasy soon turns into a hate-filled reality that relentlessly preys on the person, allowing the effects of the poison to destroy its victim. And destroy it does, sooner or later.

"Wake up you, son of a bitch," screams Dillon. Using both hands, he's lifting Gibby by the lapels of his jacket, shaking him violently.

He's in a dead sleep as he's jostled awake by the stings of hard slaps across his bare face.

"Wake up you little bastard," shouts Dillon as he continues slapping first one way and then the other across the face of a semiconscious Gibby.

With the residue of the drugs still in his system, he resists being fully awakened. His head is snapping under fist-driven blows, first in one direction then the other. His involuntary reactions kick in with his arms flailing like an automaton, at the same time, he continues struggling with consciousness. Once Gibby has come to enough to begin to ward off Dillon's advances, Dillon takes his rage to another level. He begins to increase his closed- fist assault on, the still defenseless, brother.

"You wreck everything you ever touch, you goddamn, rotten bastard!! Now you've wrecked the most beautiful thing on this ranch!!!"

Dillon's fists are bleeding, as he continues to beat his brother back into a state of unconsciousness.

"Stop! Stop! Stop now!" comes the uninitiated imperative from his father. Norbert is wrapping his arms around,the still swinging arms of, his eldest son. "What in the name of God and all that's holy are you doing?" implores Norbert of Dillon.

"I warned you Dad! You should have thrown his sorry ass out of here a long time ago!" shouts a defiant Dillon, still trying to get at his, now unconscious, brother. Gibby's face is a pulverized mass of blood and swelling. With himself between his sons, Norbert turns his attention to Gibby, letting Dillon storm off in another direction.

It seems that Dillon had gotten word from one of Jed's buckaroos, "Rumor has it ole Gibby has knocked up Jed's daughter." Dillon didn't wait to have it verified, but remembering April's visit the night before, and how despondent she sounded was enough for him. His hate for his erring brother became unbearable. Rage soon possessed him. Gibby had spoiled the purest being that Dillon has ever imagined. Dillon has placed April in the same category as the Virgin Mother of Jesus. Someone to be held in the highest esteem, never to be sexually spoiled. With this mindset, its amazing Gibby is still alive.

Norbert calls out to several of the buckaroos now gathering around.

"Give me a hand here boys. Help me get him back to the house."

It's obvious that Norbert is shaken to his core. Nothing like this has ever happened in his life time, brother turning on brother in such a violent and destructive way. A ranch hand has quickly filled Norbert in on what has provoked Dillon. Nothing stays private for long in such a small community.

"What in heaven's name has happened!" Joanie stands with her hand over her mouth as the men carry the listless body of her youngest son. No one is giving her an answer. Instead Norbert barks a command.

"Get a pan of hot water and soap!"

Obeying, Joanie immediately brings a dripping pan of water, a bar of soap, and some towels.

"What happened Norbert? Did a horse kick him?" Joanie is not getting answers, her hysteria is increasing. "Norbert, I demand an answer."

"I'll tell you in a bit, right now lets work on getting him cleaned up." Not wanting to discuss this private family matter in front of the men, Norbert thanks them and at the same time dismisses them. He then barks another command "Get Rob Roy in here!"

Heart broken, he hesitates to lay this family catastrophe at the feet of the mother of the perpetrator. His thoughts are jumbled "I'd rather have my tongue torn out than have to tell Joanie about this." He wishes he could carry the entire burden of sorrow without their mother having to be innocently drawn into this kind of filial carnage. While continuing to wash Gibby's wounds, Norbert, nonetheless, tries to unravel as much as he has heard to Joanie.

"It seems April is pregnant. Supposedly Gibby is responsible. April had told her parents about her condition. They in turn, promised not to make an issue of it until she had talked to Gibby. She came home last night distraught after talking with him. Evidently one of the ranch hands overheard the conversation, and by morning, it had spread around the ranch. Dillon got wind of it and went ballistic."

Rob Roy is quickly found and brought to the main house. He's the closest thing the ranch has to a medical doctor. He's the ranch's resident veterinarian. He's attended every kind of cut, broken bone, concussion, even planter warts that this ranch has ever encountered. Within minutes, he's pulling the last stitch through Gibby's shredded lip.

Turning to Norbert and Joanie, he says assuring, "Other than looking like he's been run over by a stampede, he'll heal up pretty fast. Most of these bruises hurt worse than he'll like, and he'll have a couple of shiners.

All in all, he's taken quite a beating, fortunately nothing is life threatening." With that Norbert thanks him, and Roy makes his way out the door.

By now, Gibby is ready to get up and move around. Walking to a mirror, he examines his wounds. His mother is right behind. Under her breath she is muttering, "I knew that girl was going to be trouble, I just knew it."

Being only heard by Gibby, he pathetically looks to his mother for an ally and sympathy. It begins to flow from her like lava.

Having heard the outcome of April's scandalous pronouncement on Gibby, Jed and Karen by now have made their way into the Geiberson house. They have gone through a gauntlet of emotions since their daughter revealed to them the cause behind her strange flu like symptoms. One look at them tells the story.

Not sure where he's going to land in all this, Gibby retreats to his room.

Norbert, meantime, motions Jed, Karen and Joanie into his office, closing the door behind them. Both Karen and Joanie are trying not to catch the others gaze as they search for a chair that doesn't force an unwanted confrontation.

"Is what I'm hearing true that your daughter is pregnant and that my son Gibby is the father?" asks Norbert.

"Short of a paternity test, I'll have to say that I believe my daughter when she tells me she hasn't been with anyone else. So my answer is, yes it's true," says Jed, with an air of reluctance. His sad expression, along with his thick, drooping mustache, adds to an already comportment of forlornness.

Once this question is finalized, and taking Norbert a moment to digest its reality, he then motions for Jed and Karen to take a seat. He in turn, sits where he's most comfortable, behind his massive, worn, hand carved desk. Beginning to look a bit worn himself, he takes a moment to search his mind for insights.

Norbert begins. "I want to believe my son will be the man I believe him to be. I've always held out, that in all of his horse shit, there has to be a pony somewhere. But in the event he doesn't, I want to assure you as grandparents of this child, we will support your family in anyway we can to see this thing through to its' rightful end."

Jed and Karen look at one another with a look of relief. They had both hoped Norbert and Joanie would share their desire that April chooses to go full term. Now they feel they can rely on an ally to help them with whatever the future holds.

Sympathetic hugs and a promise to co-operate are exchanged. These parents know there is going to be some trying times for both families. Norbert can not envision a perfect world. He is much aware that to wish this is to want no world at all. On the other hand, a close attainable facsimile in this world, at least in his estimation, is to be ready for reconciliation and give forgiveness.

With Jed's and Karen's departing, the attention turns once again on Gibby. He has heedfully made his way back down stairs.

"Dad can I talk to you alone for a few minutes?" asks Gibby through a obvious swollen mouth.

"Certainly" says Norbert, motioning Gibby back into his office. He can't help but look with sympathy on his son. This, however, does not negate his fatherly responsibility to hold his son accountable, especially in this latest fiasco with the Landers family.

Gibby slumps down in a big leather chair. Norbert forgoes his desk chair for one placed more intimately with his son.

Gibby sits for a moment staring at the floor. Norbert is patient, bending his look directly at Gibby, waiting for him to begin.

"Dad I know this business with April has got everyone turned in every direction. I know everyone is looking in my corner, but right now I just can't come out. I've got to have some time to figure this all out."

Pause.

"Dad I've got to get out of here. Dillon is making it impossible for me to stay," laments Gibby. He's visibly shaking as tears begin to streak his tanned, swollen, doleful, face.

Stunned to his core, Norbert swallows hard. He envisions his family hanging precariously by a thin thread. His sense of powerlessness overwhelms him, as he tries to form words that won't form.

"Where would you go? What would you do?" replies Norbert. There's a distinct heaviness in his voice.

"You know I've been spending my weekends in Vancouver lately. What I've been doing is flying some charters for people. They have a helicopter and I've been busy carrying fisherman and hunters up north," lies Gibby.

Norbert's world is collapsing down around him. All of his hopes for his sons seem to be disintegrating. It's as though The Six Horsemen are galloping at a breakneck pace directly toward his family. Gibby definitely has his father's attention.

"What I would like is to have my inheritance."

Norbert's heart is breaking under the weight of such a foreign request. It's like taking punches without a defense. *"But then, how does one plan for this"*, is Norbert's second thought.

"What in the world would you do with it," says Norbert as calmly as he can.

"I've been thinking, I'd like to start my own charter service with my own helicopter."

Gibby managed to get the words out as he glances out of the corner of his eye for his fathers response. Looking directly at his father is too embarrassing.

Norbert would rather take any kind of beating than see his family fall apart. Pulling himself together he thoughtfully states, "Gibby you know you can depend on your mother and I to support you with any reasonable request. What we are particularly concerned with is, regardless of where this relationship with April may go, we hope that the two of you will consider the two sets of grandparents in this mix. I guess what I'm asking is that neither of you choose abortion. Gibby lifts himself from his chair, leaving Norbert with the implied idea that he won't pursue the abortion way.

Gibby's request is giving Norbert something to think about, and Norbert's request is giving Gibby things to consider. Heading straight for his bedroom, he opens his window and lights a joint. He's got a lot to try and forget about as he watches the smoke drift out into the darkened loneliness of his world. After leaving Gibby, Norbert heads out to find Dillon. He finds him busying himself in his office.

"I wondered how long it would be before you made your way over here," says Dillon plunking himself down in a chair behind his desk. Dillon's intuition tells him that the intense way his father is entering, that any vindication he may come up, with will not, in his fathers eyes, justify his actions.

"In the name of God Dillon, what prompted this insanity?"

Dillon has been his father's son for twenty four years, and in all that time, he has never seen his father this intense. He feels a wave of fear coming over himself as he stumbles for the right words and the right tone of voice to justify his actions. In the presence of his father's concern for the good intentions of his sons, he feels even more so, the contrast between himself and his father. He's left wanting.

"I know what he did to April and I just lost it!" He knows this is a weak reason to present to his father. What he won't reveal is an even weaker reason, that he is secretly in love with April and that he beat Gibby in an 'out of control' jealous rage.

His explanation, as predicted, burdens Norbert. This has gone way beyond normal sibling rivalry. The want of righteous principle in Dillon's reaction toward his brother, has thoroughly stretched his father's mental energy.

"You almost killed your brother. What's behind this Dillon?" Norbert feels strongly that Dillon is not leveling with him.

Dillon understands his father's penchant for truth better than anyone. He feels himself being closed in on. He quickly attempts to throw this hound onto another scent.

"He's a thief, dad. He stole a bunch of scrap and sold it without letting me know."

Hoping to appeal to his righteous indignation, he continues, "You know I've always hated a thief. When I confronted him, he lied. I don't like a liar any better."

Norbert is disheartened by the bitterness flowing from his oldest son. What hurts even worse is that this hate is directed at an equally loved son. Not satisfied with any explanation that Dillon has given him, he begs him to search his heart. His intention is to not alienate either son, but rather bring them to their senses.

On the other hand it is becoming apparent that Dillon has set his teeth in ridding the ranch of his brother. As for his request that he "search his heart," he is taking a perverse satisfaction in hardening it. The evening is especially difficult for Norbert and Joanie as they review the day.

"I'm having a hard time with Gibby's request for his inheritance. He's unwavering in his insistence that Dillon's behavior is driving him out."

"I don't doubt Dillon's behavior is a great contributor, yet after all is said and done, I wonder how much of it has to do with April?" says Joanie. She's sitting up in a bed unable to make any clear sense of her questions.

Iinلا

"I don't know. I don't think I'm getting straight answers from either of our boys. I think their both telling us what they believe we'll buy."

Norbert embraces his wife. It's as much for his comfort as for hers. They said the "Our Father" together and begin to drift to sleep. The nights are dark this time of year.

CHAPTER 9

THE MOVE TO VANCOUVER

"So the father agreed to divide the wealth between his sons. The younger son took his inheritance and went to a far away land." Luke 12:13.

It's the next morning. Dillon is up and in his office before the rest of the family has awakened. It's as much an avoidance issue as it is his way of dealing with stress. On the other hand, he's far from being finished with Gibby.

Norbert is facing Gibby at breakfast. It's awkward at best. Gibby's face is a gruesome reminder that no one need pinch themselves for the reality of this scene. Looking back at his father through two blackened eyes and swollen lips, there is nothing daunting his resolve to give up his, even more persistent, effort to leave the ranch.

"Dad you didn't answer me yesterday about giving me my inheritance. Can we talk about it today?"

Norbert has given himself a day to resign himself to this new reality. *"It's hardly enough time for so many life changing decisions,"* is his thought.

"I have Gibby. Your mother and I discussed it. We aren't opposed to it, but I'd like to see a business plan."

"Dad you know I'm not like Dillon. I can't plan my whole life out the way he does. I'm asking you to trust me to do it my way."

Norbert doesn't need his son to point out the differences between himself and his brother. What is distressing him is that he hadn't prepared himself for this day. Loosing both his sons, although in different ways, is like loosing two vital organs.

His prayer is that this is only a set back in a bigger picture, that his sons will come to their senses and return to their values as a family, where there is an ultimate concern for the welfare of one another.

None the less, the genuineness of his youngest sons request haunts him. It seems surreal. Norbert is an abundantly wealthy man, not only in material goods, but also spiritual principles. Both of these riches are willingly shared, not only with his family, but as well with any number of hired hands over the years. There isn't a person in the region who would not describe Norbert as a generous man.

Knowing he can't hold his sons to values they have not yet embraced, he relents.

"OK Gibby, if you're sure this is what you want," says Norbert calmly, and cautiously. To Norbert, this decision is short on good logic and long on patience. Hoping for Gibby's success, is certainly not a prevention against him failing.

"Thanks dad, I know this is not the way you like to do things, but it's something I have to do," says Gibby trying to find some honor in his selfish request.

It's not that Norbert is missing the self-serving nature, possessing both of his sons, but its that he's wise enough to realize they will have to experience life's failures themselves. At this point, the dollar cost is irrelevant to Norbert. His thought is, the quicker his son comes to the failed end that his request is destined to bring, the better.

"How much do you figure you'll need for this venture of yours?"

Norbert patiently mulls over his sons wild idea, hoping he will be able to reconcile going along with them. As remiss as Gibby is to come up with a business plan, Norbert calculated for the type of helicopter he needs, along with a hanger and an unforeseen cushion for incidental business expenses, they settled $1.5 million.

A sense of security, whether real or imagined, that so often accompanies a privileged life, is now making it's way into his thoughts. Within days, Gibby has moved from the stability of his father's house into, what he perceives as a security offered in, an upscale condo in Vancouver.

The problems that had formed in his life from living on the ranch are soon distancing themselves from his consciousness. He has chosen to ignore April, being content in letting her pregnancy remain her problem. He's also fully embracing his liberation from, both, a doting father, and a bullying brother. He's becoming quite confident in his abilities to manage his own life. For Gibby, truth and reality have become nothing more than what he fantasizes *to be* truth and reality. His own subjective conceit has altogether besieged him. In this same period he has established himself as a "player." He is noticed for his high-rolling life style. Eventually resulting, with a girl who works as a stripper in a local strip club, moving in with him.

He has traded his signature Dodge Ram pickup truck for a new silver B.M.W. He's become quite the rambler. Money, booze, cocaine flow like water with this prodigal.

In the ensuing weeks the Chinese underworld is also taking notice. His reputation as a dependable and capable drug runner is supplying him with enough work to more than support his life style.

The purchase of his own helicopter is finalized. The special ordered Robinson R44 Clipper has arrived. It's a beautiful blue, capable of 200 knots and possesses the maneuverability of a cat. Everything someone in his trade needs.

The pot growers in British Columbia have discovered that the remoteness of the many slopes and valleys are ideal for growing their crop. Consequently, there are tons of pot that needs moving. A local boy like Gibby, who knows how to fly in these hidden areas, is soon in demand by every pot grower in the region.

Much of what had been picked up by the quad runners and snowmobiles, can now, with a skilled helicopter pilot, be picked up in the field, and within a couple hours be on the street.

Even in this short period of time, Gibby's piloting skills have become legendary. His claim to fame has become his ingenuity in landing in less than helicopter friendly areas, and in addition, which also goes without saying, avoiding the provincial police.

Money is never the main issue as he takes more and more risks. The more exotic the challenge, the more he finds himself drawn to do it. Gibby is plunging into each new adventure like any adrenaline junky worth his salt.

Christmas and New Years have passed. Gibby has avoided any family contact since he left home. Nonetheless, back on the ranch Gibby's escapades have not gone unnoticed. According to Dillon, Norbert and Joanie have opted to "bury their heads in the sand." Dillon, on the other hand, has been vigilant in his efforts to find out exactly what his brother is up to. His resentments continue to run long and deep. He not only wants to undermine anything Gibby may be doing, he wants him destroyed.

April has opted to go full term and keep her child, much to the relief and liking of both sets of grandparents. Also, and certainly not least, she is holding on to the hope that she and Gibby will find their way back into each others lives.

Dillon looks on April's growing belly with disgust. His resentment toward her and Gibby continue to grow. She's damaged goods. He avoids her, and when he can't, he doesn't acknowledge her. This is fine with April, as she finds him weird and at times even scary.

By any outside observer Gibby's life is envied. Internally his life is not that pleasant. His efforts to discard his life on the ranch, and his obstinate refusal to maintain any connection with his family is beginning to catch up to him. It's presenting itself in the form of depression. He's hoping his new stripper girl friend is the distraction that he needs to pull himself out of this funk.

Gibby isn't exactly sure how old she is, although, she claims to be twenty five. Her name is Rachael Vanderhoff. She originally came from a small Dutch community on the west shore of Michigan. Rejecting her strict Calvinistic upbringing, she left for Hollywood hoping to make her fortune as a model. Like many before her, having the looks, but not the savvy to survive that industry, she eventually found herself depending on men who promised to advance her dreams, only to find herself being used, and then quickly discarded.

Eventually finding her way to Vancouver, she has these days become skilled at turning the tables. She is no longer allowing herself to be preyed on, but has become the predator. Along the way, she has had some good teachers.

Rachael promoted herself to be Gibby's girl friend and suggests to him that she move in with him. She does this, not because of his cavalier attraction, but because of a vulnerability she sees in him.

He, in turn, is convinced that he has captured a trophy. She dotes over him and gives him the impression she is willing to put up with and live in the shadow of his exploits. To Gibby, it's a dream come true.

Before she moved in, Gibby had installed a large safe in the basement of his condo. He had it cemented into the wall behind a locked door, making it, for practical purposes, impenetrable and immovable. The only access is through an electronic state-of-the-art combination. It's the only interior door within the condo that remains locked.

"Whadda ya got behind the door Gibby, another girl?" teases Rachael "Worse, I got snakes," he teases back.

Knowing no one locks doors if there is no valuables, she is willing to wait as a spider waits, until its victim is hopelessly tangled. She is confident that she will soon know it's secret.

Rachael does not lack in physical attributes. She is strikingly beautiful, casting a perfectly poised shadow across each male she encounters. What average physical attributes she may have had, she has had enhanced by the best plastic surgeons a boyfriend's money can buy.

It didn't take her long to learn that men are basically simple creatures. The only thing required is there egos be constantly stroked, a full belly and empty balls. She has become a specialist at fulfilling these requirements.

The amenities that have come from living with Gibby has prompted her to give up the strip club for the time being. Now she can focus all her time and energies on gaining Gibby's trust.

"Gibby, honey you look tired," she says running a red -polished finger nail down his chest. "Why don't you let me give you a massage."

Placing him on the bed, she straddles him as she mischievously tugs on his shirt.

Laying out the lines of cocaine, they take turns snorting through a shared straw. Her long, slender fingers are soon massaging areas of his body he would find difficult to say "no" to as they float into a phantom world that to them, has no beginning nor end. The world is not hesitating to give him all it has to offer. It's always ready to up the ante with new and more exciting distractions, always pretending to be his friend and lover. The distractions are designed to divorce one from ones past.

For Gibby, it's to help him forget April, the ranch, his parents. To accomplish this, his highs need to be higher, and his thirst for adrenaline rushes becomes more intense. But then his lows are also reaching new valleys. Lately it's taking more and more to pull him from his funk.

"Thank God my phones ringing." It's a day later and Gibby's uneasiness has made him a prey to boredom.

"Tommy here, how you doin?"

"Doin' is about what I'm doin'. So what sup?"

"Got a big one if you're interested," chuckles Tommy.

"Oh ya, how big?" questions Gibby. Gibby's "how big?" question has more to do with the challenge than the money.

"We'll discuss it later. Meet me at my cousin's." Aware of phone surveillance techniques authorities are able to use,Tommy avoids all, but clipped conversations.

When Tommy says "meet me at my cousin's" Gibby knows he means the pizzeria.

Immediately, Gibby slips into what, he now refers to as his, "doin' business" out fit. He's traded his jean jacket, off the shelf boots, and straw-style western hat, for custom made western boots, black leather pants, long 'stage coach' styled black leather coat, and a black leather hand crafted western hat. In his pocket he carries a pistol, it's rarely away from his side. It's a .380, small, but deadly.

He's no longer the kid from the backwoods who can fly a helicopter. He's gained the respect and confidence it takes in this business to be in high demand.

Sauntering into the pizzeria, he takes his usual seat as a waitress brings him his usual, an ice tea with two shots of Jack Daniels. Doing what he does,and doing it well, the underworld treats him like a rock star.

"So whadda ya got for me?" asks Gibby. He lights a cigarette, takes a long drag before exhaling. His cool factor is high.

"There is a client who wants 75 kilos of coke delivered out east," informs Tommy.

"How far for how much?"

"Saginaw, Michigan for $200,000."

Gibby pauses for about thirty seconds. The last message he wants to convey is that his adrenaline just pumped enough to blow the average man's head off. Quickly, he turns his excitement into the appearance of annoyance.

"You want me to fly across the border and another 2,000 miles with a cargo, that if I'm caught will, at minimum, cost me a 1 million plane and twenty years of my life. Are you nuts? You tell them I'll do it for $600,000 plus $100,000 for expenses and that's a bargain considering what it's going to take to deliver."

"Let me make a call. You know I can't make these decisions," says an uneasy Tommy as he leaves the table and exits the front door.

Gibby can see him through the window negotiating. If they only knew, he'd do the job for a dollar. "God, I hope I haven't pushed too hard," he thinks. Although, he knows he has probably royally pissed off the Chinese gangsters. He is also much aware that money is the only language that gives one respect in their world. If they only knew that his need to live on the edge of life, and his addiction to adrenaline, that would be enough for them to play him the fool. He has played them to their edge. Now he must deliver.

The world these men create for themselves is where they are most at home. Their lives are full-featured films that each personally creates, produces and directs. In order for them to live, they must deliver an Oscar every time.

Soon Tommy is back.

"They think you're getting to be a greedy bastard. They'll OK the deal for $600,000 but no expenses and you'll only get $150,000 up front and the rest on delivery. I think you pissed the client off," chuckles Tommy sporting his signature grin.

"Yah I 'spose I have, but then I've been pissin' people off my entire life, so what's new with that," says Gibby sarcastically. He smiles to himself, confident he's pulled another one off.

"Ya OK. Gibby, pissin' these guys off is one thing, but getting pissed on is another. So what do you want me to tell them?" says a reluctant Tommy.

Flippantly twirling his cigarette lighter around in his fingers, Gibby finally responds. "You tell them they got a deal."

Gibby has smuggled million's worth of drugs throughout Canada. He has crossed the boarder into the United States only a few times, but each time he crosses requires two crossings, once over, then once back. Each time exacts quick, precise decisions, along with nerves of steel.

"There is no room for shouldas," admits Gibby.

After he meets with his Chinese clients, the particulars are left up to him. He knows this job is a big deal. It's one, that under no circumstances, can ever be screwed up. This is a multimillion dollar deal that is going to make him or break him, enhance his life, or possibly, even end it.

"Tommy I know these guys are cousins of yours. I'm going to need extra hands I can trust. I'm willing to bring you in for $100,000 if you'll work with me."

Gibby is straight forward. He knows Tommy has done successful smuggling into California. There's no question in his mind that Tommy is mentally capable.

Sitting across from Gibby with a blank stare is Tommy. Obviously, Gibby trusts Tommy's abilities, but Tommy is wondering how much of a risk this rising star could pose. He has never worked with Gibby "on the road" so to speak.

"You're right. Gibby. The Triad is made up of all relatives, and it's true

I do work for them, but they don't own me. I contract outside as long as it doesn't cause a family conflict. All though working where it conflicts with their work could suddenly make me, a non-relative."

Tommy snickers a nervous laugh, then adding, "But back to your offer. I'll say if the deal makes sense, and we can work together, I'll do it but not for $100,000. I want half and I want Mooch as part of the deal."

For the period of time Gibby has known Tommy, he has heard Mooch talk only a couple of times. He's decidedly more than just another cousin, he's Tommy's most trusted confidant.

"I got no problem with half. As far as Mooch goes, he's on your payroll," says Gibby clearly and as straight forward as any wise guy would negotiate.

Tommy agrees with a hand shake. "Somethin' else I gotta get settled with you before we get started. You ain't as clean as you think you are," says Tommy with a rather hard stare.

Gibby nervously lights up another cigarette, taking a deep drag, "What the hell is that supposed to mean?"

"You know we've got people down town. It seems your name has come up as a person of interest. Someone they are being advised to pay extra attention to, especially your comings and goings."

Gibby nervously takes in another drag, looking puzzled, to say the least.

"It means you've pissed somebody off and they're trying to get even," continues Tommy with his stare continuing to search Gibby for any undisclosed hazards.

"What the hell could these bastards possibly have on me?" questions Gibby clearly agitated. This mystery is making him extremely uncomfortable.

"It's my understanding from one source, that they really don't have anything concrete. Usually the way this shit goes down is, you'll be put on the back burner until you screw up and get noticed," says Tommy with the air of one who's been there, done that, and got the t-shirt.

With not much relief in Tommy's effort to put him at ease, Gibby shouts back, "I sure as hell hope your right."

"Yah, well in this business you're always going to have enemies. If you're going to survive you have to be offensive. It's necessary 'to do unto them' before they 'can do unto you'," says Tommy with the same practical air, taking poetic license with the Golden Rule.

Confident this problem will be worked out soon, Tommy agrees to begin to work out the details for their new alliance. Much, of which, is being done in the backseat of the Escalade. Mooch's job, among other things, is to drive.

Part of being a driver is noticing who's noticing you. He has begun to notice a particular car more often. It's a white, late model Ford. It has recently been in the vicinity of them too often to be ignored. Finally being in a position to get a license plate number, and after giving their information to their informant, it comes back as that belonging to a private investigator. Mooch waits until he and Tommy are alone, he then informs Tommy of this unsettling development.

"Whenever Gibby is with us, this guy shows up, so I had him checked out. He's a Private Dick named Bartrum Bayliss. What I found out, is that he's a high-rent guy that works for high rollers. They say he's got a good reputation for getting the job done." Mooch pauses for a moment with more than an ordinary pensive glare, then adds, " I don't think we should take this guy too lightly."

"Thanks, Mooch. As usual, you've done damn good," says, as yet, a mystified Tommy. Nonetheless, getting even a small picture of the enemy is more reassuring than none at all.

The next morning Tommy decides, as a precaution, to change some of his methods of operation. Before leaving the parking garage, he has Mooch survey the neighborhood. While waiting for an all clear, he makes arrangements with Gibby to meet him at the public library, giving him some odd instructions.

"I want you to come in through the library front door and quickly leave by the back door. I will be waiting for you directly in front of that back door. I'll be in a blue Ford van with hockey stickers covering the windows. Get in the open sliding door as fast as you can."

Always ready for an adventure Gibby makes his way to the library. Following Tommy's instructions to the letter, he's in the front door and out the back door, entering the waiting van in record time.

This task completed, and hopefully leaving this "Dick" with his dick in his hand, they leave undetected.

"Gibby, you got any idea who you pissed off enough to hire a private detective to follow you around?" asks the other voice in the backseat.

"There's no way I could possibly know that Tommy. This is your turf, I'm just a new kid on the block," says a heedful Gibby.

The last thing a guy like Gibby would fain to happen, is to be out maneuvered by an unknown adversary, and not know why.

Tommy brings his finger down tapping on his cell phone. "Before we go any further we have to find out what this dude is up to."

In a matter of a minute he's on his cell phone talking Chinese. Gibby can hear the voice of the person on the other end also talking in Chinese. The language always sounds to him as though everyone has a sense of urgency.

Completing his call, Tommy turns to Gibby with an earnest perspective.

"We're going to get to the bottom of this." His eyes stare straight ahead as though he already sees the end result.

Sensing they're unrestricted, and with deep resolve to end this uninvited threat, Gibby is happy to be on the side he's on.

"Who's we?" questions Gibby.

"We have family who have special skills."

Gibby has learned that the old Chinese man they met when he and Pete first came to Vancouver is not only the grandfather to Tommy and Mooch, he is also the oldest of this family of smugglers.

Their legacy goes back several generations into China when the black market supplied the peasantry with goods and services. For various reasons intrinsic to the communist government, they alone could never supply all their people needed to survive. The only slogan they have incorporated from the "Mao period" into their way of life still prevails; "power grows through the barrel of a gun".

Meanwhile, Mooch has circled around in front of the library. As expected, the white Ford is parked with out an occupant.

Tommy motions for Mooch to park the van in a spot where they can keep an eye on the Ford. Within a few minutes an unassuming middle-age man, wearing a sweat shirt and baseball cap, exits the library. He appears to be somewhat frustrated. Continuing to glance around, he casually walks by Gibby's car as though convincing himself his prey has not left, but is only alluding him. He finally returns to the white Ford, seeming content to wait for his mark to reappear.

Turning to Gibby, Tommy asks, "You recognize this dude?"

Shaking his head from side to side, "I've never seen him before in my life."

Confident before tomorrow they'll have the answer, Tommy motions for Mooch to drive on.

CHAPTER 10

IS THAT YOU GIBBY...
"Still a long way off." Luke 15: 20

Back at the ranch life goes on. It's neither hidden, nor surprising, that Norbert's thoughts often turn toward his younger son. The suffering he and Joanie have endured since that rift between their sons, is immeasurable.

Norbert finds himself unconsciously looking out the kitchen window, down a long the two track that leads out to the highway. "I sure hope that boy is OK," he can be heard saying.

"I think we should go into Vancouver and bring him home," says Joanie in a despairing, motherly voice. Her eyes fill with tears whenever she thinks of her youngest son.

"I know how you feel, Joanie. I'd like nothing more than to see that boy coming down this driveway." Norbert pauses long enough to let his words create their impact, still staring out the window he adds, "We can't force him home. It's going to have to be his idea." As a father he has committed his life to continue to love his sons, even when they reject it.

Dillon enters the room in time to hear his parents lament over his brothers absence.

"Why the hell don't you just make a shrine to that asshole. I'm surprised I don't hear you praying to 'St. Gibby'," blurts out Dillon. Adding yet, more pain to his parents loss by his selfish arrogance.

It's obvious to Norbert that his eldest son is loosing himself to his bitterness.

"Dillon please, I've lost one son to wantonness, I don't want to lose another to vengefulness," pleads his father

"Dad, I don't think you and mother get it. I'm 100 percent dedicated to this ranch. When I see the two of you fawning over someone who can drain the money right out of all my work, I get upset. Unless you can show me I'm wrong, I figure I've got a right to feel the way I do," shouts Dillon, slamming his fist into the door jam as he stomps out.

Norbert sees his older son burying himself in self righteousness. He is opting to step back, as he has with Gibby's unrighteousness, and let each find their bottom.

Dillon continues bullying his way through his office shouting at everyone he perceives to be in his way. Seeing April working horses in the corral brings out another wave of hatred toward his brother. "*That bastard ravaged her like an uncivilized heathen. He should have known how I felt about her. Now he's ruined her. I'll never forgive him.*"

To him the world is to be graded. Who better to grade it than him. His family has failed, April has failed. He is convinced his vision is the best of all worlds, if only the world, and the people in it would just stay put.

"What a terrible waste of time and energy," says Norbert, reviewing Dillon's behavior. He and Joanie are trying to find a foothold where they can begin to restore a relationship with Dillon.

"Maybe we haven't given Dillon his due," says his mother apologetically. "Maybe we've been so consumed with Gibby's behavior that we've neglected him."

Norbert acknowledges that he heard her, but remains deep in thought. Joanie has grown used to this habit of Norbert's and is willing to give him a pass.

After a few minutes of quiet reflection, Norbert suddenly leans forward in his chair, as though he has had an epiphany.

"You may be right about how Dillon may feel, but I'm not so sure that his feeling reflects the facts. Dillon has always liked his ducks in a row. When they're not, he gets insecure and takes it out on Gibby."

"You're probably right, Norbert. I guess I just miss those days when the boys were little. I could hold them in my arms and rock them to wellness. Now they seem so far out of reach."

Joanie sighs a sigh of reluctant acceptance,and soon begins her daily routine.

Norbert continues to watch out that kitchen window. He can almost see his boys, arm and arm, making their way up that long road back home.

"April I wish you would not climb on your horse," says her mother somewhat apprehensively.

"Mother, just because I'm pregnant doesn't mean I have to stop living," replies April, just short of scolding her mother for her uninvited intervention.

Karen, watching her only child, remembers her own sense of independence when she was pregnant, and how an overwhelming restlessness also compelled her to do foolhardy things.

"April, I'm not trying to interfere with what you consider 'normal activities', but stop and think, do you actually believe that a five-month pregnant woman should be riding a horse," interrupts her mother.

For good or for bad, her mother continues a reluctant defense of her "mother knows best", inch by inch, until she has her way.

"Alright, all right mother, you win." Throwing the saddle to the stable floor. Her frustration with life is coming out sideways as she bursts into tears.

"Honey, I know you feel overwhelmed at times, but you,re going to have a beautiful baby. Things will change for the better, just you wait and see," says Karen stroking her daughter's hair, holding her close. Tears,are also coming to her own eyes, as she senses her own powerlessness to make her daughter's life okay.

Breaking loose from her mother's, near death grip, April blurts out, "I need to go for a ride,"

Tilting her head back, she gives her daughter a squint, "I thought we just settled that."

"Oh I don't mean on a horse, I'll take my Jeep," assures April, wiping the tears and her running nose on the wrist portion of her red and black-checkered flannel shirt.

It's a cold February day, but to April it feels good to be outside. Turning the key in the ignition, the Jeep bursts to life. Feeling a sense of freedom, she waves to her mother, leaving her standing by the horse barn.

"Don't worry, mom, I'll be back soon," she yells out through her open window.

She slips in her favorite CD and begins to sing along. Whether it is a conscious or unconscious decision, she soon finds herself on the road to the cabin. Pulling into the opening like driveway, she shuts off the engine and lets out a deep sigh.

She's been here many, many times. She has always felt it to be her place, a place where she can think and be calm. It's a place she doesn't want to ruin by having her good memories of it turn bitter.

Purposely walking past the cabin, she feels drawn to the lake. The path is still snow covered, but not as much as fills the thick growth of alpines. Making her way through the snow, she tries to bring back to life the perfect evening she had had only a few months ago with just her and Gibby.

She remembers that even as children, she liked being with Gibby. Her feeling is that of all people involved in Gibby's life, she knows him best. Knowing the real Gibby Geiberson, she tries to reassure herself that it will not be like him to stay away too long.

"I just know you'll be back," she finds herself saying to, as yet, an absent Gibby. This reassuring hope gives her comfort.

It's beginning to get dark as she looks out over the frozen snow covered lake. The alpines contrasting against the snow give the world a black and white appearance. Looking at her watch she realizes it's only 5:30 pm. There is something foreboding about early darkness, but along with it can also come, a quiet comfort.

Making her way back up the path to the cabin, she enters, going directly to where she remembers leaving a lantern. In a minute the light is on. In another moment, she ignites a fire in the stone fireplace.

Between the lantern and the flickering of the fire, she recalls the last time she was in here. The smell of the wood burning only serves to tease memories of her and Gibby. One voice tries to convince her that what they may have had was, at best, just pretend. *"You're the one who wanted to play pretend. You're the one who cleaned this little cabin all the time pretending you and Gibby lived her."* The other voice says, *"It was not pretend. It was real. It's as real as sunshine, as moonlight, as new, and as pure as that first, fresh snowfall."* Her thoughts assure her once again that Gibby will be back. *"After all when we held one another didn't we delve deep into each others soul, didn't we sense a oneness between us."*

The cabin has warmed up. It's quiet except for the crackling of the burning wood. Occasionally the beams above snap and creak as they expand when the heat hits them. The warm, yellow glow of raw fire cast a cloak of serenity around the room.

April looks at herself in her oversized, flannel shirt, brogan boots, her hair pulled back and tucked under a bright, red stocking cap. She gives herself a little titter. *"Good grief, I look like some kind of a poor, pathetic immigrant just getting off the boat."*

April has been lost in her day dreaming, failing to hear the vehicle coming down the lane. The door suddenly opens startling her. *"Gibby?"* she utters almost inaudibly. That question had not been thought out, rather it burst from some thinly, veiled hope.

"Oh my gosh you startled me." Grasping her chest with both hands, she stares at the figure standing in the door way. The orange light flickering off his face gives him the appearance of a much younger man. It seems to have smoothed the weathered creases of fatherhood.

"I thought I'd find you here," says a much relieved Jed.

That illusory arrival of Gibby has left her with a renewed sense of loneliness. Her whole body is still quivering as she gives out a sigh.

Making his way next to her on the couch, Jed runs his hand across the fabric as though he is caressing an old friend.

"This is the same couch your mom and I had in our first house."

"Yes, I know, mom told me that when I pulled it out of the shed." April is tentative. She's wondering what her father has in mind to bring him out looking for her.

"Your mother thought you'd be here" says her father with a knowing smile.

"She sent you out to hunt me down?" asks April.

Being familiar with his daughters sense of independence he picks his words with caution. Pausing for a second he continues his thought.

"Moms worry, you know."

"Ya, I know," says April trying to sound flippant.

Jed continues to look at his daughter with a gaze that suggest he's struggling for words. "Do you?" he asks.

"Do I what?"

"Worry", repeats her father.

"Sometimes," states April as a matter of fact, somewhat validating her own emerging motherhood.

April perceives her father's difficulty. She's willing to leave him with it. She's fears if she cracks the door of communication too far, he'll barge in. There is still that three-year- old-inner child declaring, "I can do it myself, daddy."

Over the years Jed has found that unsolicited council will often lead to a defensive counselee. He sits quiet for a moment, staring down at his hands, lost for words.

April breaks the silence.

"Daddy, I really appreciate you driving way out here, but I think I want to stay here for the night. I need to have a little uncluttered time alone."

Her father continues to be quiet. His first thought is to tell his daughter to quit being silly and get in her Jeep and follow him back to the ranch.

As his second thought emerges, he finds himself saying "Well, if you're going to insist, and it sounds like you are, I want you to take my rifle."

"OK daddy, if it will make you feel better," she says trying to sound sarcastic. Secretly she's actually relieved as the nights often brings mountain lions, bears and an assortment of other predators. Jed soon returns from a quick trip to his truck with a fully loaded 30.30 Winchester.

Giving her father an assuring hug she thanks him, "I hope you and mom understand that I'm grateful for everything your doing for me." Pausing for a moment she adds, "I just need some time to think things out."

Heading back to his truck, Jed returns, sticking his head in with one last fatherly thought, "Use your cell phone if you need anything."

"Scout's honor," promises April holding up two fingers. "I love you, daddy" along with the thought *"More than you'll ever know"*.

With that Jed heads back toward the ranch. He's not looking forward to coming home alone. Its going to be a long night with Karen.

Soon April cannot hear her father's truck any longer. It's been less than five minutes since the cabin was alive with the cadence of father and daughter conversation. Now it's conspicuously quiet.

Never really thinking of herself as glamorous anyway, this physical change hasn't really been the dramatic melodrama it could be. Sitting cross-legged on that old, worn out couch spreading her fingers across her belly, she stares at her protruding bulge. It reminds her of a Buddha. She wonders to herself if her mother, while sitting on that same couch twenty-two years before, looked at her protruding belly when she was pregnant with her, also had the same thoughts.

The temperature is is quickly dropping and as the cold mixes with the moisture in the air it begins to create a frost on the windows. She comforts her self by placing another log on the fire. The next challenge is to curl up and get comfortable. Unanticipated, she feels a distinct protestation from her prodigy, a kick in the ribs, then a kick to the back. She has opted not to know the gender of this seeming cage fighter, but does from time to time refer to "it" as a 'tough little buckaroo'.

Searching through her hand bag for something to satisfy her hunger, she comes up with two power bars, a small bag of sunflower seeds and a liter of bottled water. Deciding on half tonight and half tomorrow she washes down the first half with a slug of the bottled water.

Morning comes soon enough. It's time to leave, but not before she kicks enough snow aside out side the cabin door to squat down and relieve a bladder that her 'little buckaroo' has been laying on all night. The cold wind hits her bare butt cheeks making her all the more glad to get back in the warmth of the cabin.

Tiding up the cabin a bit, putting out the fire, taking the last bite of her morning ration of power bar and sunflower seeds, she slurps down the last of the bottled water, then hops in her Jeep and heads back to the ranch.

As expected her mother is silent. April ushers herself to the refrigerator, pours herself a glass of milk and sips it while, watching her mother try her best to act as though she's going to ignore her daughter, continuing her task of impulsively wiping off every table and counter in the kitchen.

"Sorry," says April taking another sip.

"Oh it's OK. I guess."

April can detect the pout in her mother's voice. Still nervously sipping she finds herself saying, "I had to see how I do alone."

"What! Now where are you going?" Her mother's pout quickly turns to a near panic.

"Nowhere now, but someday. You and daddy don't want me here forever do you?"

She gives her mother a little whimsical grin hoping to disarm the howitzer of anger and frustration her mother has aimed at her.

If eyes alone were a gun, Karen's are cocked and spring loaded in the pissed off position.

"All night I sat up worrying with all these questions. What happens if she goes into labor? What happens if she has that baby out there alone in that shack? What happens if she falls or is attacked by God knows what?"

Karen's frustration finally peaks as she blurts out her final epitaph, " I hope someday you have a kid just like you!"

"Ma, you just did it."

"Did what April?" shouts out Karen defensively, throwing down her dishrag.

"You just gave your grandchild the curse." April deadpanned her mother for a moment then broke into a grin.

"April what are you talking about?" Karen finally caught the jest of the curse. Since Adam and Eve and their sons Cain and Able, seemingly parents have been passing on the curse. It's usually done with exasperation. "I hope some day you have a kid just like you!"

The irony of it all hit them at the same time. They both begin to laugh and cry, they hug each other and cry, then laugh and hug and cry some more.

"Oh baby, I hope we can get through this together," says Karen dabbing her eye with her dish rag, then dabbing April's.

"Ma, get that dirty thing away from me," says April swatting good naturedly at her mother.

CHAPTER 11

DON'T MESS WITH THE TRIAD

The Vancouver Chinese Triad is made up of several families who have married in order to promote mutual interests. It's created a brotherhood that positions itself with differing levels of competence that one could find in any well-run corporation. There are those available and trained to address any problem that may pop up.

The problem that posed itself yesterday, as to who is interested in Gibby's coming and goings, is being addressed today. Tommy's cousin Randy Chang is head of the Triad's surveillance unit. The fact that he is also working for a large corporation as a software salesman does not present a problem. Family business can always be worked in.

Randy and the surveillance boys are now tailing Bayliss. The hunter has become the hunted.

By phone, Gibby has just been instructed to leave his condo then drive to a parking garage across town. As expected the white Ford begins to tail him. Following orders, he drives to the top of the parking garage, parks his car and exits it.

The white Ford also parks. The short, stocky man, still wearing a sweatshirt and baseball cap, exits hurriedly.

Suddenly from nowhere, a car with markings on the sides saying "security" pulls in front of Bayliss. He's quietly and quickly grabbed by two men, and forced into the backseat. Less than five seconds have elapsed leaving Gibby the only witness to this whole affair.

Bayliss is quickly hand cuffed with a black bag immediately placed over his head, but not before forcing a piece of duct tape across his mouth.

His sense of fear cannot be mistaken as it's physically and verbally expressed through his jerking, wriggling and as the muffled sounds force their way back through the black hood.

No one is speaking to him. It's all silent except for the noise from this four wheeled trammel carrying him to where God only seems to know.

Bayliss served as a detective for the Canadian Mounted Police long enough for a retirement. Still relatively young and healthy, he took a position as head of security with a large Canadian corporation. He soon grew tired of that. Longing for intrigue, he found that his former position allowed him to breach many different corporate security systems. These, he found provided him access to closely held corporate secrets. He in turn found selling them to the highest bidder, a lucrative endeavor.

In his own way, he shares much with Gibby. Even though money, and lots of it, is his only demand, the thrill, the intrigue of the case is what he seeks.

On the other hand, this predicament is more than he had bargained for. There is no thrill in being captured and rendered powerless. That thrill has now been transferred to his captors.

He soon resigns himself to that fact. Shifting into a survival mode, he begins to recall his early training in survival tactics; listen for street sounds, for smell, even bumps in the road, anything that will help tell him where he may be.

The ride is less than fifteen minutes. Abruptly the street sounds end.

The sounds of an electric motor closing a garage door behind him brings him to the realization that things are about to change.

His car door flies open, a voiceless hand jerks him stumbling from the back seat. He is being half pushed, half dragged down a long flight of stairs with the bag still over his head. Coming to, what he assumes to be the bottom of the stairs, he is dragged across the floor and slammed down, face up on what feels like a narrow bench. His hands are still cuffed behind his back, but now something else is going on. Straps of some sort are being strung and tightened across his knees and chest. The hood and piece of duct tape covering his mouth is left in place with an additional material that feels like a wet rag now covering his nose.

Without a single word being spoken he feels the sensation of water into his nose, quickly running down his neck and behind his head. Still not able to see his tormenters and the hood soaking wet. Gasping for air, panic completely takes him.

"My God, they're drowning me!" Comes his panicked thought. He has no defense against this finality of himself drowning. He panics even further when his manacled hands prove to be useless. The silence is broken by a voice. Not a normal voice but one disguised – a mechanical voice. It's a voice spoken through a device used by those without a larynx. It asks a question.

"Mr. Bayliss do I have your attention?" the tape is removed from his mouth as he begins to cough to the point of regurgitation.

"Yes, yes," gasps the panicked dupe.

"Good," comes back the monotone of the machine, "because I am going to ask the following questions only once. Who are you presently working for?"

"I'm working for several clients, which one do you mean?"

Again Bayliss is gasping and gagging as the deluge hits his throat blocking any chance of air to his lungs.

The contents of his stomach are soon mixing with the water entering his airways causing him to struggle, yet even, harder against this indefatigable predicament.

Coughing and gasping for air, the fear that he is indeed drowning is real, but, at least for the moment, he can breath nearly normal once again.

"Think hard ,Mr. Bayliss," returns the monotone voice once again, "When I ask a question of you, do not answer me with a question of your own. It's a simple question, maybe you should answer as directly as it's asked."

Bayliss is frantically trying to recall the question. His thoughts are racing, *"What did he ask, what did he ask?"* *"Oh yes,"* suddenly remembering the question *"who am I presently working for?"*

"I'm working for a Mr. John Sawyer in Vancouver and a Mr. Dillon Geiberson from the Circle G. Ranch. And a Mr. Julius Poullion from Seattle, Washington," answers a cautious Bayliss.

How long have you worked for Mr. Geiberson?"

"At least a week," says Bayliss, a tiny bit more relaxed for not having an immediate recrimination for his unacceptable responses.

In less than a second the water is coming heavier in what seems like an eternity.

This time Bayliss lost consciousness and had to be resuscitated. After regaining his breathing, he's questioned again by the mechanical voice.

"You're a hard learner, Mr. Bayliss. If you recall I didn't ask you for an approximation of your employment with Mr. Geiberson. I'm sure you can give me the exact answer I asked of you."

Taking a moment to think and not sure whether this may be his last moments, Bayliss, in a hoarse voice compromised by his stomach acid bathing his larynx, discloses, "He signed a contract with me last Wednesday."

"Thank you Mr. Bayliss. I see we're on the same page once again."

Knowing better than to feel relieved Bayliss guardedly waits for what may come next.

"What exactly did Mr. Geiberson employ you to do?"

"He wants me to find out what his brother does with his time and who he does it with."

"What exactly have you discovered?"

"I discovered that he has a live-in girlfriend who's a stripper. That he spends a lot of money. That he has a expensive helicopter that he paid cash for, and he has Chinese friends."

Again the mechanized voice penetrates the small room, "Of all the information that you've uncovered what is the most pertinent to Mr. Geiberson?"

"I believe he'll want to know about his Chinese friends."

Bayliss is violating every rule of client confidentiality, but when reality comes between living and dying, his client quickly takes second place.

"Who do you believe these Chinese friends to be?" continues the disembodied medium.

Bayliss wishes,for the first time in his career, that he hadn't been so damn thorough.

"I believe them to be part of the Chinese Triad operating here in Vancouver," divulges Bayliss beginning to shake. His fear has completely over taken him.

"That is a astute observation Mr. Bayliss, but now we have to become pragmatic. From my position you are posing a threat. I don't sleep well with an unresolved threat.

My first thought, of course, is to just eliminate you, and the threat disappears. What do you think of my first thought Mr. Bayliss?"

Bayliss is shaking uncontrollably. He has already lost control of his bowels and bladder.

"I'm begging you to let me live," whimpers Bayliss.

"Do you have a family Mr. Bayliss?"

"Yes I do?"

"How many in your family?"

"Including myself, five."

"That's truthful Mr. Bayliss. As I have already mentioned, my first thought is usually my best and the one I have come to rely on, but I'm going to give you a break, and one break only.

"I want you to listen to me carefully. I want you to have no contact what so ever with Dillon Geiberson or his brother. That means no phone calls, no emails- nothing. You will return whatever amount of money he has paid you, with no explanation. If you see him coming in your direction, I am strongly suggesting you run the other way. Now if you should break any of these stipulations, one of the five members in your family will disappear, then another and another. Do you understand me so far, Mr. Bayliss?"

In a barely audible voice Bayliss whimpers, "Yes sir,I understand."

"I see your capable of making wise decisions Mr. Bayliss so I'm giving you one more to ponder. If the thought should cross your mind that you have a civic obligation to report this incident to the authorities, then once again, one by one your family will disappear. Are we clear Mr. Bayliss," pauses the baleful voice.

"Yes, yes sir," sighs Bayliss.

"The tone of your voice leaves me somewhat unconvinced."

"Yes sir, I understand," shouts Bayliss mustering up all the strength he can push through vocal cords that are barely hanging together.

Just as suddenly, the straps are released from his knees and chest, although, he remains handcuffed and hooded. Wet and stinking, he is led back up the stairs, put back into a car and driven back to the location where he was abducted. The car comes to a halt, the handcuffs are removed and he is shoved out an open door onto the pavement.

Still hooded, he lay motionless unable to decide what this means. Having heard the car speed off, he finally embolden himself to remove the hood.

He finds himself laying alongside his own vehicle. A man with a concerned look is making his way across the parking ramp.

"Are you okay, mister?" shouts the excited good Samaritan, halting in his tracks as he gets a whiff of what is beginning to look and smell like it could be the last stages of incontinence.

The last thing Bayliss wants or needs is a curious spectator. "Thank you sir, I'll be fine," says Bayliss waving him back. Finally able to fish his car key from his soiled clothing, he's in his car putting as much distance as he can between himself and this horrific mortification.

Two days later Dillon receives a large manila envelope from Day Star Detective Agency. Hurriedly opening, expecting an update on Gibby, he is surprised to find his contract and check returned with the wording, "canceled due to illness."

Standing near a window in his office, contemplating his next move he allows himself to be distracted by the persistence of a red-tailed hawk being out maneuvered by a wily flicker.

His intuition tells him there is something enigmatic about this whole affair with Bayliss. Bayliss had assured him that he was capable of any challenge and had the credentials to back it up. Now out of the blue he sends back a $5,000 retainer and feigns some nebulous illness. All in less than a week. Puzzled by it all ,he continues watching the hawk until it finally snatches the fatigued prey.

Not about to be dissuaded, he tosses the envelope on his desk and grabs the Vancouver phone directory, opens it to the Yellow Pages, running his finger down the page, he stops abruptly then punches the number into his cell phone.

"Hello, Cobra Detective Agency. My name is Dillon Geiberson. I'd like to make an appointment with one of your associates.

CHAPTER 12

A ROAD TRIP PLANNED

The three young men had little in common six months ago, but now are sharing a growing trust.

"What did your cousins find out about that asshole following me?" asks Gibby.

Tommy contemplates the question for the moment, rolling his cigarette around in his fingers. He finally comes back with a question of his own. "What do you know about a 'Dillon Geiberson'?"

Taken back, Gibby ponders this question. *"I can't believe Dillon is behind this,"* is Gibby's first thought *"but then I'm not too surprised that he is,"* becomes his second thought. He has mixed feeling of sadness and animosity.

His eyes meet Tommy's. "He's my brother," says Gibby trying to conceal his embarrassment.

"What the hell is he doing? Trying to play some kind of joke on you," says Tommy, "he's the one who hired that bastard."

"My brother doesn't joke. That's one thing I can say for sure about him." says a reluctant Gibby.

Feeling desperate about this new dramatic turn, Gibby ventures to get it dismissed.

"Tommy, forget about my brother. He's a horse's ass. We've got a lot of work to do."

"Yah, right Gibby, I'll do that as soon as you tell my why your brother should be forgettable." Tommy is purposely squinting at Gibby, nervously juggling his keys.

"What do you want to know?" Gibby is resigning himself to the fact that this new development cannot go away without some explanation.

"I want to know why he makes you nervous, because when I see you nervous, I get nervous," says Tommy.

There are certain things Gibby would just as soon not have Tommy know about his family, this being one of them.

"Be sure of this Tommy, my brother could care less about you, it's me he's nosy about," says Gibby. He's purposely trying to down play his brother's sudden concern about the Triad.

Gibby can hear his heart beating. This whole conversation is becoming confrontational.

In spite of his brothers undaunted contempt for him, he still feels a need to protect his family. The last thing in the world he wants to see, is his parents hurt any more than he is already hurting them. Fate is moving in on this meeting. This time it seems to be on Gibby's side.

The dingy coffee shop where they are meeting is in a different neighborhood. It's a Vietnamese neighborhood. They watch out the window as an old Vietnamese woman pulls her small, two-wheeled shopping cart through a slushy sidewalk.

Gibby, seizing the opportunity to turn everyone's nervousness in another direction, says "The only thing I'm nervous about right now is why you want to meet in this neighborhood. I thought the Vietnamese don't like you Chinese."

"They don't," says Tommy. "It's just the way we let them know who's boss." Pausing for a moment not letting Gibby's ploy change the subject he continues, "You need to do something with your brother." Tommy continues to look Gibby square in the eye.

Gibby's mind is searching for a precautionary way of explaining his brother and their relationship. The last thing he wants is unnecessary suspicion in the direction of his family.

"My brother gets carried away sometimes in his big brother role. Really, it's nothing to worry about," says Gibby trying to chuckle.

Still keeping his gaze on Gibby and making one last point, Tommy says, "Gibby, my family will take care of this only once."

As usual, Mooch sits with nothing to say, but is far from not being busy. He continues a vigilant watch for anything appearing out of the ordinary. He never carries a gun rather preferring numb-chucks. The butt ends are apparent under his coat.

The air being somewhat cleared of this "Dillon" problem for the time being, they are soon absorbed in their plans. So absorbed they fail to notice the coffee shop is beginning to assemble a group of young Vietnamese men. By the time Mooch can respond four males making their presence known by standing in a menacing position, circle their table.

Mooch responds by opening his coat, positioning himself to get up fast if need be. His expressionless hard glare serves as a warning, strongly suggesting that they really don't want him to get up.

The ringleader is a young Vietnamese man in his early twenties, slight of build, sporting a military haircut, accompanied with a weak looking beard. His tattoos indicate he is a gang banger. With arms crossed, he defiantly holds his ground, returning his own challenging glare.

Tommy slowly and purposely stands up and walks boldly toward the ringleader, he says something in Chinese. The Vietnamese gangsters look at one another, then without comment they turn and leave.

"What the hell did you say that made them leave like that?"

"I mentioned my grandfather. They know they are here only because he allows them."

Shaking his head in disbelief, Gibby confesses, "Your family never ceases to amaze me. Is there any place in Vancouver they don't have eyes and ears?"

Tommy, in an unaffected manner, shrugs his shoulders and gives Gibby his little grin, replies, "Not too many."

The "dark" side of life is after all, the normal way for those who have spent all their life in its shadows.

The preservation of the family's way of life is at the cost of getting rid of any outsider who may be a threat. Allegiance to the family is not debated nor questioned. It's a normal expectation. Ridding the family of any real or perceived threat is, therefore, considered an honorable pursuit.

On the other hand, Gibby's family is a cause for confusion with these Chinese. His brother Dillon's intent to destroy his younger brother, is viewed as, highly dysfunctional. Tommy finds it difficult to connect with any family member who does not respect its own members. This dynamic only tends to increase Tommy's concern. Engaging in any activity with one who arises out of such family mayhem could be risky. But like the young in any culture, he is willing to compromise a staid and true value for the expedience of the moment.

Once the Vietnamese gang has left, they're back to business. The challenge is to get 200 pounds of cocaine from Vancouver to Saginaw, Michigan. Their challenge is going to be to move this amount of drug quickly and with minimal risk.

As usual, Gibby's exuberance overcomes a multitude of doubts. His mind is in high gear as he takes the lead.

"You and Mooch trailer snowmobiles across the border. You guys could be the typical vacationers going into the States for a winter snowmobile event. Once there you will then drive east to the small border town of Night Hawk. On arrival, you will unload the snow machines, and be prepared to move. With G.P.S. I'll get you to where I need to meet you. I'll be arriving by helicopter with your 100 pounds.

The decision is not to risk them carrying the cocaine through customs, but rather split the 200 pounds of cocaine with Tommy and Mooch after they cross to the U.S. side of the border leaving Gibby on the Canadian side. Gibby has a spot in mind to make the drop. It's a remote location on the border along the Okanagen River.

"I've flown over this area before and made a drop. It's remote and has an area that's clear enough to land."

The expectation is that he can repeat the maneuver. The principle part behind splitting the dope is that it reduces the risk of losing it all in the event of some kind of law enforcement intervention.

Tommy and Mooch have been together since birth. Their fathers are brothers, although these two are cousins, they have been raised as close as any brothers. These boys have, in the family tradition, honed their smuggling skills to a level that brings honor.

Another cousin, a young lawyer, has managed to get the paper work arranged indicating that they are delivering two snow machines sold to an eBay account in Saginaw, Michigan. The paperwork is skillfully prepared along with the proper permits to cross the border.

Gibby has also been busy. He's made arrangements with a Triad-owned upholstery shop to build snow mobile seats matching the make of the two snow machines as well as the helicopter passanger seats. Instead of using ordinary seat forming materials, the inside will be formed of cocaine. It's an ingenious process. Even an outside layer of Caspian chili pepper is used to surround the cocaine to discourage any chance of a drug-sniffing dog's ability to sense its true contents. He has quickly caught on to the idea that a successful smuggler is one who pays attention to details. He also needs a flight plan and a purpose for the flight. This decoy has to be convincing enough to avoid suspicion. This must be the kind of decoy that cannot easily be penetrated, enabling only the most highly trained to uncloak the deception.

Since his cargo is also concealed in the five passengers seats, he needs a false cargo that will draw attention only to itself.. The purpose for his flight is worked out. Ostensibly, he will be delivering a bogus cargo of sensitive computer equipment to an address in Saginaw.

Rachael has been with Gibby for more than a month. Despite her rather sordid past she nonetheless possess many of the same ordinary wants and needs as other women, building what can be described as a "nest" in Gibby's condo. The plain spartan appearance of his "man cave" has been transformed into, now what Gibby describes as, some place a gay guy might live.

She has wreaths on the walls of grape vine, and various wheat-looking plants, and little pots of dried weeds by doors. She has not removed his black leather chair and ottoman, but has added chairs with floral patterns and area rugs with an art deco theme.

Rachael is a girlie girl. She has girly things that Gibby has never seen before and she is much aware of the feminine power she has over Gibby, especially in her ability to manipulate him.

In spite of his new "Rock Star" image, he in turn, hasn't had the experience to deal with such a devious woman. She generally gets what she wants.

"Gibby, you're getting ready for something big aren't you?" questions Rachael. Both her hands are on her hips giving her a rather defensive, hostile persona.

"What do you mean," comes back an undaunted Gibby, continuing to fidget with some container.

"You go away for days at a time. Leaving me practically penniless. If that weren't enough in itself, I get scared being alone," says Rachael as she wraps her arms around Gibby's neck, pressing her breasts against him.

With no noticeable defense, he's dropped what he's doing.

"Rachael, you know I won't leave you without cash." Digging around in his pocket, he pulls out a roll of paper money, handing her ten $100 dollar bills.

"Thank you Gibby, you're so kind," she says holding the money as she purses her mouth and kisses his lips.

Appearing to be content, she sits on the couch with her long, naked legs curled up under her chiffon robe, twirling a strand of her long, blond hair. All the while watching Gibby continue to fuss with supplies, she plots.

"What's all that stuff?" she asks extending a lean leg, and poking at his paraphernalia with one of her painted toes.

"It's provision I would need it if I survived a crash," says Gibby.

Seizing the opportunity, Rachael leaps off the couch, wrapping her arms around him while professing, "Don't talk like that Gibby. I don't think I could live life without you."

Laughing a little manly laugh, he grabs her, drags her to the floor and strips her of her robe.

She is an absolutely willing partner.

"I don't think you'll have to worry about that" he says. At the same time he has produced a small satin jeweler's box. Opening it, he looks directly at her. There rests a full two-carat diamond ring, letting the light from the window, dance through its cuts.

Without looking at Gibby, as though mesmerized, she reaches for the box. "Is this for me?"

"Whadda ya think, I'm gonna wear it on my big toe?" says Gibby, confidently slipping it on her finger.

Coming from somewhere, with absolutely no warning, a flash of April shoots through his mind. Quickly trying to dismiss it before this image bores its way into his conscience, he picks Rachael up, cradles her in his arms, carrying her naked body into the bedroom.

Rachael has replaced Gibby's barrack-style bedroom outfit with a luxurious oriental design. She has, in a little over sixty days, turned Gibby's bivouac into girlish interior. Her potions of lotions, trays of various shampoos, conditioners, lipsticks, hair dryers, and curling irons have overflowed the bathroom counter tops.

Each of them snort a line of cocaine, ultimately giving the drug their full permission to wrap itself around e little neuron in their body.

Playfully running her finger over his lips says, "What do you want Gibby?"

"everything you got, baby," replies Gibby, feeling the drug's effect getting stronger.

The drug induced love-making leaves both of them exhausted. They lie in silence. The drug leaves them only aware of their own person and their own high. The reality being, that there is never a perception of "the other" in drug-induced sex. It remains, as it can only be, a selfish, self-centered act.

As they begin to come down, Gibby notices Rachael's ring is continuing to play with light coming from everywhere. He picks her hand up to his lips and kisses her fingers. He can't get over how damn beautiful she is.

The learned behavior of Rachael is to play along with the different men in her life. Always giving them the impression that she cares about them. What she is beginning to have difficulty with is, as much as she tries to continue acting, is that it's becoming easier to admit to herself that Gibby becoming much easier to like. He's generous, faithful, kind, thoughtful, and making it even more difficult, he's also good looking.

She quickly tries to excuse her feelings by reminding herself that some of her other men also possessed some of these attributes. She knows herself well enough to realize, she will at some point, be moving along. For the present though, she'll enjoy this ride for a while longer.

"Whadda ya think babe, ya like the ring?" asks Gibby with a hopeful smile.

"I love it," pausing for a moment, "but what does it mean?"

"It can mean whatever we decide it means," says Gibby still smiling. He senses that both of them are a little more nervous about making too much of a commitment over all this.

Always maneuvering, she already knows where she is going with this. "I think it means we should take our relationship to another level of trust."

"Why, are you afraid I'm seeing other women?" says Gibby with a questioning look.

"No, not that kind of trust, but I do feel you're holding back a lot of what your life is about," says Rachael as she moves closer to him, placing his head on her lap. Staring up at her bare breasts he contemplates the tiny scares where she had implants. If the end result was to re-arouse him the surgeon did a good job.

He crosses both his arms and legs as an unconscious gesture of defense.

"Furthermore, what's that locked room in the basement about? You want to know what scares me when you're gone? Part of it's because I don't know what's lurking behind that damn door and it frightens me. Don't even tell me that it's snakes, that just makes it worse." She has secretly searched every conceivable hiding place for a key, but to date, has found nothing.

The sex is great, Rachael is a beautiful woman, and for now that's all Gibby wants from her. He is not yet ready to bring her into the basement of his life, nor the basement in his condo. "In due time babe, in due time."

He rolls over and began to kiss her inner thigh. In a matter of moments the subject of the basement door is no longer on either of their minds.

CHAPTER 13

ON A ROAD TRIP

It's the last weekend of February. The days begin gray and end gray, but the good news is the days are gradually getting longer. The roads are showing damage, all the result of an early thaw. The frost pushes its way upward through the asphalt, breaking it up with each rolling tire, eventually, leaving a crater behind. Tires rolling through pot holes make an unmistakable sound, more often than not, accompanied with a vulgarity or a curse.

As Gibby makes his way to his hanger, he's making mental notes of all that he needs to do. The placement of the small gym bag with a few changes of clothes, a shaving kit, along with his survival kit, but most importantly, the seats containing the cocaine are finished, have been delivered, and are ready to install.

Arriving early at his hanger, everything is morning quiet, thus amplifying his tinkering. He is making sure e aspect of his machine suits him. His movements are swift, but sure. His fuel stops are planned, the seats go in with no problem. And the weather forecast is for clear skies, warming temperatures and low wind velocity. everything is on schedule. All he needs to do is place the bogus computer along with the reupholstered snowmobile seats into the cargo hold and he's ready to fly.

Meanwhile, Tommy and Mooch are making their way to the border.

It's early in the morning as they hope to mingle in with the rush of morning commuters crossing to Seattle. They have all the paper work they need, but it's still best, not to encounter the border guards.

"So far so good," says Mooch as they have pass through the Canadian side with no problem.

"Hey Mooch," says Tommy, "you know what the guy who fell off a twenty story building said as he passed the fifth floor?"

Mooch turns and looks at his cousin with that "What the hell are you talking about" scowl.

"Hell no, what kind of stupid question is that?"

"He said 'so far, so good,'" says Tommy, sporting his usual smirk.

"Damn it, Tommy. This ain't no frickin' time for jokes," says Mooch.

The lines of cars filled with commuters are moving swiftly, working to their advantage.

In minutes they are being confronted by a border guard.

"Are you citizens of the U.S.?" The voice is firm and authoritative.

"No," says Mooch, "We're both Canadian."

"Do you have your passports?" returns the same no nonsense voice.

The guard is handed the passports and without looking up he furthers his questioning, "What's your purpose for entering the U.S," now asks the guard who looks directly at them.

"We're delivering these two snow machines to an eBay account in Saginaw, Michigan," reports Tommy in a matter of fact voice.

"Pull over to the side," orders the official pointing to a parking area with several other vehicles in various stages of inspection.

Soon there arrives a couple of new officials. One asks to see the paper work. The other is circling the trailer and S.U.V. with a drug sniffing dog.

Two Chinese men, with gang tattoos, in their early twenties, wanting to cross the boarder, sets off a couple of red flags. As much as both countries deny profiling, it is a certainty that with some people, due to race, gang affiliation, common sense prevails and consequently they are given a harder inspection. Within fifteen minutes the shake down is complete. Nothing illegal is found. The next fifteen minutes are spent in putting things back together, and they are grateful they followed Gibby's suggestion not to carry the cocaine across the border. The fees for the snowmobiles are paid and they are soon on their way.

A call is made to Gibby to let him know how their border crossing went. After hearing about drug sniffing dogs, he too is relieved that his plan didn't include the extra risk of replacing the seats before making the border crossing.

"You guys have about a six-hour drive. Get used to driving the speed limit, and for God's sake don't do anything stupid," says Gibby.

Tommy is careful not to say too much, realizing that cell phone conversations are often monitored around border crossing areas.

"Don't worry about us. Be sure and keep in contact."

As they swing onto Highway 5 heading towards 20, Tommy confidently breaks out into his special little smile he reserves for when things are going right.

"OK, Mooch let's rock and roll," giving Mooch a wink he adds, "So far, so good, ay Mooch?" Mooch gives him a blank a stare in return letting Tommy know that in spite of his efforts at humor, that he prefers to remain humorless. Nevertheless, satisfied they are all on the same page and they continue to have high hopes that this adventure can be pulled off without a hitch.

After the border incident, both agree they need to change their image. Stopping at the first shopping mall in the States they have substituted their baggy gangster pants for Cartharts and hats with ear flaps. They spend a few moments every so often, looking each other over and coming up with unflattering nicknames. "You look like the lead singer in a hillbilly band", says Mooch. "Ya, well you look like the lead man in a "C" rated porn flick," says Tommy. They shake with laughter as they come up with name after name.

Back at the hanger, Gibby continues to ready his flight. Fully fueled, he's capable of nearly 300 nautical miles. The destination point for both Gibby and Tommy is the lonely outpost and border crossing at Nighthawk, Washington.

Nighthawk has been described by some as the border crossing time forgot. It's secured at night by only a few removable traffic cones. The wild country around both sides of the border and the lack of security make it a perfect location for smugglers. Civilization has by passed many of these lonely outposts along a 4,000 mile border. Homes that were previously built for settlers, and gave promise that more families were on their way, are now all abandoned and in various stages of decomposition. The ridges are speckled with Ponderosa pines and abandoned mines, a left over from previous days of glory, when silver and tungsten ruled the area.

A few weeks ago, Gibby had made a drop in another area where two logging roads ran parallel. A fence separated the two roads. On one side of the fence is Canada, on the other, the U.S. He was able to land and throw his cargo over the fence. His contact in turn threw the money back over. Both parties were on their way in two minutes.

The size and weight of the cocaine-made snowmobile seats prevent this same kind of drop. Using a computer Gibby and Tommy discovered a satellite view of a remote area beyond Lenton Lake near Night Hawk. "Look dude, it's only yards from the Canadian/ U.S. border," said Gibby that day weeks ago, as he and Tommy began this scheme. It further indicates the area is covered with snow, posing no problems for the snow machines. They are depending on this high-tech information to be accurate.

Tommy has been driving, while Mooch reads the map. They have G.P.S. in the Escalade as well as a hand held G.P.S. but Mooch prefers a map.

"It gives me a bigger picture," he declares, defending his aversion to all this high tech "bull shit".

Tommy continues to readjust his seat. Despite of its numerous settings, he can't get comfortable. All this fidgeting with seats and G.P.S systems is making Mooch come unglued. "Dude, pull over and let me drive," says an exasperated Mooch. Tommy doesn't hesitate. The next opportunity soon becomes accessible and he is onto the shoulder of the road.

Both decide to relieve themselves behind the trailer before switching. Neither has finished when a deputy sheriff drives by. Within a second he "u turns" and pulls up behind them.

Shaking his head in obvious disbelief to what he has just witnessed he says "Could I see some identification." Both hand him their driver's license. "You boys been drinking?" is his first question.

"No sir, not at all," both say in unison. The questions keep coming. "Who's the owner of the Escalade? What are you doing in the States and where are you going?"

Soon satisfied things are in order the deputy asks the simplest of all the questions, "Do you know why I'm here?"

"Because we were pissing in the road" they both stammer over one another.

"Close," replied the officer. "but not concise enough. If you would have turned your back on the passenger side we wouldn't be having this conversation, but you gentlemen chose to incense the entire state of Washington by exposing yourselves while pissing directly into the line of vision of every man, women, and child passing by. It's called indecent exposure."

"You're right, officer, I wasn't thinking," says Tommy, punishing each of his pockets, as he jams in his hands, nervously looking for a cigarette lighter.

"I don't know what you do in Canada, but in my state you don't stick your dicks out in front of anyone. If you both can agree to that I'll cut you a break."

"Yes sir," both say together. This is exactly the foolish misadventure they cannot afford. There is absolutely no room for this kind of carelessness in this line of work.

The officer, satisfied, returns to his squad car. Both Tommy and Mooch feel a tremendous sense of ease as his car pulls back onto the road and drives off without them.

Both look at one another in disbelief. "How in the hell could we be this stupid?" It is the question that so far remains to be answered.

Tommy stares out of the window on the passenger side, as Mooch drives with a death- like stare into the eternal gray of this late February afternoon. The silence is broken only by the flapping of windshield wipers. These boys are city boys. Their notion that once in the country, the city laws go away has to be revisited. "Hey Mooch, lets keep this dumb ass move to ourselves," says Tommy, "I don't think Gibby has to hear about this."

Without answering, Mooch lets out a huge sigh, hoping he's recovered some of his lost common sense. He shuts the flapping windshield wipers off.

"I hope, to God, we got every stupid thing we're going to do, done," says Tommy still staring, but seeing nothing out of the window.

The ringing of his cellphone finally intrudes enough to bring his vision and brain into the same reality. Glancing at the number he says it is Gibby."

"How far you guys from point 'A'?" questions Gibby. Point 'A' is the code agreed for Nighthawk.

"About two hours maybe two hours and fifteen minutes," replies Tommy. Then muttering to himself, "If everything goes right."

Gibby weighs the information against his time in the air. "OK," says Gibby pulling everything out of his mind that can be perceived as litter, "From here on we need to be focused."

After a few more details are finalized and they agree to call Gibby back in an hour.

The huge Rolls Royce engine pours its energy into the rotor blades, lifting the six-seat cabin into the air. He has checked and rechecked his agenda. At this moment he feels confident, warm, excited, sanguine, ardent, fiery, wild, bold, daring, and connected.

He is oblivious to any thoughts, other than the task at hand. To contemplate anything other than success is never brought to mind. Gibby remembers something he must have heard, or made up himself. *"For those who live in fear, miscalculation will turn into hopeless and vain expectations. For those who live for fear, the hope, the trust, the contemplation, the prospect is to foresee triumph."*

Everything is subtly different in the air. It's here that safety lies in the shadow of danger. The duality of this kind of life is the order of things for Gibby Geiberson. Trusting his skills to over come fears that ultimately tame dangers, unites him as a yoke fellow, to his chosen purpose in life: to overcome trepidation but also to possess the ability to discern the fine line between foolhardiness and courage.

Gibby begins his restless quest as always, pushing man and machine to their limits. It would never occur to him to operate his helicopter at anything less than its limits. He has calculated his speed on every maneuver within a hairbreadth of flipping and crashing. He tolerates nothing less than top performance, both from himself, and his machinery. As always, he teeters on the cusp of vanity, or, merely using his God-given talents to their limits. The cautious consider him foolhardy. Those few, who, along with himself, find their life lived mostly on the edge, consider his skills quite common. All in all, he's true to himself.

As the crow flies, Gibby is only 150 miles from his target. The fluidity with which he enters and exits narrow turns between solid rock walls, only heightens his endorphin discharge. His adrenaline is producing a euphoria with which no opiate could ever hope to compete. It's during times like this, that peace and excitement overlap, in a nameless sense of, only "being".

Tommy and Mooch have traveled twice as far by land, optimistic they are within a half an hour of their destination. Contact is made between the air and ground travelers.

"We're within just a few miles of point 'A'," reports Tommy. This is the signal that they will soon be unloading their snow machines for the final rendezvous with the helicopter.

The town of Nighthawk, predictably of no consequence, now lies behind them as they make their way to Lake Lenton. Finding a spot that permits easy access to the lake, yet remote enough to work undercover, is easy enough. The plan is to race the snow machines across the frozen lake to the north end where they will find a clearing. If all goes as planned, they'll converge with the helicopter at the designate 'point A'.

This area is a not contiguous with any roads, so the chance of a border agent appearing is slim. But none the less, it's ill advised to let one's guard down. Each of these actions must be conducted with 100 percent professional proficiency. And at the same time hope that the god of thieves and smugglers is smiling on them.

"OK, Mooch, it's show time," declares Tommy leading the way to the lake. In minutes the machines are on their way, making the whining noise that distinguishes them. In the process, they kick up a plume of snow behind them, emanating raw power as they streak across the snow-packed lake .

It's late afternoon approaching dusk as they sight the helicopter. Running wide open, these snow machines will do 80 miles per hour. They soon find themselves running parallel with, what appears to be, a giant dragonfly.

The end of the lake is approaching. Tommy, in the lead, catches sight of what he discerns to be a two-track, unplowed road. Closer inspection shows it angles to the north toward their rendezvous point. A split second decision finds them plowing through the soft snow on the two track.

The whine of the snow machine begins to make a cacophonous discord with the thumping rotor blades. The two differing machines, try, as best they can, to synchronize their unique distinct sounds. This horrible symphony is tolerated by these operators only because of the significance in their arriving at the same spot at the same time.

With little fanfare these rehearsed operatives begin their work. Mooch produces a battery-operated power drill with an attached socket wrench. In less than a couple minutes he has proven his proficiency with both snow mobile seats and detached and replaced with the cocaine-filled replicas.

The next leg of their journey is to get across the mountains safely and into the Midwest plain states. Even though meandering is not the preferred travel mode for this sojourner, the mountain range offers little options. The air above for Gibby, and the road below for Tommy and Mooch, prove to be nothing like a cake walk.

Most of the mountain ranges run north and south, giving evidence to the earth's plates slamming together. Not finding valleys that run east and west, takes much of the helicopters energy, as well as for the Escalade, with their added weight of two snowmobiles and a trailer. All having to be powered over one precipice after another.

Constant snow banks lining these narrow roads, narrow them even more, reminding these travelers that there will be ascents and descents that require chains on the tires.

In spite of the boys growing up in the city, it's still a Northwest city and they learned early how to deal with winter's angry days. Although, the snow mobile trailer is enclosed, securing their cargo from the elements, a "shear" wind blowing up the mountain side, can jackknife a trailer in a heartbeat. This kind of road trip is not for the faint of heart.

Stopping and sleeping is not an option. Settling on taking turns at the wheel, while the other sleeps, has become the rule of the day.

The goal for Tommy and Mooch is to reach Manitowoc, Wisconsin and to board the ferry for the 60 miles expanse across Lake Michigan.

Gibby, meanwhile, is able to find enough fueling stations at out of the way private airfields, to complete about 1,500 miles before curling up in his sleeping bag. He's rigged a piece of plywood across the two, facing one another, cocaine-made passenger seats, creating a platform bed he can comfortably stretch out on. The night passes without incident.

The next morning Gibby is relieved to find, at least, a privy on the grounds. Along with a few more bites on a ham sub he picked up the day before, and a few slurps from his thermos of cold coffee, he's ready to meet day two. By 7 am he's airborne. Heading along the Canadian – U.S. border he steers east. The next line of business is to contact Tommy and Mooch.

"Where are you guys this morning?" asks a rested Gibby.

"We're just coming into Wisconsin on Highway 94," comes back a more lethargic voice, "We've driven nonstop since our pick up 20 hours ago with you."

"Good, you guys are right on track. Let me know when you get to the boat landing at Manitowoc."

Gibby calculates the trip across Wisconsin, plus the ferry ride across

Lake Michigan, then the trip across Michigan from Ludington to Saginaw, should be another twelve hours of travel time.

Gibby is opting to stay at this "po dunk" air strip until sometime later in the day. Pouring over his maps searching for the optimum point to cross the border he comes across a strategy that looks interesting. It's in a place called the Lake of the Wilderness on the border with northern Minnesota. It's a porous border for any kind of traffic. Much is left to the honor system. He has concluded that if he leaves in the evening after all of the first shift border workers go home, and stays below 900 feet, chances are, he'll go undetected.

Gibby has found that by drawing and redrawing his charts, he can more easily commit things to memory. It's difficult to refer to a map when a split second decision has to be made.

He knows that once safely across the border, he can travel the northern States without much problem. It's his estimation that the time and energy the U.S. puts into drug control is directed primarily toward the southern border states, leaving these areas relatively unguarded.

Gibby amuses himself by watching a pair of coyotes stalk a fox. It didn't take the coyotes long before they closed in on the fox and killed it. He finds it surprising the fox didn't at least try to live up to his name and find a way out of his dilemma. It was almost as though he knew he was done and surrendered without a fight. Gibby found himself sitting for a moment, contemplating the poor fox's demise. Definitely glad he's not the fox, he shrugs his shoulders, ready to move on.

Tommy and Mooch have made their way across Wisconsin without incident. They have finally arrived in Manitowoc. The huge car ferry named "The Badger" awaits, loading its cargo of automobiles. Originally, this behemoth of the Great Lakes was used to transport rail cars between

Michigan and Wisconsin. In recent years the rail traffic has given way to a burgeoning need for truck and automobile transport.

This monster was built in the early part of the 20th century. So far, and despite its age, it has withstood even the most severe weather. Especially this time of the year, weather patterns on the Great Lakes are unpredictable.

The purser sells them their ticket and points them to a traffic director who places them on the apron to await loading. Adding to their heightened anxiety from these unknown procedures, someone else asks them to exit their vehicle, and then leave their keys in the ignition. The reason, as explained to them, is in order to have their vehicle and trailer backed on to the boat by the professional loaders.

Being asked to leave their vehicle unattended,then and to board on the top deck, further increases their misgiving. They look at each other wordless, hoping the other will solve this dilemma.

This is the stuff that marks a professional smuggler, different from a paranoid. This trade demands the discipline to quickly discern the purpose for a succession of new events, without panicking. In this case, as they look around, men are scurrying from vehicle to vehicle with only one purpose...to load the boat.

After handing the keys to the attendant, Mooch asks, "Tommy, did you keep the key to the trailer?"

Tommy winks as he twirls the trailer key around his finger.

They soon find themselves in a large room on the main deck. The room is packed with truck drivers and other travelers. Large enough to seat 50 people comfortably.

"Think we should give Gibby a call," questions Mooch.

"Yah, if for no other reason than to find out where he is," says Tommy.

Tommy pushes Gibby's number. One ring and he can hear the familiar thumping noise of the helicopter rotor blades.

"Let me get back with you, I'm kind of busy right now. If I don't get back tonight I'll get back in the morning," assures Gibby.

As Tommy and Mooch are preparing for a night trip across Lake Michigan, Gibby is making his way into the U.S. through the Lake of the Wilderness. The area is remote, except for an Indian Reservation, and its few small villages.

In Canada, because of the lack of infrastructure, thousands of air craft, of all shapes and sizes, fill the air routes everyday. Hunters, fishermen, skiers, and commerce use air travel much more liberally than in the states.

Gibby is depending on this congestion. Also, he is depending upon lax border patrol during the day. A single, low-flying helicopter flying below radar may be heard at times but seldom is there the man power to follow up.

Just over the border lies a small airfield. It's 8 pm and dark when Gibby lunges his chopper forward. The fog is rising off from the melting ice on lake. Consequently, he's depending, mainly, on his instruments. Suddenly the fog breaks just as he reaches land. Still depending on the chart he's committed to memory, he knows that there will be the familiar green beacon marking the airport soon. Soon comes soon. He's about five miles inland when he spots the rotating beacon.

Preparing to bring the chopper down on the airport's only helicopter pad, he begins to wonder about this airfield. It's much larger than the map indicates appearing to have a half dozen run ways.

Abruptly a voice comes over his radio, ordering him to remain in his seat. This is not expected and of course it's the first time he has, in his short career, experienced anything like this. Quickly rechecking his maps and charts it indicates a small municipal airport.

Looking around he notices the word "Federal Homeland Security" on one of the signs near the office. Something has obviously changed.

Within minutes of being ordered to remain in his cab, a Federal Homeland Security vehicle approaches and stops next to him. A young woman, ten years his senior, exits the driver's side. Adjusting an official looking hat that matches an equally official looking uniform, she approaches Gibby's chopper. With a wave of her hand, she motions him out of his cockpit.

Meantime she is looking directly at the numbers on the tail and recording them on her clipboard.

With Gibby out of the chopper, she steps on the foot peg with a flashlight scanning the interior then retreats to the locked cargo hold ready to repeat the same routine.

"Where are you a citizen?" she asks.

"Canada," replies Gibby.

"What's your address?"

"Circle G Ranch, British Columbia."

"Where are you going in the U.S.?"

"Saginaw, Michigan."

"What's your business in Saginaw?"

"I'm delivering computers to Gold Tone Software."

"Let me see your paper work."

By this time Gibby has become aware in this short encounter that this lady is definitely out of his league. Nonetheless, he knows he isn't going to last if he doesn't think on his feet. Gibby has given her all his paper work. She doesn't hold a steady gaze for more than a few seconds before she fires off another question. This agent is making it quite clear that she doesn't intend on allowing Gibby to get comfortable.

What further complicates this interrogation, is this female interrogator is down right pretty. She has dark eyes and full lips. Pretty can be a fatal distraction if he doesn't hold his focus.

So far, he's remained all business. He is relieved that she has limited the cockpit area search to a quick look with her flashlight and is concentrating next on the cargo hold.

"Have you ever been arrested?" she presses further. It's clear, she is mixing her questions, obviously hoping to confuse him.

"No," shoots back Gibby in his clear, most non evasive voice.

"Are you transporting illegal drugs today," his time pausing, letting her gaze purposely meets his. She is trained to notice any changes in the rhythm of Gibby's responses.

"No," replied Gibby deliberately.

Her dark eyes, though beautiful, have a coldness about them. In the process, she continues her unblinking gaze straight at him.

"Would you please unlock your cargo hold?"

Anticipating this request, he already has the key in his hand.

"Sure thing," he says unlocking the compartment door. Her flashlight quickly illuminates the entire interior. She skillfully makes an inspection in the most interior box. Satisfied, she steps out and away from the chopper. "Follow me to the office so we can finish," came the next directive.

The greater the distance she places between herself and his machine, the better he feels. Back at the office, she filled out a few forms, without reading them and he signed. The next thing he knows he's handed his paper work, plus a writ of inspection, stating that he had complied with U.S. border regulations of his own volition.

As much as he had tried, for the last 2,000-miles to avoid this kind of inspection, he is relieved that he has a free ride, at least from here to Michigan.

In the true Gibby Geiberson mode, this glitch is quickly part of his past. After all, he hadn't really envisioned any other scenario than a successful out come. Back in the air, after refueling, he takes a long pull on a fresh Marlboro. He's so pumped over having both his and Tommy's inspection go so smoothly, that he can hardly wait for the next leg of this tour de force.

Back at the ship Tommy and Mooch have embarked. This time of year Lake Michigan does not have that blue green color seen on postcards. Rather it's going to be 60 miles of unscripted black water, separating them from the affectionate attachment they both claim to share with dry ground.

"I sure as hell hope these guys know what the hell they're doing,," says an uncomfortable Tommy looking around at multiple number of deck hands. They are totally in the hands of about 30 different personnel doing various tasks.

Both of them finally relax enough to try and doze while other passengers pull out laptops as young people either, chatter on their cell phone or give their thumbs a workout as they text. Still others are reading, while young parents try and and get their children to sleep.

It's going to be a four-hour trip at best. Everyone is trying to do familiar things that make them as comfortable as possible.

It's clearly an alien environment for all but the crew. The adventure of a Lake Michigan crossing soon gives way to tedium. Once one has walked around the deck, there is nowhere else to go. As the bow slices through its sign-less path, the path remains indistinguishable. Only the autistic can find water parting for four hours interesting. For most, the first glimpse of the lighthouse beacon in Ludington, gives promise that this quest is over.

As the car ferry makes its way between the break waters and into the harbor, it's horn sounds a low, but euphonious signal to any that may be in its path.

"Wake up,Mooch, I think we are about to get off this old tub," says a yawning Tommy, poking his sleeping cousin.

Mooch wipes a bit of drool from the side of his mouth, simultaneously trying to slowly move a stiff neck. "Shit man, I can't move my freakin' neck," says Mooch sitting up straight in his chair from a slouched position.

Tommy is paying little attention to his cousins whining. His mind is already working on getting through the next phase of this expedition.

They can barely wait to get off the boat. It's 2 am by the time they dock. The next step is to wait for the dock hands to drive the Escalade and trailer off. At last they see their vehicle making it's way out of the belly of this colossal coal fed whale.

Both sets of eyes are set squarely on the trailer. Satisfied the lock has not been tampered with, they move along the short distance to downtown Ludington and pull into a supermarket parking lot.

"Before we go any further I think I'll check in with Gibby," says Tommy, flipping his phone open, expeditiously selecting Gibby's number.

"Yo Tommy," comes the familiar voice.

"Where in the hell are you?" says Tommy, half laughing. He's relieved enough to be off the boat, and by sheer gratitude of this fact alone, he's regained at least half his sense of humor.

"Better yet, where the hell are we?" adds Tommy, still trying to battle his fatigue with wit.

"I'm in a small airport 60 miles north of you, named Frankfort, Michigan. How was your boat ride?"

"Damn miserable, it's about three hours longer than any boat I've ever been on."

"Well at least you didn't get sea sick."

"Thats about all we didn't get," comes back Tommy, "I think we're going to get a motel. I can't stand how bad Mooch is starting to smell."

"OK, guys, I'll talk to you in the morning," with that, Gibby hunkers down a little deeper into his make-shift bed. Even the humblest of warm accoutrements on a February night in Frankfort, Michigan are as equally appreciated as, any luxurious villa overlooking a warm beach on the Mediterranean.

By morning, and having an overwhelming urge to empty his bladder, Gibby steps out of his cocoon long enough to dispel the urge.

Looking around in the morning light, he can clearly discern the snug valley he landed in, last night in the dark. It's truly a winter wonderland. The hills stand as glacial engravings, bearing leafless trees, contrasted as black, naked sentinels, against a glistening white blanket of new snow.

The next urge he experiences, is an urge for steak and eggs. His curiosity is piqued in the direction of a lone pickup truck parked in front of a small building, loosely described as the "Frankfort Air Terminal." Butch Reed is the airport manager. He also digs graves for the township cemetery. He has an affable demeanor and is capable of carrying on endless conversations about anything and nothing. Even though he lives across the road from the airport, he prefers to drive his 1973, half-ton Chevrolet pickup the 150 feet.

"Nice whirley bird ya got there mister. Nicest and newest that's been here in a while," greets the affable Butch, just as Gibby enters the office.

"Thanks," says Gibby. Without hesitation, he continues, "I need fuel and, hopefully, a ride to and from the nearest restaurant."

"I can do both," says Butch, peering through a pair of yellow aviator glasses, simultaneously he lifts the phone, and begins to dial. Gibby has never seen a phone that dials. He wonders to himself if this is some new U.S. invention.

"Hey Milly you still planning on goin' into town for groceries?" Butch pauses as he waits on his wife's answer. "Good, 'cuz I got a guy over here needs a ride." Another pause. "OK good, just pull on over here and pick him up."

Turning to Gibby, Butch reports, "The ole lady's goin' into town grocery shoppin'. She'll drop ya off at Dingy's Restaurant and pick ya back up when she's done."

"That sounds good, and you'll fuel her up for me?" follows up Gibby.

"Consider it done. That gonna be credit card?"

"No. Cash," says Gibby.

Butch looks startled. He's not used to that kind of cash. He begins to calculate the amount and how he's going to have to get to the bank and make a deposit.

Frankfort is a sleepy town this time of year. For years its neighboring village, Elberta served as a port for a railroad. Its car ferry's carried rail cars to ports in Wisconsin. With the death of the railroad, its content to come alive only between Memorial Day and Labor Day catering primarily to tourists and fishermen.

Milly has dropped Gibby off at Dingy's bar and grill. In the summer months, Dingy's draws a down state Yuppy crowd, who find rubbing elbows with the local crowd a kind of avant garde experience. In the winter months, Dingy's personnel have to be content catering to locals. This experience includes men who have never been seen out of bed without a hat. Men who are willing to risk having everything they own stolen in order to have the luxury of bragging, "I don't lock nothin'. I ain't taken the key outta my truck since I bought'er."

Gibby has come in on such a crowd. After their initial period of silence as they look this stranger over, they resume their bantering.

"Think the lake level's gonna come up this year?" asks Lester Olson to anyone willing to answer.

"All depends," comes back Coonie Vigland.

"Depends on what," says a curious Ernie Sorensen.

"Depends on how many ah' them down staters put their boats in this summer," says Vigland with a wry grin.

"What the hell you talkin' Coonie," heckles Skeezer Anderson.

"Just like this," he says taking a piece of his pickled baloney and plops it in his beer. "See how when I put this little hunk of baloney in my beer how the level comes up. Same damn thing when them down staters plop them big-ass yachts in the lake, they bring the level up. The more ah them boats, the higher the levels."

The whole table is just sitting and looking at Coonie in disbelief as he deadpans them taking another sip of beer.

Finally a voice from somewhere in the group speaks up, "You're full of shit Coonie, you know that?" The table's occupants break out in a roar of laughter.

By now Gibby's steak, two eggs, home fries, whole wheat toast and coffee have arrived and dominate the table and his attention.

Within fifteen minutes the only thing left are empty plates, as the matronly waitress, bar keep and cook, returns with her accommodating smile.

"Can I get you anything else honey," she asks, affably holding a coffee pot.

"No thanks, I'm just fine," says Gibby holding his hand over his cup.

Noticing Milly has pulled up out in front, Gibby pays his bill and exits to the waiting "de facto taxi" this diversion is exactly what he needed. He feels as good as if he had finished a month in Hawaii.

Arriving back at his helicopter, he answers his ringing phone.

"Good morning Gibby," says Tommy on the other end.

"Good morning. Did you boys get your beauty sleep," quips Gibby.

"I don't think so. Mooch is still ugly, but he smells better. So what's up," asks Tommy ready to take on the day.

"You guys take Highway 10 straight east to the Tri-City Airport. I'm about an hour of flying time from there and you're about two hours driving time. I'll be waiting for you. What ever you do, don't go over the speed limit."

Tommy takes the phone from his ear and looks at it disdainfully. "Whadda yah think, I'm nuts," he yells back in the ear piece.

"No, but we're too damn close to blow things now," says Gibby in a more or less apologetic tone.

It is the usual luxury of youth to pass worry off to old people, but this crew doesn't have that luxury. They share the same danger, demanding the same discipline, as that of trained combat soldiers. One false move and they're whole mission is done.

The trip across Michigan takes them through towns like Reed City, Clare, Sanford, Midland, and at last a sign declaring "Tri-City Airport."

From the air, Gibby is also making this trek by following Highway 115 from the north and then Highway 10. His arrival is a bit more complicated. He must radio the tower asking permission to land. He's then directed to a helicopter pad on the perimeter of the runways, well out of the way of commercial planes. He makes arrangements to be fueled and waits to hear from Tommy and Mooch. Meantime, he loosens the stitching in the seats. No sooner finishing this task, his phone rings. It's the now familiar voice of Tommy.

"We're in the parking lot. What's our next move?"

After getting the parking section information from Tommy, he says, "Stay where you are. I'll be there as soon as I get through the terminal."

Within minutes, he's knocking on the window of the Escalade. The familiar click of the electric lock, unlocks the door allowing him inside the S.U.V.

"Pretty damn good so far, eh guys," says an excited Gibby giving high fives.

Tommy, Mooch, nor Gibby have never been this far from the safety of their home turf. They soon settle down and get back to business. A healthy fear begins to set in. It's the fear of things yet to come. It's the kind of apprehension that send the irresolute fleeing. For young men like these, it actually sharpens and quickens their perception. Not a bad thing in their business.

It's agreed to leave the trailer with Mooch. He is to cut the stitching on the snowmobile seats, while Gibby and Tommy take the Escalade through a freight gate back to the chopper pad to pick up the smuggled contraband from the chopper seats. In a matter of minutes, they have returned to Mooch and the trailer.

They are aware of security cameras everywhere, so being as "routine" as possible, and blending in with other freight traffic, is the name of this component. The only thing that sets this whole sink-or-swim adventure apart from "routine" is two million dollars. Otherwise they're just three guys taking care of business, along with a few hundred others.

"OK guys we need to move on," says Gibby, pulling out his phone together with scrolling down his numbers. Gibby not only feels the adrenaline in his body, he can see the pulsating blood pushing its way through his wrists as he punches in the phone number.

"Hello," says Gibby, "Your pizza is cooked. Where would you like it delivered?"

This is the predesignated code agreed on weeks earlier with the reputed boss of the Hess 13 gang. His name is Raphael. The Hess 13 are attempting to make their mark in the clandestine world of young gangsters.

The voice on the other end has Gibby frantically writing on the back of his hand. Finally the conversation ends with Gibby agreeing on a designated location near M-13.

Saginaw is a city with high unemployment. Overflowing with the dregs of left over, unemployed auto workers, with no place to go, nor any hope for jobs. This disenfranchised group of young men is the fodder gangs feed on, rapidly advancing their numbers.

This gang is a new development in Saginaw. The younger Latinos are finding a charismatic leader in this Raphael Moreno. He has broken alliance with an older, established gang called the Vatos Locos lead by a less charismatic and more ruthless young gang boss named El Gordo.

Still pulling the trailer, Mooch weaves it through the streets, aware that a black Escalade pulling a trailer with lettering "TEAM 1" on the side, could be attracting attention from those other than intended.

"Turn left here Mooch," says Gibby as the street sign agrees with what he has written on his hand.

Mooch responds making the turn, which leads past a group of abandoned factory buildings to a lone parking lot. There is no threat of security cameras in this configuration. It's now late in the afternoon. The lot is snow covered, but not deep, maybe three to four inches. There are only one set of car tracks crossing the fresh snow. They lead to the back corner where is sitting a late-model, tricked-out blue, Lincoln Town car.

"Stop here Mooch. Lets not get too deep in to this before we know where we are, and who this is."

Again he punches in the same numbers into his cell phone. He can see the person in the back seat answer the phone. It's a young man about 20 years old wearing a distinct blue hoodie. There are three others in the car, all wearing the same colored hoodies.

"Lets get this done," says Gibby to the yet unmet, cowled ring leader.

Before an answer comes back Mooch sounds the alert that they have visitors. They are being pinned in by two other vehicles. Almost as quickly as they have arrived, Gibby has pulled a .380 pistol from his coat pocket. Mooch and Tommy are also in high alert.

"What the hell is going on," shouts Gibby into the phone.

"Don't worry about it," comes back the faceless hood, "They're here to increase security. We don't want any unwanted visitors. Pull up next to the Lincoln and we'll get this done."

Gibby thrusts his pistol back into his coat pocket, positioning it for easy access to the trigger. As Mooch moves forward, the entourage of Raphael's security stay put. They are clearly made aware they are on Rachael's turf.

Stopping next to the Lincoln, Raphael emerges as though it were a chariot. He immediately begins to shout orders in Spanish. His underlings react as commoners do in the presence of one who is titled. They position themselves as guardians, ready to defend to the death the crest of "Hess 13" and its leader.

Adding to his pomp, is a quick smile of self-confidence, and a display of gold bling on all his fingers, as well as gang tattoos on his hands and neck. None the less, throughout all this pageantry is a sense of deadliness. Looking into the face of each of these young men, the same message emerges, "Mess with me and I'll take you down."

The transfer is quickly made. Both sides are satisfied they have received what was pledged. A promise for another future business venture is assured, then quietly and quickly, they disassemble.

Gibby's whole body is wound up like an eight day clock. All the while Rachael's entourage is leaving his eyes flash in every direction, as if he were watching a tennis tournament,. Precaution cannot be measured out enough. They are left alone in a city, that in so many ways, look for ways of disposing people like them. The police and rival gangs are certainly on the top of the list to accomplish this, not to mention the latest weather forecast. Nature is flexing its muscle, threatening an arctic blast, with temperatures dipping below zero, accompanied by a foot of snow.

The relief accompanying the smooth transaction, is quickly replaced by a concern to protect their ill-gotten gains. Getting out of Saginaw with out incident, is the trio's immediate concern.

It would be naive to imagine, they have crossed the turf of rival gangs without being noticed. Time, so far, has been on their side, operating so quickly so as not to give any rival gang the luxury of slowly processing their presence and their purpose.

"We need to fuel up and get the hell out of here," says an alert Gibby. "So far we've had lady luck on our side, I don't want to start pissin' her off now."

There is no way this trio can overdose on alertness. As they pull into a gas station, Mooch notices a tricked out black 1978 Gran Torino shadowing them.

Turning to Tommy, he says, "I think we have some new friends," tilting his head toward the car load of hooded males parked across the street.

Gibby and Tommy cast a casual glance. A new shiver of concern over take all three of them. No one is saying anything. Finally Gibby speaks up.

"I think it's the trailer they want, at least I hope that's all. We may have to drop it." He has silence from the other two as they look at each other.

"You sayin' give these assholes a trailer and two snowmobiles," says a defiant Tommy.

"You got a better idea," shot back Gibby, "We've got a couple million dollars we need to deliver. A trailer and a couple of snow machines are chump change. Think of it as the cost of doing business."

Tommy mulled the thought for about a couple of seconds, catching the continued vigilance of the punks across the street.

"OK," he agrees, "Where we gonna drop it?"

"The next parking lot," says Gibby, nervously assessing this new threat.

Within two blocks after leaving the gas station, they come across a Walmart.

"Perfect," says Gibby.

Mooch wheels the column away from the main parking area. The Gran Torino is right behind him. They all know no one can predict the outcome of this encounter.

People are coming and going about their business, oblivious to what is brewing in this remote corner of this parking lot.

Hearts continue to pound. Adrenaline is forcing its way into every available artery. The expectation is that one is soon going to be running or fighting.

Tommy and Gibby unhook the ball and hitch, leaving the trailer and its cargo as a gesture of peace , while Mooch, ever attentive to all that's coming down, keeps watch.

Gibby makes a nod to the Gran Torino in the hopes they will accept this as payment for trespassing across their turf.

The answer becomes clear as the three of them suddenly find themselves encircled by the five Gran Torino thugs.

"Give it all up dude. Anybody doin' business with that punk Raphael gonna have to give it all up to the V. L.," declared an oversized Mexican male weighing at least 400 pounds. It's obvious to the three they are dealing with El Gordo, the leader of the Mexican gang, Vatos Locos.

El Gordo stands confidently with a smirk, showing off a gold tooth with a red ruby in the center. He's surrounded by trusted gang members, anxious to do whatever it takes to reach their objectives.

"We know you done a dope deal with Hess 13. Now you gonna give it all up." El Gordo gives out a little confident laugh.

Gibby grips his pistol inside his coat pocket. Before he can react El Gordo is on the ground with Mooch's numb chuck embedded in his fat forehead. He went down like a pole axed steer.

Tommy, has also moved like striking dragon to the solar plexus of

this, unsuspecting adversary. During this lightning fast ploy, his opponent doubles over, with crushed bones in his larynx. In another calculated
move, he then gouges out both of his eyes,then slaps both his opponent's
ears with cupped hands, breaking his ear drums.

Another moves forward drawing a pistol. Mooch has rebounded with
cyclonic speed, and he has broken the pistol arm of the would be shooter
and then his neck. The other two marauders seeing three of their homies,
including their leader, either dead or dying and flee across the parking
lot on a full court press.

Surprise always proves to be a formidable weapon on a more formidable foe.

The proficiency with which Tommy and Mooch executed this maneuver suggest to Gibby they have done this before.

Gibby could barely get a word out before both Tommy and Mooch had
opened the back of the trailer, dumping two of the, either dead, or soon to
be dead bodies, into the enclosure. El Gordo, who actually has his name
tattooed across his forehead, proved to be a dead weight and impossible
to move, even with the efforts of all three. They settled on simply rolling
him behind the trailer.

In another calculated move, Mooch removes the license plate from
the trailer and slits all four tires on the Gran Torino.

"Come on Mooch, get your ass in the wind, and get the hell out of
here," commands a still-stunned Gibby.

Barely five minutes have passed before the Escalade is mixed in with
traffic.

Mooch and Tommy are talking fast in Chinese.

"Alright," shouts Gibby from the back seat, "You guys quit talkin'
that shit and speak English so I know what the hell is going on." Gibby is
clearly frustrated. "This was not supposed to happen," he continues. "I'm

not blaming you guys. It's just that I never thought this part into what I would call a 'needed response'."

"It's a damn good thing we did," says Tommy, "or that fat bastard would be driving an Escalade with a couple million dollars and we'd be locked in the back of that van waiting for someone to come and throw our dead asses out.

Gibby continues his stare. He still trying to digest the last fifteen minutes of his life.

"I'm only saying that I never thought this part into what you guys did. I'm damn glad you two were there. I may have shot a couple before they got me, but I'd sure as hell be dead."

Mooch remains quiet the rest of the way to the air port. As quiet as he is, he always seems to be two steps ahead of both Tommy and Gibby. He led the way in this unplanned stratagem. They both thank God he did.

The next thing they realize, is they are pulling into the Tri-City Airport. By this time they have settled down. What's assured, is that twenty miles behind them there lay three dead men. Without a doubt, there is a high police priority on the killers, if for no other reason than to keep gang violence down.

The Vatos Locos would certainly not be cooperating with the police. With a little luck, the cops will be looking for the perpetrators in the next neighborhood . It'll take a few days before the street info works its way into any precinct.

The Vatos Locos gang knows what happened but for the present they are leaderless. Word has gotten around in the gang world, that a couple "chinks" and a "white guy" are responsible for all the havoc. They're driving an Escalade with Canadian plates. Word like this spreads through out the gangs pretty fast. The police get some info from informants, but it usually takes a few days to sort out the facts.

Power is supreme with these young men. It's sought after and respected. Above all, they'll risk dying for it. It's a silent commodity that's won with money and bullets. Violently gained money is the only money that's respected. Earned money gains no respect. Money must be gained through power and its loss must result in the misery of the donor.

Three lone foreigners have, unwittingly, changed the balance of gang power in Saginaw. Now it looks as though a successful escape is within their grasp. Sitting relatively safe in Tri-City Airport, the trio are offered a relaxed intermission. This interlude is not wasted but used to calculate their next move.

The money is stacked into two equal piles of a million. The idea is to protect as much of the money as possible. Gibby will take half by air, Tommy and Mooch half by car, thus reducing the risk of loosing it all to some unforeseen incident.

"Tommy, you and Mooch back track across Lake Michigan. This time avoid any large cities. The last thing we need is to risk breaching somebody's gang turf or catch the attention of some cop. Head north and we'll meet up at Hurly, Wisconsin. I think, the quicker we get out of the States, the better."

"Do you know how much we hate going across that damn lake," laments Tommy, "but you're probably right."

Mooch, as usual, goes along with whatever program is in play. He usually just adapts with little or no comment.

Mooch's demeanor has always been a point of fascination to Gibby. How Mooch's face always has the same scrunched features in spite of changing circumstances. When he's angry it looks like it fits the occasion but when he's relaxed, it also looks like it fits that occasion.

He's in his relaxed mode at the moment. Looking rather lumpish as he yawns, shakes his head a bit and wipes his eyes down. It's hard to believe he can be this calm after taking the lives of two human beings just a few hours ago.

It's not that Mooch is slow or dull witted, it's that he has accepted his role as Tommy's body guard. In the world of his own mind, he knows no one else can do this job as well as himself. He has found purpose in this role and will faithfully remain loyal to Tommy, regardless of where that may lead.

The more Gibby contemplates this strange creature, the happier he is that they are both on the same side.

"There *can* be honor among thieves," thinks Gibby still contemplating how he's shaping his most recent life's course.

"I want to thank both you guys for joining me on this job. I don't believe I could have had two angels cover my back any better than you two," declares Gibby.

Neither Tommy or Mooch are given much to mushy sentiment.

"Let's cut the bullshit Gibby and get on the road. We don't get paid for standin' around holdin' hands," says Tommy.

For a farm boy, Gibby has gained a lot of street smarts in the past six months. When his frontal lobes aren't screeching out of control, his thoughts find their way back to the ranch. He wonders about his parents and more than he cares to, about April.

For reasons unclear, he has kept a picture of her in his billfold. It's her graduation picture. He avoids looking at it for fear of the feelings it brings up. Quickly occupying his thoughts in another direction, these thoughts of home soon fade away.

The trip from Vancouver to Saginaw had been full of apprehension. For the return trip, other than protecting the money and getting out of the

States, it should be a road trip with minimal stress. For most, this would be a welcome relief, but not for the likes of men like Gibby. His thoughts have already turned to his next exploit.

Tommy and Mooch have arrived at the boat landing at Ludington without incident. The weather, as predicted, is bitterly cold. Preparing to go through the routine of loading, they overhear the conversation of a couple deck hands.

"Captain says we gotta get this tub across the lake before the storm gets too damn bad."

"The only reason he wants this boat in Manitowoc, is because he lives there. He thinks if he doesn't get on the water soon, he'll be stuck on this side for a couple days," says another crew member.

Not knowing what it means to experience a storm of this magnitude, on the Great Lakes, Tommy and Mooch pay little attention. At this point, all they want to do, is get as far away from Michigan as they can. Water is not the place they feel most comfortable, so the sooner this trip is over, the better.

Anxious to get started, and already knowing the routine, they willingly hand over the keys to the dock hand. Not constrained in their trust of these dock hands like the previous trip, Tommy grabs the duffel bag with the million dollars, as they head for the deck top.

Along with the temperatures dropping, the wind has picked up. It's the kind of wind that stings the face, soon causing frostbite to any skin left exposed.

Unimpeded, the old coal steamer muscles its way out of the harbor, directly into the storm. Just like it has so many times in the past.

Tommy and Mooch, after having a sandwich served them in the galley, settle down in the main deck lounge ready to endure four more hours of boredom.

The ship seems to be laboring as the seas begin to swell, amplifying the boats pitching and rocking. The wind is unfettered in displaying its force. The single deck hand scurrying around the outside open deck, displays a white zombie like appearance against the darkness of the night, as the spray carried by the wind, freezes on his clothing.

Within an hour the sou'-wester has kicked up 30-foot swells, pitching this mega-ton behemoth like it were nothing more than a bobber on the end of some ones fishing line. The whole lounge area, forgetting about sleep, are beginning to suffer from either, seasickness or anxiety, as the conditions worsen.

The growing chaos is soon broken by the sound of the captain's voice coming over the intercom."This is Captain Bishop. We are in no immediate danger, but because of high seas, and for the sake of passenger safety, we are asking that everyone remain seated until we reach calmer waters. We thank you for your cooperation."

Mooch is sicker than he can remember being. "If I could heave I know I'd feel better," laments Mooch.

Tommy automatically puts the duffel bag with the money tightly between his legs.

Without notice, Mooch grabs his hat off his head, using it as a basin, he empties his guts into its concavity.

Most, as hard as they initially try not to be discovered by their neighbor, have none the less become impervious to any embarrassment, with their sickness taking on a life of its own. There have been several others who have, within the limits of their best efforts, also given in.

The,not-so-discreet, smell of vomit has forced Tommy, with a few others, to risk moving toward the lounge doors, hoping for a burst of fresh air. Others are tending to the needs of their sick children or spouses.

Over the next hour, things are worsening. It's apparent that the ships bow has become thick with ice.

Tommy tries to open the door leading to the deck. At first he assumes it's been locked, but soon determines it's frozen shut. No matter how hard he and a couple other men try, they can't kick, bang or force the frozen doors open. With every crashing wave, the freezing water relentlessly adds inches of ice, glazing the passengers into a frozen cocoon.

What has not become apparent immediately, is that a loaded semi truck has broken its anchoring in the ship's hold. This has unwittingly started a chain reaction by one pushing into another and another until the trucks and cars are being pushed forward toward the bow, adding to the already, several tons of ice building on the entire front of the ship. The bow is slowly being forced lower and lower into the water, exacerbating the icing problem.

Without warning, the whole ship begins to shake and roar with vibration. This is a sound that no captain ever wants to hear. It is now evident that the weight of ice on the bow, and the displaced vehicles shoved to the front of the boat, have lifted the huge propeller directly in the back of the boat out of the water. The boat has now become like a giant see-saw. The 410-foot ship is no longer being steered. It is now at the mercy of the raging 60-knot winds and temperatures at -10 degrees Fahrenheit. Everything is sliding forward. Passengers are screaming as they are thrown on top of one another, as huge waves continue to pound the floundering ship. The lights begin to flicker and then suddenly go out. The sound of the vibrations are beginning to take on a more muffled sound, as the ship surrenders itself to the rush of incoming icy waters.

It's become black, and cold. Everyone is aware of only themselves, presently dominated by their own despairing struggle against what has become obvious.

Soon all is quiet, leaving the raging storm far up above to rage on alone.

CHAPTER 14

FOOTPRINTS IN THE SNOW

"... and he took a trip to a distant land, and there he wasted all his money on wild living." Luke 15:13

Gibby has unsuccessfully tried to contact Tommy by cell phone. Oblivious to the dreadful tragedy his two comrades have suffered, he sets the effort aside for the time being. After all, Tommy and Mooch didn't just fall of the turnip wagon, they're capable of handling most anything that pops up.

They have agreed to meet at the small town of Hurly in northern Wisconsin, but he has been forced by the same storm to land back at the same small airport at Frankfort.

Puzzled, but not overly concerned as to the 'why' Tommy is not answering his phone, he is sure that a reasonable explanation is forthcoming.

Butch Reed dropped him off at the Harbor Lights Motel and agreed to pick him up in the morning. He's quite content to have a warm motel room in close proximity to a restaurant and cable TV.

By morning the storm has moved on. Still not able to reach Tommy, his frustration level is mounting.

"Where in the hell are you boy," he says out loud, while snapping his phone closed.

Optimism is not completely gone but is diminishing with his thoughts turn to pessimism. *"The police have them for those murders back in Saginaw."* It's much more satisfying to imagine them being neglectful out of a disregard for timeliness than it is to imagine the worst, nonetheless, pessimism is creeping into his thoughts.

After giving Butch a call to come pick him up, he switches on the TV. The news of a Great Lake ferry sinking is the lead story and rescue efforts have produced no survivors. All are presumed drowned.

Not having an event like this even cross his mind, he stares at the TV dumbfounded. This is the first heartfelt failure he's had to deal with. It's hitting him with a force strong enough to knock the breath out of him.

A sense of loneliness and despair over take him. It's the kind that's deep and dark. Insensible to everything but his powerlessness, he barely responds to Butch's knock on the door.

He remains downcast on the ride back to the airport. Finally, he finds an overwhelming need to talk about this.

"Butch do you mind me asking you something?" He poses this question trying not to sound distraught.

"Go ahead. If I get it right, do I get a big cash prize," he says with a laugh.

Gibby gives an anxious smile, trying as best he can not to fall apart.

"What do you know about that lost car ferry out of Ludington?"

Butch is looking back at a man with the seeming weight of this whole affair on himself. Not knowing quite how to deal with this kind of intensity he measures his answer.

"What would you like to know?" Butch asks now with a more serious tone.

"Have they found any survivors?" Gibby's voice has a quiet quiver that pleads Butch give him the answer he hopes for.

Suspecting there is more to this question than a passing inquiry, Butch measures his response. "I haven't heard that there has been." Butch is looking hard at Gibby's response to his answer. He then adds, "Why do you have someone on that boat?"

"Yes I think so," says Gibby. He finds a moment of relief in discussing this with someone.

"Is it a relative?" Butch inquires further.

"No," says Gibby, fixated on a torn piece of vinyl on the truck's dashboard, "They're two close friends."

"Hey man, I'm really sorry to hear that," says Butch reaching over and touching Gibby's shoulder.

Butch's hand has the scent of Dove soap left over from his morning shower. It's the same scent Gibby's mother always has. He finds a moment of welcomed comfort in this compassionate gesture.

By this time they have arrived at the airport. "I want you to come into my office and have a cup of coffee before you take off," says a concerned Butch.

Gibby, having at least momentarily lost his impetuous nature, agrees and finds himself pointed to the most comfortable of Butch's office chairs. It's an old leather that at one time was as comfortable as it still looks.

Gibby finds himself backing into the chair. He sinks nearly to the floor with his arms parallel with his armpits, resting them on the chrome strips running the full length of the chairs arms. He is suddenly conscious of their conspicuous coolness and roundness.

Butch clears a spot on a coffee table, littered with magazines, setting down Gibby's freshly, poured brew within easy reach.

"Thanks, Butch," says Gibby waving off the offer of cream and sugar. Taking a sip he comments, "I don't normally act like this but this has hit me on my blind side."

"When I saw you back at the motel, I thought to myself that you looked like you had lost your best friend. Now I learn that you lost two."

Gibby tries as best he can to control the tears, but he may as well try and control diarrhea. If he were asked if his tears were for his friends he would say "yes." At the same time, he knows these are also tears of frustration. Frustration with dealing with the loss of his two friends, plus the money he pledged to return. Both these losses have his head going in several directions. The Chinese guys don't take any kind of loss kindly neither money or their cousins. *"This is my deal. I know damn well they'll hold me to it one way or another,"* he reasons.

"I appreciate you givin' me a few minutes of your time Butch," says Gibby wiping his tear-filled eyes with his sleeve. "I'll be alright once I get home."

With that, he's regains his composure and he thanks Butch Handing him his empty coffee cup, he takes a deep breath and heads for the door.

Butch didn't bother Gibby with the details of his own retirement off the Great Lakes. He had once been stranded in a similar boat, caught in an ice pack for thirty days. This suddenly seemed pale compared with Gibby's losses. He kept it to himself.

Back in his chopper he shivers as he waits for the engines to warm, while staring out at a future that looks bleak. Trying to get a hold on himself, he talks out loud.

"So Gibby, the world ain't ended yet, so, lets get your ass in gear."

With that, he flips a few switches. The big rotor blades begin to turn. Now that he's safe in his cockpit, the world is soon left below. The Earth always looks so innocuous, so manageable from 5,000 feet.

At times like this, Gibby can't help but find himself thinking about home, recalling how his father would patiently encourage him when he was in the dumps.

"Where the hell are you when I need you?" he says out loud. It's like he's blaming his father for his own failure and upset because he's not being rescued. He definitely feels as though he has drawn the short straw. In more ways than one Gibby is finding himself in a distant country, physically, mentally and spiritually. A country that is beckoning him to ignore all, but those things that intoxicate, stimulate or arouse him. Things that molest any decency his father may have left with him.

What is beginning to surface instead of the swashbuckler is a frightened little boy, who is losing his self assurance, while being slowly boiled like a frog in this disastrous, self-destructive but chosen lifestyle .

At times like this he finds himself thinking about his father.

"I gotta get over this. That old man is crippling me," he thinks as he tries to shove his father's influence out of his mind and force his own agenda back to the forefront.

He stubbornly pushes on, confident that he can make life on his own, convincing himself he doesn't need his father's love. He can't control the entrance of these thoughts but he can willingly resist them. Nonetheless they continue to plague him

It's up here, 10,000 feet about the Earth, where he maneuvers this million dollar chopper. It's up here that he feels confident in his proficiency. High above the Earth, and its endless, senseless drama, provides Gibby the escape he yearns for. It's up here that he can make perfect sense of his every decision. Looking down from above on the wonders of God's artistic work has never been a chore. The mountains, the clouds, the green forests, the crystal-clear glacial lakes are seen in a perfect mosaic. And best of all, there no people to ruin it all. It's truly heavenly.

As much as he would prefer to remain orbiting the Earth, the truth remains that more sooner than later his fuel runs out and forces him back to the ground.

The big storm that claimed the lives of Tommy and Mooch has passed. Having to fly so high so as not to encounter the winds has taken its toll in extra fuel, forcing Gibby to make fuel stops every 100 miles. Not wanting to risk a border crossing at this time he finds himself over a small airfield in North Dakota.

Radioing ahead to insure they have his fuel octane, the voice coming back on the other end also insures him the planet is still inhabited.

"Yah, it's a big ten four on the fuel. Set her down on da north end," comes back a male voice.

Gibby makes a visual of the helicopter pad. Within minutes he's parked and out of the cockpit. Charging down the runway is a tanker truck that's at least 25 years old, piloted by what appears to be a man somewhere between the ages of 50-70 years.

Stepping out into the sunlight is a grizzled old fart, dressed in a sheepskin parka, trimmed with what in years past, may have been white fur on the inside, cascading in yellowish brown panels onto the outside collar. On his head is a coonskin hat, complete with muzzle, eyes and tail still intact with the front paws holding an innovated ear muff. It could almost be described as a functional costume.

More startling than this, is the cigarette hanging from the corner of the man's toothless mouth. It too, is surrounded by what may at one time been, white whiskers, now deeply nicotine stained. He seems to be oblivious to the hazard a lighted cigarette creates around high octane fuel.

"You're the fella 'at wants the fuel," he asks. The cigarette wobbling in rhythm with his words.

"Ya, I do," says Gibby still watching the lit cigarette curling smoke up and around the man's mustache. It affirms a fact he likes to ignore while in the air; that in spite of his lofty travel path, his feet are firmly planted on this earth.

The man continues to ready his equipment, finally to the relief of Gibby, he discards the cigarette on the concrete pad, putting the final touches to it with the toe of his boot. Now he's all business. Within minutes the plane is fueled.

Paid in full and ready for takeoff, he glances out the side door window. He spots the grinning, toothless man pointing his two fingers to the coon hat eyes and then the same two fingers pointing back at him as if to say, "I see you."

As goofy as this man is, Gibby's second thought is "I hope he gave me the right fuel!" As a friendly gesture he returns the "I see you" gesture. This leaves the toothless man slapping his thighs in laughter. Obviously, pulling this prank, highlights this man's day.

Everything seems colder, with the rotor motor whipping the blades around the cockpit. Finally in the air, this big flying dragon courses to the west.

The quick money, the excitement this trip initially promised, has swiftly retreated, replaced with a strong sense of desperation. The only bright spot is that he still has half the money. On the other hand, he still has half the trip back to Vancouver, and with it, all it's unmet hazards.

Gibby is resigning himself to making the best out of a bad situation, but he can't help but have uneasiness about the way things have changed. He's experiencing first hand Murphy's Law, anything that can go wrong will go wrong.

His thoughts are not his best. Loosing Tommy, Mooch and the money has thrown him off his game. "If I were merely adjusting to some new innovations to get the job done, it would be no problem but this is as tough as it gets and it stinks," he thinks.

For a guy like Gibby to fall short is an admission of powerlessness. In this world of gangsters, power is the measure of success. To demonstrate powerlessness,or failure in any area, means the person loses any respect. In the past, he has always faced his insecurities head on by throwing caution to the wind. He does not mean to make today the exception.

He has made his decision to re-enter Canada in a remote mountainous area, thus hoping to limit detection. This is not the time to give in to helplessness but to gather the troops, renew with vigor the objective and trudge on.

Peering out the plexiglass window of his chopper, he is drawn to a soaring eagle whose territory he's assaulting. The big bird is not giving way to this motorized interloper. Its demonstrates a defiance that could spell disaster for both bird and man. Since survival is the prize, neither wishes to pay the final penalty for their indifference. The eagle capitulates. "Smart bird," says Gibby out loud.

He can't help but wonder if he is as smart as that bird. "Do I know when to lay down and deliver up my own obstinacy. Will I know when I'm up against unbeatable odds?" He can't rightly answer.

Checking and rechecking his maps, Gibby soon finds a favorable point of entry. At last the terrain meets his criteria. It also insures that only the most competent, the most expedient of pilots would dare such an endeavor. A momentary lapse in focus or judgment, or for that matter, even a limited hand-to-eye dexterity can prove to be a pilots undoing.

Gibby is confident that his own natural wariness is enough to make him cautious. But even though caution is relevant, it is also relative. Wanting to be the best, he more often pushes himself outside his comfort zone. Some would say that times like these are not times to experiment. Gibby, on the other hand, is always pushing for ways to improve his flying skills. His ability to weasel his way through narrow gorges, all with unforgiving solid rock facings, has for him become routine.

A twist of fate brings the unexpected. Not only are dense mountainous rock walls looming in every direction, but a dense fog is added to the mix.

It's easy enough to fly into thick fog but the odds change fast when it involves flying safely out. Attesting to this fact, are the wrecks littering the landscape that every pilot becomes disconcertingly aware during any routine fly over.

Torn between crashing if he risks the fog, or detection if he goes over the cloud, Gibby can't risk being torn for more than a brief moment. Quickly calculating that making the wrong decision can be fatal, he chooses the lesser of the two evils. He's going over the top.

"I hope the birds are singin' for somebody somewhere, cause they ain't singin' for me," he thinks to himself.

"Fate has dealt me a loser's hand here but I gotta play it out," he further speculates.

He makes his move. The fog is becoming more dense as he increases his altitude. The only relief he feels is the silence of his radar alerting him of crashing into a mountain. At the moment his visibility is zero, at the same time, he also knows when he breaks through this ceiling his visibility will be endless.

Patience is how he must deal with this unseemly turn of events. Impatience in bad weather can be deadly. Add to this the thinness of the air at this elevation. This causes the helicopter to loose power and quickly becomes the written recipe for calamity.

Nonetheless, Gibby remains dauntless. He has a centrality of purpose and remains faithful to its end. Some could easily say that he's, "doing all the right things for all the wrong reasons."

At last he breaks through this fog ceiling into the brilliance of the sun's light welcoming him to its heavenly domain. The beauty above the foggy clouds can be mesmerizing. Up here the sun never stops shining.

What a few minutes ago had been formidable foe, now gives an inviting sense of softness. It's as if the chopper could bounce from one white, fluffy cloud to another.

He entertains himself with the notion of seeing a passenger aircraft buoyed up by one of these formations with its passengers standing beside it and waving. He chuckles to himself at the prospect.

His chuckle is short lived, from out of nowhere he spots a fixed-winged plane dogging him. The words "police" inscribed across the tail section cannot be misinterpreted.

In the next moment a voice comes over his radio identifying itself as the police requesting he identify himself.

Quickly checking his fuel gauge, "Damn, I used more gas getting up here than I realized," he mutters to himself. Running is hardly going to be an option.

The only option he has is to break down through the cloud bank.

He finds hes talking to himself. "OK, Gibby don't panic, stay focused!"

The choice becomes evident, as a hole in the clouds manifests itself about a mile ahead. He doesn't know the wind conditions or the terrain below this mountainous haze, but he knows fixed-wing planes cannot maneuver as close to the ground, nor can they stop in mid air as can a helicopter.

The mile gap closes in a hurry. The chopper seems to be taking on the thoughts of its pilot as it responds to his every move. Suddenly Gibby stops the flying dragon and begins to drop straight down through this mile-deep trough. The plane is forced to give up the chase as it unable to manipulate these kinds of maneuvers.

Visibility, between the walls of this cloud-like worm hole, is two hundred feet at best. It's requiring every bit of attention Gibby can muster just to stay on focus. Not aware of the terrain below, he has the concern that unless he breaks through soon, he may find himself crashing into a mountain or at best, some tree tops. But as is the usual for the cavalier types like Gibby, they are never surprised when things work out to their advantage.

Without warning, he suddenly breaks through the cloud about 200 hundred feet above what appears to be a several acre opening in a wooded area. It's snow covered and flat. Almost too perfect.

Visibility at this altitude is still less than one mile. It's unsafe to travel forward as the mist is hanging loosely over this de facto airfield.

"OK, Gibby go easy. Hope for a solid, level spot."

The danger of this kind of landing is that the pilot has no real idea what he is landing on. In this part of the world many planes, as wells as pilots, have been lost after landing on a glacier only to discover that the snow has covered a hidden crevasse that swallows plane, pilot and cargo.

Gibby surmises from the chopper's altimeter that he is setting down in a small valley, at least 1,200 feet above sea level.

"Good landing, Gibby" he declares to himself as the landing rails of this giant bird only sink ankle deep into the snow.

Having an overwhelming call from nature, he exits his cockpit and relieves his overextended bladder. After lighting a cigarette, he begins to examine his private airfield, noticing immediately that there is not a single shrub, or for that matter,no vegetation growing at all. Finding this phenomena odd, he then digs his heel into the packed snow to examine it's footing. His reaction is near panic.

"What the...this crap is punk ice!!" he shouts, with nothing but the scrub pines surrounding his landing site as his only listeners.

At that moment he hears a loud crack. Turning in time to see his helicopter spitting water in a fountain of spray as it disappears. It's being swallowed by a glacial lake that in this early March thaw it's ice has been forced to give up its strength.

Gibby stands motionless and unblinking. It's as if what he has just viewed is a dress rehearsal for something, and in a moment everything will return to normal.

Though it is enough to hear it once, the void in this amphitheater echos every death gurgle and belch this lake can produce as it digests its victim with nothing less than a firmly committed sense of finality. A small expulsion of soothing mist from this gaping hole falls down as though it's fulfilling an unwritten obligation in its attempt to heal over the lake's open wound.

For all of Gibby's careful preparations, this is another one of the unknowns that have escaped his ingenuity. He is left totally destitute. His emergency kit, with all his food, water, matches, and his sleeping bag, are gone. A million dollar helicopter and a million dollars in cash now resting at the bottom of a 500-foot lake. Certainly resting more comfortably than himself.

What is galloping toward him at breakneck speed is dusk, with temperatures beginning to drop. This occurs during this time of year: temperatures above freezing during the day but then drop below during the night.

Being a slacker under these conditions are for those who have given up. Gibby is determined not to amble down this path to his own death.

Without the pressure panic *can* produce, but definitely with urgency, he examines the contents of each of his pockets. Then clears a spot in the snow with a gloved hand, as he lays out their contents.

A half package of cigarettes, three pieces of chewing gum, a small buck knife attached to his belt, a cigarette lighter, a hundred dollars in twenties, fives, singles and a handful of change, an energy bar and an odd assortment of tissues and napkins left over from some previous lunch, and his small pistol still in his inside jacket pocket.

A measure of gratitude accompanies each of these discoveries as well as having the presence of mind to have worn a jacket, hat and gloves. But he does find himself lampooning his negligence at leaving his cockpit door ajar, thus hampering any chance of recovering the planes contents. "*God only knows where that money will drift to,*" ponders Gibby.

He begins to scan the landscape. He needs shelter, or at least as close as he can come to some adequate protection against the meanness brought on by this fateful change of events. Scanning the landscape once again, he chooses what appears to be an adequate campsite. The fog still hangs, seemingly to further chasten Gibby for his unwelcome intrusion.

Among the scrub conifers, he cuts a few dead branches. The wood is damp. Tearing a small scrap from a napkin with a few dead pine needles, one flick of his lighter catches the pine resin. He soon has a fire that insures him that, at the least, he will be able to survive the cold.

Though he doesn't expect any company, this is the time of year that bears emerge from their winter nap, not to mention, roving bands of skinny wolves. They're all hungry, and generally not too fussy what they feed on. The small caliber pistol is hardly a defense against a 300-pound bear, or pack of hungry wolves, so building a large fire becomes his immediate focus of defense.

The dark is beginning to thicken, exaggerated only by the brightness of his fire. His thoughts remain remarkably focused and relatively calm considering his present surroundings. He vigorously turns his attention to cutting enough pine boughs to serve as insulation against the frozen ground and hopefully enough to pile on top of himself.

"This is going to be a different kind of sleep tonight, but I'll survive," he tells himself, poking around his fire one last time before crawling into his pile of pine boughs.

For each of his encouraging thoughts, he discovers there is an equal number of negative thoughts to battle through. He can not remember spending a night in the cold this unprepared,or in this matter, being this vulnerable, to only what God knows of dangers that can lurk against the improvident.

What Gibby has on his side, is a better than average physical fitness, along with the natural thinking agility that accompanies his youth.

These alone may allow him a night or two. Then considering how relentless the environment is in its attempts to reclaim those who can't defend themselves against its harsh dominion, he is also going to have to withstand more than deficient shelter when he encounters the phantom enemies his own thoughts can produce.

Morning arrives with no fanfare. Gibby immediately gathers more fire wood. His fire is not completely out yet but it has severely reduced its B.T.U. out put. Next he has hunger and thirst to deal with. Thirst is the least of his concerns, considering there is, yet, plenty of snow to melt. Food on the other hand, is going to present a problem, that is, unless he can in a timely way find his way out of this mess.

In some ways wanting to finalize his losses, Gibby makes his way back to the hole in the ice. He notices his slushy foot prints had frozen through the night. He finds himself wishing they belonged to someone else, someone who could rescue him.

The scent of gas is detected long before he reaches the still unfrozen gap in the lake. The broken surface reveals a mixture of fractured ice and gasoline, much like when a dead whale gives up its body fluids.

The cold is not as oppressive as it was during the night. The sky is still over cast ,and the fog is reforming itself as the warmer temperatures pull moisture out of the melting snow. The lack of sun leaves Gibby puzzled over directions. So far he has seen no evidence of human activity in any direction.

Surmising he is stranded in a valley of foothills in a larger mountain range, he chooses to explore what he senses to be, a southerly direction. Other than being hungry, he feels hopeful he'll find his way out.

Returning back to his campsite, he rubs his cold hands over the last flicker of flames from his fire, hoping to soak in as much heat as he can.

Anxious to get on his way, and after kicking snow on the still burning logs, he contemplates his final moments in this campsite. The heat from the logs releases steam from the melting snow giving off a hissing final good-bye. He's cut himself a six-foot walking stick, sharpening one end to add to his "bear and wolf kill" arsenal.

Now facing the most challenging leg of this escapade, he sets his feet toward the north face of what he hopes is a southerly direction. It appears to be a 1,000-foot incline. What becomes conspicuous as soon as he enters the wooded area off the lake, is how many wild life tracks there are. The white snow defines them perfectly making them easy to track.

Almost immediately, a game trail reveals itself. Wild life are creatures of habit and follow the same trails for many years. Not knowing exactly where these game trails lead, one can be sure that these indigenous critters take the path of least resistance around these highlands, that most assuredly lead to water.

Some of the rock formations bear witness, corroborating that a past civilization did some mining for flint in this area. The evidence becomes visibly apparent in more and more locations along this trail.

Even though people no longer need or use flint tools, this gives him hope that he may be near an Indian reservation. Many of these areas are considered sacred home lands and preserved by many of these native cultures.

On the other hand, the anemic pallor of the landscape is not what indicates hopeful expectations. The human brain yearns for color. The best nature can produce in March in this part of the world is black and white. Even that is rendered to a pale gray created by the mist hanging in the air.

Four hours later Gibby's clothing is sticking to his body, giving way to the natural adhesive nature of sweat. He's trying to convince himself that he must be near the summit. An hour later he arrives victorious.

Drained of energy, he grabs a glove full of snow and presses it into his open mouth, thawing out enough to begin to trickle down his throat. This is hardly the hardy gulps his body craves. Almost involuntarily he searches his pocket for his lone energy bar. This is the first time he wishes the fat content were higher.

He knows he is going to have to stop soon and build a fire to dry his clothing. Taking a chill under these conditions is not the way to conserve energy. Keeping dry is imperative with the limited amount of clothing he has. He cannot afford to be irresponsible about stopping and taking care of this.

From the leveling landscape, he surmises that he has at last reached a plateau of sorts. The mist is left below, being replaced by outcroppings of smaller hills and alpines, making it difficult, if not impossible, to see distances.

It's been a long, hard trudge up from the valley below. Taking a bite of his precious energy bar, he carefully rewraps the remaining contents and zips his jacket pocket closed.

The advantage, he soon discovers of being on top of this 1,000-foot foothill, is that it is much more wind swept of snow and easier to gather fire wood. Stripping naked, he soon has his clothing hanging on sticks angled over a roaring fire releasing the trapped moisture. The temperatures have dropped at this elevation, pushing temperatures down below freezing.

Gibby's mind is still sharp enough and as his body still renders enough reserve energy to give him a needed supply of adrenaline when his system calls for it. Dressed again in warm, dry clothing, he attempts, with what these overcast conditions allow, to calculate a southerly direction.

Determined not to allow his situation to spread a shade of gloom over him, and sure that he can weather this uninvited trouble, he attempts to lift his spirits by singing.

"You better not shout, you better not cry, you better not pout, I'm tellin' you why. Santa Claus is comin' to town."

It's one of the few songs he has ever mastered. Louder and with great vigor, he sings his song as he continues his trudge. As loud as he bellows out each verse, he can't quite rid himself of the over-bearing concern that things have gone terribly wrong. What is keeping him in the "now" is the awareness that his survival is going to depend on his next move.

Nonetheless, there is a mind spot where hopelessness begins its bid for domination. It is never satisfied with anything less. It's a place where a thin wall separates confidence from melancholy. Once it penetrates his psyche it will result in an over-powering force of lostness. There is always a feeling of despair that accompanies the loss of confidence. It usually terrifies the person enough to cry out for help, hoping some divine, or cosmic force will intervene.

Gibby has never been in a place where a weakened disconnect has made its way into any happenings surrounding his life, that in some measure, he couldn't quickly rectify. This time, because of these extreme circumstances, relief may or may not come. It certainly doesn't appear to be around the corner anytime soon.

As the day wanes on, the reality of his situation continues to infiltrate his mind, he's finding it more difficult to remain pollyannish. His heart pounds with a mixture of fear and apprehension.

He knows he must continue to hope for the best outcome, but must also mentally prepare for set backs. Death is not something that can be prepared for in this ballgame. It just happens.

"So you want to kill me," he questions, with a bit of bluster, while scrutinizing his environment. "Don't count on it." Humming confidently to himself, he goes about finding a suitable place to find shelter.

Darker clouds have been forming for the past hour suggesting that

210 The Prodigal Father

the weather is not standing still. Something is changing. Early March in the northern hemisphere is always tumultuous. Old Man Winter grows long of tooth this time of year, refusing to die easily, his death throes can prove to be fatal.

Without warning, Gibby feels a cold, stinging sensation on his bare face. It's a mixture of rain and ice. He knows from experience this weather pattern is going to leave a coating of ice on everything that's not covered. It's predictable and treacherous.

As fast as he can work, he cuts alpine boughs laying them over a fallen tree, shaping and weaving them into what, he hopes, to be protection against this assault. The last thing he can afford to do, is to waste energy trying to warm up a cold, wet body.

Not having a fire is, completely out of the question. Under these conditions survival depends on conserving energy. There's plenty of wood, rich in pine resin and tar-like creosote. The downside is this wood burns hot and fast, therefore, requiring continuous attention.

Gibby is exhausted. He's been without food, other than a couple bites on an energy bar, for two days. He's also limiting his desire to eat snow for fear of using precious calories to warm it back up to body temperature.

Closing his eyes comes easy. Sleep comes quickly, but fitfully. In his dreams, he imagines himself trying to dance in the dark. Once awake, it leaves him shaken. The anxiousness the dream produced renews itself, then morphs into fears that are leaving him frightened. Gibby has never had a problem with distinguishing an encounter with a perceived physical nemesis, then again, the attack from these fears are not produced by the seen forces, rather, by unseen adversaries.

Gibby may not have perceived himself to have had much experience with a higher power, but as his circumstances continue to torment him, he's becoming well acquainted with a lower power.

By morning light, he's awakened by the familiar sound of cracking limbs trying to shed themselves of unwanted layers of thick ice.

The only wood left dry enough to burn are the pine boughs he slept on. Being too tired to try and scout for more dry wood, most of the night was spent shivering. The quick, hot fire they produce hardly lasts long enough for him to adequately warm up.

"Damn this weather," mutters Gibby, moving about his camp preparing himself to step out into this unkind, brutally dangerous landscape. He can't help conclude how terribly unprepared he is to meet these new challenges.

The early morning sun is creating a beautiful crystal garden, leaving every branch and tree regally adorned in a glistening array of dancing light. On the other hand, he is much aware of how the beauty of this sight assails the mind in its attempt to minimize its hazards.

He is not looking forward to stepping out, but knows he needs to get moving. His shivering is involuntary to the point of being unable to manipulate the zippered pocket containing his last bite of energy bar.

Deciding not to wait until he thaws out, he begins his trek. With everything covered in ice, his walking stick becomes the third leg he needs to stay upright. The cold has zapped much of his body's energy supplies, leaving him feeling particularly vulnerable today.

Another downside is steadily developing. The wind is picking up, causing already stressed ice encrusted tree branches, to be pushed to their limits. Some are already beginning to rain down shards of broken ice, indiscriminately pelting everything below. Gibby's greatest concern is being struck with a broken, ice-laden limb weighing several hundred pounds.

"Stay focused, stay alert," is his forced mantra. He is barely able to hold this thought for a few minutes before his energy starved-brain begins to wander leaving him little choice, but to hope he can react to hazards without an accident.

The line of trajectory he is attempting to follow, has led him to an unforeseen narrow ledge, with a drop of about 60 feet to, what appears to be, a creek. Judging from the direction the water is flowing, he assures himself that he's heading in the right direction.

Without notice, his heels slide out from under him and finding himself in a free fall, he tumbles down the steep embankment. Not able to get a hold on anything, he's stopped only when he reaches the bottom, finding himself laying face down in an icy mountain stream. Its bone-chilling water refuses to grant him even the slightest amnesty. With out exception, it continues to cascade over this latest victim, soaking him thoroughly from head to toe.

If there was anyone to listen to him rolling down the ice covered slope, all they would have heard is "shit, shit, shit, oh shit!" in a riveting fashion making the hearer wonder how many of God's children enter eternity with these lesser songs than a doxology.

Immediately this shocking sensation sends his body into uncontrolled shivering. Everything he is wearing is sticking to his body like pliable sheets of ice. This horrific mishap has, in a matter of seconds, brought this nearly-managed predicament, to a death- threatening emergency.

For all of his physical prowess and youthfulness, all bets are off for his survival. This new situation is leaving him mentally and physically exhausted, as he thrashes around, sloshing himself out of the stream. His thought process, what is left of it, has been abandoned somewhere between the ledge and the stream. He is now acting on pure instinct.

Mustering every ounce of energy he has left, he quickly stands up, involuntarily shaking his arms and hands as though this could complete a drying process. With reason all but gone, he begins to claw his way, by blind impulse, out of this gorge, grabbing at anything that looks like a hand hold. What he hasn't noticed, is that in the flurry of tumbling, he has lost his hat, gloves and pistol.

Finally reaching the top, the wind is intensifying. The chill of the water is still stubbornly bathing his body. Frost bite is already beginning to ravage his skin. His body's futile attempt to warm itself throws him into more uncontrolled shivering. It isn't going to take long to thrust him into irreversible hypothermia. His core temperature begins to plummet. His cognitive abilities have been replaced by confusion. Not fear, apprehension or doubt, but pure unadulterated confusion.

Compartmentalization training can prove to be quite effective, but even that, along with physical fitness, youthfulness, or even mental toughness, finally succumb to a relentless Mother Nature. The end result, is that the human mind and motors skills are finally forced to agree, that man is still at best only a part of nature and far, far from being its vanquisher.

After about twenty minutes of confused, unrestrained frenzy, he finds himself hobbling down a ravine to what appears to be a clearing. Beyond tired, succumbing to his fatigue, he collapses under a lone tree, laying his head back for just a moment. His exhausted brain and body are only asking him for a few minutes of sleep.

CHAPTER 15

THE BRUDERHOF

Just a mile down a lane from Gibby, past several open fields, another way of life is being lived.

"Can I take Jacob with me?" asks Henry Wultman in a dialect of German that has not been spoken since 18th century Germany.

"No, I need Jacob over in the hog barns." He is answered by Reinhardt Wirt in the same ancient dialect.

Reinhardt is the Farm Boss or Weinzedle, as its referred in this ancient German dialect, on this 10,000 acre farm owned by a colony of Hutterites.

The Hutterites made their way to the New World beginning in the 19th Century. They had their beginnings in the Protestant Reformation as a sect referred to as Anabaptists.

Being persecuted, by both Catholics and Lutherans for their strange religious beliefs, they were forced out of Germany. Finding a brief reprieve in Russia, only to be forced out once again, they at last found religious freedom in North America along the U.S. and Canadian border.

They formed themselves into communal colonies numbering approximately 120 men, women and children per community. This particular group identify themselves as Schmiedeleut. So named after one of their early leaders.

They practice a form of communal living that resists any personal ownership and insists on absolute pacifism. Firmly positioning their place in the world on the New Testament and in particular the Biblical book of Acts 2:44 "having all things in common."

On this particular March morning and after a short communal devotion, Reinhardt is delegating the work for the day. Henry has been delegated the task of bulldozing brush off a 100-acre plot at the northern border of the ranch. The process is to break off the brush while its still frozen. This is the first phase in reclaiming an overgrown field back into a tillable crop producer.

Henry is towing the dozer on a low boy trailer along a still frozen over farm lane that leads to this morning's project.

Getting the dozer off the trailer is quickly and efficiently completed. With the same expedience, the big diesel engine is brought to life. His attention is abruptly refocused from his task at hand to a staggering, limping man emerging from the brush.

The man stumbles to a scrub oak, plops down and leans his head and back against its trunk.

Henry doesn't recognize this man, suspecting him to be a non Hutterite or "English" as they are referred to.

Something about this situation is not clear to him. The man, from his first impression appears to be drunk. It's not uncommon to have some wild-eyed mountain man, imbibing in his own home brew, come staggering out of the woods. But this man is too young, and other than a few days stubble growing on his chin, he's too clean cut.

By this time Henry is only within a few feet of this disabled figure. The man is not moving nor is he acknowledging in any way that he is aware of Henry's presence.

Dismounting his dozer, he approaches what he discovers to be a man, completely covered in icy clothing.

"Hey mister you OK?"

The voiceless man lays motionless along with his life slipping quietly away as an unusual sleep is overtaking him.

"O mein Got im Himmil," blurts out Henry in his most familiar language. It's a prayer for help.

He feels for a pulse. It unusually slow.

Grabbing this lifeless victim under the arms, he drags him to his dozer, at full throttle makes his way to his truck. Loading the still unconscious mystery man into the cab, he fires up the engine, turning the heat up as high as it will go. With one hand on the wheel, he swings the big truck in the direction of the colony, with the other, he holds his cell phone, shouting into the ear of its listener of this new dilemma.

By the time he returns, word has spread, bringing out a reception of a couple dozen men and women. Irene Wildermuth is the female in command. Besides serving as a midwife for the birth of most of the children, she is also a trained nurse. Irene has probably bound up more wounds and broken more fevers than most physicians.

Her husband is Wilhelm Wildermuth, the colony secretary. Traditionally, she is also the colony shneider or seamstress.

Two men have wheeled out a modern gurney to receive the half-frozen body being hoisted out of the truck.

Frau Wildermuth is mincing no words in issuing orders to these men

"This man is going to die of hypothermia if you don't get those wet clothes off him. Fill the tub with warm to hot water and lay him in it. We have to get his temperature up."

Searching through his wet clothing they come across his pilot's license.

"It says here his name is Marlon Geiberson and he's from British Columbia," says one of the attendants.

"Henry did you happen to see any type of air craft when you came across this fella?" asks Wilhelm.

"No, when I first saw him, he was staggering out of the brush and come to rest against a tree. I didn't take the time to look any further," he replies.

"It's no wonder he was staggering, look at the size of that ankle," says another attendant.

The ankle is swollen almost twice the size of the other, taking on a blue, yellow color.

Within a short time after Gibby is placed in the warm water, his core temperature begins to rise. Following this phenomena his cognitive skills are also improving.

Coming to in a strange bath tub, surrounded by strange looking, bearded men, startles Gibby enough to cause him to make an effort to exit the tub.

One of the men attendants alerts Alex Hofer, the head minister, also known as Predigor. He is also the chief executive of the colony. By the time he arrives, the men have Gibby out of the tub and into a pair of black home spun trousers, socks and shirt.

In the brief period of a couple days, Gibby has traveled from a world concerned with possessions to a subculture that rejects almost every western value. Little does he know that he is embarking on an experience that has eluded the rest of the western hemisphere for hundreds of years. By virtue of a good Samaritan action on the part of these Hutterites, he has gained entrance into a community where in many ways, time has left them unchanged, religiously and socially, for almost 500 years.

Gibby has always been aware of Hutterite colonies in British Columbia, but as most "English" do, he marginalized them.

As for the Hutterites, "the less we have to do with the English, the better." This phrase is echoed throughout the colonies.

When criticized by other Christians for not being more ecumenical they unashamedly admit that "If you truly seek God, you will find us."

"Mr. Geiberson how are you doing?" inquires Minister Hofer.

"I must be doing a lot better than I was," says a perplexed Gibby.

"You were close to saying hello to your Maker," adds Minister Hofer. He says this with the tone of a man who is comfortable with his Maker.

Gibby drops his head in an unusual gesture of agreement. Not at all accustomed to the feelings that accompany defeat, he's having a moment of confusion in both labeling it and really not a clue how to fight against it.

Looking down at his ankle, he tries to stand. The pain is more than he wants to deal with, forcing him back into his chair.

Frau Wildermuth has appeared with two stainless steel pails. One contains ice water and the other hot water.

"Put that foot in this pail," she orders. The tone of her voice is not mistaken. She's definitely not offering a choice. It's a command she expects to be followed.

The freezing content of that pail gives Gibby a momentary flash back to the earlier epoch accompanying his fall into the creek. This forced alliance with cold water and the circumstances encompassing it, are giving Gibby an unusual pause. It's certainly not the kind of pause he's ever had to deal with before.

"Holy shit, that's cold," shouts out Gibby.

Frau Wildermuth, not used to vulgarities mixed with the word "holy" feigns a giggle, not knowing how else to respond to this irreverent English.

"Now put it in the hot water," she orders. She only retires when the dinner bell rings, but not before prescribing "you alternate your foot in each of these for 5 minutes."

Gibby finds himself nodding in a most obsequious manner. He has never been so totally dependent since he was an infant.

An element contributing to Hutterite stability is their attention to order. The dinner bell has rung. It's purpose is to announce the noon meal. All drop what they are doing and make their way to the "essenzimmer" or the dining room.

Shortly, a young girl wearing a black head scarf with large white polka dots appears in Gibby's room. She's carrying a TV-style tray with a hot pork sandwich between slices of home baked, whole wheat bread, smothered in pork gravy, an ample cup of apple sauce, and a cruet filled with steaming coffee.

Without hesitation his primary concern switches from the pain in his foot to satisfying a two-day hunger.

The diehn, or young lady, places the tray directly in front of him. It's all he can do not appear as a gluttonous lout, so with great restraint, he waits for her to leave. Within minutes he has consumed every morsel, hardly finding a place between bites to take a breath. With gravy sticking to his several days old beard, he embarrassingly looks up to see the young lady returning for his empty tray. Sheepishly wiping his chin, he attempts a polite smile toward his server, thanking her as graciously as he's able.

"You're welcome" she says nervously blinking only adding to her attractiveness.

She's a simple, natural beauty, about twenty years old. Her long, plaid cotton dress fits her young curves perfectly. A crisp, white vest top gives her a strange, but tender, innocent appearance. She's a flower the outside world could never appreciate.

"I hope you enjoyed your lunch."

Her innocent small talk is strangely confident, reflecting an honest humility. Gibby finds her naivete strangely attractive. It seems to add to her charm.

He feels embarrassed by her kindness.

As soon as lunch has passed, Frau Wildermuth returns. Slightly turning his ankle one way and then another.

"Aahhgg," he lets out a gasp.

Looking directly at him, she rises to grab a roll of heavy gauze and begins to wrap his swollen appendage. "Your going to have to stay off that foot for awhile. You've gotten yourself a bad sprain."

Gibby, with a "doe in the head light look," and exhibiting a defiant tone asks, "How long you talkin'?" It's apparent he is not, at all, used to having his foreword motion curtailed, especially by some strange women.

"At least a couple weeks," she replies meeting his defiance with a sympathetic but firm voice.

This is not what he wants to hear.

"I can't do that," says Gibby as though Frau Wildermuth has the ability to heal him sooner but is choosing to restrain her healing powers.

"God does the healing and He won't be rushed" says Frau Wilder-muth, matter-of-factually.

Something in the body movements, along with looks on the faces of his rescuers, tells Gibby he may want to tone down his disappointment and maybe show a little appreciation.

Most people who arrive as guests at the Bruderhof come because they are looking for God. Gibby entered in an attempt to escape God. Curious as to how Gibby has come to cross paths with them, Minister Hofer's sense is that God is somehow involved in all of this and for the time being he is willing to wait for His intentions.

"Not to be forward son, however I'm curious, what events lead you to our door step?"

Gibby carefully crafted his tale leaving out any incriminating details.

"I was flying back from a business trip when I hit bad weather forcing me to land on, what I thought was, a clearing. It turned out to be a lake with a thin layer of snow over half thawed ice. My chopper went to the bottom. I'd of gone down with it if I hadn't gotten out to smoke a cigarette."

Minister Hofer glanced knowingly at the other men. "That lake is over 500-feet deep. Your helicopter is probably there to stay," he says with a tone of finality.

Gibby's mind wanders back to knowing he had left the chopper's door open. Even if he could send divers to recover the money, chances are it separated from the helicopter.

Now that the threat of death has passed, a fuller impact of the last week's happening are hitting Gibby hard: the loss of two friends, the loss of his helicopter, compounded by the worry about people who don't care about you -only the loss of their $2 million.

Frau Wildermuth soon returns with a "state of the art" pair of crutches.

Bruder Joshua Wipf was the last person to use these. He fell reshingling the barn roof. We've saved them especially for you Mr. Geiberson. This is as close to humor Frau Wildermuth will allow herself.

He has been assigned a small, one bedroom apartment in a larger complex with several other families. Carefully lying on the twin bed is the clothing he had on when rescued, all washed, dried and folded. The room is clean, but noticeably bare of any wall or window treatments. All the furnishings are wood finished with a clear varnish. What is conspicuously absent is a television or even a radio. On a small table, with a lamp next to a comfortable looking rocking chair is a Bible.

Out of curiosity and boredom he thumbs through it. It's written in German. He tosses it back and peeks out the window. The late afternoon sun is wrapping everything in a golden glow. Silence suddenly surrounds him. He takes a deep breath and utters a most more of a pitiful plea, "What the hell am I going to do?" It's as much a statement of his present place in life as it is a question. His life has been disrupted by uninvited tragedy. As well rehearsed and planned out that he imagined this adventure would be, it has turned into a reckless disaster. This turn of events has left him ill equipped for the present circumstances and depressed.

What is making this worse for Gibby's type "A" personality is him being forced into inactivity. His first thought is to hurl himself into the wall or pick up the small table and pitch it through the window. Thinking it through for a minute, it would only convince his, much-needed hosts, that they were dealing with a lunatic. He soon forsakes the urge as an impulsive idiocy.

Without notice there are three soft taps on his door. He finds his adrenaline has at least a small out let in hobbling over to open it.

It's the same pretty young lady named Rebecca who's brought his supper, readily presenting it in front of him on the same familiar tray as the noon meal.

Wanting to make conversation and possibly flirt some with her for a moment, he attempts a bit of small talk.

"So what do you do around here for fun?" he asks, giving her his widest smile.

"We sing or go for walks," she answers unapologetically. "Why do you ask?," she innocently questions, pausing for a thoughtful moment. "Would you care to join us?"

Taken, somewhat, back by her forthrightness, he furthers the conversation without answering her question by asking another question, "What do you sing?"

"We sing hymns." Her smile is a genuine smile brought about by pleasurable thoughts at the prospect.

Gibby is moved by her truthful, unapologetic innocence. "No, I think I'll pass," still trying to maintain his boyish charms. This attempt suddenly sounds hollow and shallow when compared with this server"s genuineness.

This kind of transparency and truthfulness is not a common trait among the women, of late, in Gibby's life. He finds her behavior both attractive and uncomfortable.

Not at all convinced he is going to be here any longer than a phone call, but in a flash, remembering that his phone is at the bottom of the lake, he is forced to consider his next conundrum.

"Would you, by chance, know where I could make a phone call?" he further questions his new friend.

"Minister Hofer has a phone in his office that he uses for business calls" she replies with the same frankness.

As she turns to leave, Gibby thanks her. Once again alone, with only his thoughts, he returns to stare out the window. The sun's bright golden glow has now turned to darkness. How unexpected.

"If it could have only stayed that way. It was beautiful," are his thoughts.

Now, under its mask, darkness is shrouding everything, adding even more to his heightening bewilderment.

In his well-planned world, he should be back in Vancouver celebrating with Tommy and Mooch on the success of their latest venture. Instead, he's has two dead friends and he's he's stuck in a Hutterite Bruderhof with people who haven't a clue what they're missing in life.

"I don't think life could get any worse than this," he thinks. Managing to muster enough pleasure from the warmth his bed is offering him, within minutes he is fast asleep.

In the course of time he is awakened by what is becoming a familiar sound. A dinner bell calls the colony to breakfast. Another familiar form appears at his door. It's Henry Woltman, the young man who saved his life.

"Did you hear that noise, Mr. Geiberson?" questions Henry with a quirky grin.

"Ya I heard a bell clangin' and then someone knockin' on my door," answers Gibby with a hint of irritation.

"No, not that noise, I mean the 'crack' of dawn," says Henry triumphantly, taking satisfaction in being able to pull something on this interloper.

Henry is fond of Rebecca. He's taken special notice of her being a bit to eager to be of help to this young charmer from the English. Even people sworn to pacifism and community prosperity can't help but be agitated when something they consider dear, is threatened. Henry is found to be no exception.

He isn't resentful for rescuing this outsider, after all it's his Christian duty. However, he is finding himself resentful over Gibby hindering his courting pursuits. He is particularly fearful of Rebecca finding Gibby's innovative flirtation attractive. Henry knows this is a sign of something of which he will need to repent. In the meantime, he fully intends to squeeze as much perverted sense of pleasure as he can from his ill feelings.

Gibby faintly recognizes Henry from the day before. While pulling his trousers on, he studies him for a moment. "Are you the guy that found me yesterday?"

"You were close enough to death to have crows circlin'," says Henry still straining with being civil. "I'm supposed to show you to the dining hall."

Always conscious of God's will in his life, Henry struggles with these uninvited emotions. He doesn't even have names for them.

Rising to his feet Gibby offers his hand to Henry, clearing his throat says, "I really want to thank you for what you did for me."

Henry looks at Gibby, hesitating just short of it becoming an uncomfortable moment. Finally accepting this nonverbal gesture of appreciation, he reaches out to welcome his waiting hand.

This simple, humble, sincere symbol of appreciation shown by Gibby has somewhat defused Henry's animosity causing him to see some of its absurdity.

"My name is Marlon Geiberson, but everyone calls me Gibby," he says extending his grip on Henry's hand a bit longer, hopefully to reflect his desire to be friendly.

"I'm Henry Wultman," says Henry in a rather flat tone. He's struggling with his pride and shame for harboring hostile feelings. Being forced out of hostility by shame and guilt is often a worse "affect" than harboring its "effect." It seems the devil is never in a hurry for those he's sure of, so the young get much of his attention.

Gibby hobbles along on his crutches down to the dining hall behind his guide. A sign above the door reads" Welcomin" and then below this the words "Essen Zimmer": Welcome, dining room.

In this culture the men all sit on one side of the room, the women on the other and the children in an annex off the main dining room. Older siblings often tending to the needs of the younger. German is spoken with English words interspersed.

He guides Gibby to the side with the men, watching carefully how Rachael reacts to Gibby's presence.

Maybe Henry has unconsciously adhered himself to that old adage "Hold your friends close, but your enemies closer" as he seats Gibby next to himself.

Those on cooking duty this week are pushing carts ladened with platters of eggs, sausage, ham and toast. Each table has seating for six as the serving sizes co-ordinate with the number seated. Henry has purposely seated himself alone at a table with Gibby.

"Where do you come from?" asks Henry as he dips his toast in the soft yolk of his eggs.

Gibby finds himself unconsciously identifying himself with his ranch life. Without hesitation he answers. "We are cattle ranchers. My family owns the Circle G North of Vancouver."

This admission gives Gibby pause. He remains dumbfounded at his words. He has been running from this admission with ferocity but now discovers that admitting this has struck within him the deepest pleasure.

"Oh, so you're a farm boy," says Henry now a little more at ease at this discovery.

"You might say that," says Gibby.

"What do you do there?" further inquires Henry.

"I work in the machine shop," says Gibby.

"Your kidding me, that's what I do" says Henry jolting back in his chair, bewildered at the common bond he is beginning to draw with this alien.

"You have a machine shop here?" questions Gibby, excited by the prospect.

"We have a state of the art shop," says Henry trying to squelch his boastful tone. Hutterites are not comfortable with blustering in themselves or in anyone else.

"I'd love to see it," confesses an excited Gibby

"We'll have to seek permission first," says Henry impenitently.

This simple statement of Henry's puzzles Gibby. He's taken back by the seeming obsequious behavior of someone no longer a child. He can't imagine something as innocuous as a request to merely see this facility would provoke such a servile reaction, especially in someone his own age.

Minister Hofer is sought out and the request is made. Henry returns within a few minutes. "The Minister said he will consider it and get back with us."

Gibby says nothing for a moment still bewildered at this sycophantic posturing, nonetheless, he shakes his head affirming the decision.

As Gibby is left to finish his breakfast, Henry excuses himself, making his way to meet with Reinhardt for devotions and his work assignment.

The Minister soon makes his way over to Gibby's table noticing that he is sitting alone. The rest have all left to get on with the devotions and their tasks for the day.

"Mind if I join you for a moment," asks a congenial Hofer.

"Please sit down," says Gibby, motioning toward the chair across the table.

"How are you feeling this morning Mr. Geiberson? You look much better."

"I feel much better and I wish to say thank you for all you've done for me," says Gibby courteously. Thinking to himself how much he reminds himself of his father with all this gentility. It actually seems good for a change.

"That's good to hear. How would you like to earn your accommodations for today? After all Our Lord reminds us that 'he who doesn't work neither should he eat'," says Minister Hofer with a scant hint of a twinkle in his eye.

Hutterites tend to shy away from extremes, "Everything in moderation," that includes humor.

Gibby is left blushed. Somewhat embarrassed at this censure, realizing he had already taken so much that he hadn't earned.

"I'd be happy to help out in anyway you see fit," says a conscience-stricken Gibby.

Gibby recognizes the Minister's authority and even finds himself respecting the man. After all, there has been no shortage of kindness from these people.

"Good, follow me," says a smiling Hofer. He smacked his palms on the table as he rises, gesturing toward the door with a side head movement.

Getting to his feet, Gibby hobbles along on his crutches. He soon finds himself in a long barn. It has an unfamiliar odor, but definitely the odor of some farm animal. In a matter of moments his visual has caught up with his nose. *"I'm in a goddam' chicken coop,"* go his thoughts.

Cattle men have an arrogance within themselves, declaring that to bother with any other livestock is an inferior endeavor, remaining beneath their dignity.

The Bruderhof, on the other hand, doesn't place such restrictions on their husbandry, raising whatever livestock makes them money.

Gibby is given a crash course in egg sorting. Consequently, by the time the lunch bell rings, he has sorted enough eggs to last a life time. He's worked alone all morning, forthwith, now finding he is anxious to have Henry's company again at lunch.

Arriving at the Essen Zimmer he looks for Henry, but is met by Hofer and several other men. They assign him a seat at their table. Carefully concealing his disappointment, he graciously accepts their invitation.

Hofer introduces him to Mike Stahl. Mike is currently the assistant to Wilhelm Wildermuth, the finance manager.

"Bruder Stahl could use some assistance after lunch, so I assigned you to him for the remainder of the day. He needs someone who can use a calculator and work at some simple accounting chores. You look like you could fill that bill."

Again Gibby conceals his disappointment. He yearns to get into that machine shop, but he is a guest here and nods a "yes" to the Minister. He's resigned to help out where he can.

"I do have one request if I may," says Gibby as respectfully as he can.

"What may that be," questions the Minister cocking his head slightly to one side giving the impression of wanting to hear clearly.

"I would like to use a phone. I need to make a call," says Gibby, then quickly adds, "but only if it's convenient for you."

He's somewhat dumbfounded at how attentive he's been to others needs in the last couple days. Still if push came to shove, his own personal needs would trump over any community needs.

The Minister pauses for a moment, looking hard at Gibby as though he were watching for something that's been puzzling him. "Yes, I believe we can arrange that. Meet me at my apartment at 5 pm."

Gibby finishes the rest of the afternoon assisting Mike. His thoughts race. He knows the only way he is going to get out of here is if he can get to his money. He has $800,000 in drug earnings in his safe at his condo in Vancouver.

He is also conscious of the fact that the only person who can help him is Rachael. Up until this emergency, he considered her trustworthiness questionable. Now if he is to get out of here, he must throw caution to the wind and bring her into his trust.

As nice as these people are, and as much as he admires their honest, simple lives, he feels much more at ease in settings more familiar to him. Getting out of here hastily is quickly becoming his priority.

Knocking at the Minister's door, he is promptly greeted and cordially invited into a room that serves as the Minister's office. Its starkness surprises him. It's bare of procurements. No wall hangings, save a calender with pictures of silos. No plaques of achievement. No artistic statuary on his mantle. No overstuffed leather chairs.

Rather, there is a metal desk, a non-matching kitchen chair with an ill-fitting cushion. A metal filing cabinet, a fluorescent light hanging by chains from the ceiling and another kitchen chair for visitors. The floors are hardwood with throw rugs in front of each exterior door to catch the mud. What appears to be out of place in this parsonical setting is a state of the art computer.

Hutterites do not object to these modern conveniences as long as they will advance their community. The greater good of the community is always the overriding concern of all members. The individual is only here to serve the community. They have successfully managed to continue this practice for as long as they have existed.

Complying with Gibby's request to use his phone, Hofer points him to a black rotary dial phone setting in a prominent, convenient spot on his desk. He then pulls the other chair to the phone, cordially inviting Gibby with a hand gesture to sit if he wishes.

Obliging himself, Gibby takes the seat. He stares at the phone. Never has he seen a phone like this. Not sure he knows how it works, he cautiously pushes his finger against each number encircled in the dial. Realizing nothing is happening, and with a clear look of bewilderment, he looks to Minister Hofer then back to the telephone.

"What should I do," he asks clearly frustrated.

The Minister finally catches Gibby's drift realizing that he's helpless before this archaic piece of electronics.

"You just dial your number like this," says the Minister rotating the number to the finger stopper, muttering something about, "this younger generation."

Cautiously, but deliberately, Gibby dials Rachael's cell number. Hearing it ring raises his anxiety level for the moment.

The Hutterites don't have a sense of privacy like the "English" so Minister Hofer continues with his tasks. Gibby expected he would be allowed a few minutes alone without being overheard. It doesn't appear that's going to happen.

"Hello Rachael, how you doin' babe?"

"How in the hell do you think I'm doin', I haven't heard from you all week. What the hell is the matter with you leavin' me here and you disappearin' with no word for a week. That's how I'm doin'!"

"Yah I know I should have called you, but something have changed."

"You ain't in jail are ya?" questions Rachael

"No, no nothing like that." Replies Gibby.

"Well, I had two of your Chinese buddies come here and insist I tell them where you are. I told 'em I didn't have a clue where your sorry ass was."

Gibby is up out of his chair, clearly agitated, pacing as best he can with the limited length of phone cord and an injured ankle.

"Listen to me Rachael and listen to me close. You need to follow my instructions to the letter."

He goes on to tell her where the key to that locked room is hidden, how to disable the alarm system and the combination to gain entrance to the safe. He also gives her the address of The Bruderhof.

"Rachael, when you open the safe I want you to empty the contents into your gym bag and immediately drive to this address. Can I depend on you, babe?"

She assures him she will take care of things, promising that she will be there in a couple of days to pick him up.

With the Minister permission, he also gives her The Bruderhof phone number.

Hanging up the phone Gibby lets out a sigh, reflecting a sense of relief out of the conversation. *"I hope I haven't left anything out,"* he thinks to himself.

Hofer, without comment, picks up the phone and places it back where he is accustomed to use it.

Gibby thanks him, returning to his room to wait for the 6 p.m. supper bell.

CHAPTER 16

THE FAMINE

"... There he squandered his wealth in the wild living. After he had spent everything, there was a severe famine in the whole country and he began to be in need. So he went and hired himself out to a civilian of that country, who sent him to his fields to feed pigs. He longed to fill his stomach with the pods that the pigs were eating, but no one gave him anything.'

"When he came to his senses, he says 'how many of my father's hired men have food to eat, and here I am starving to death, I will set out and go back to my father and say to him: Father, I have sinned against heaven and against you. I am no longer worthy to be called your son: make me like one of your hired men.'

"So he got up and went to his father." Luke15;13-20

This morning is the third day Gibby has been hosted by the Hutterite Bruderhof. He is beginning to catch on to the rhythm of the colony. Much of what he hears is in an old Tyrolean German dialect. Thankfully, when speaking to him, they use English.

This morning, when the brothers received their work assignments, it was agreed that Henry could arrange for a replacement in the machine shop in the place of a brother who is unable to make it. He asked permission to use the "English" to fill the vacancy. After a brief conference with the "Gemein", or the leadership, he was granted permission.

Hutterite leaders are chosen because of their resolve to maintain the integrity of the past 500 years. When someone from the outside is in their midst they carefully measure the vulnerability of each person that will come in contact with the outsider. The colonies have been successful in keeping over 95 percent of their people in their community and with careful scrutiny, they intend to keep it that way.

Gibby is delighted. As soon as he enters the shop and catches a whiff of the distinct and odor of the cutting oils, he feels a flush of contentment that he hasn't experienced in several seasons.

This machine shop is a tribute to every piece of equipment that has ever been built. There are overhead belts driving machines that can be dated back to the 1930s. Paralleling these but not in contradiction are machines that are computerized. There are at least a half dozen brothers displaying skills from welding, to fabricating, to machine repair. Surrealistically working in concert with each other.

Gibby is placed with a brother deftly entering instructions via computer, to a router. There is the constant reminder not to hesitate to use any machine that will better do a job and advance the welfare of the colony, that includes computers.

Competition between individuals is frowned upon, however, competition among department managers is encouraged because it leads to greater productivity.

Minister Hofer has been heard to say "We do not deny basic human drives, but merely subject them all to God."

Gibby doesn't understand much of the theology of the Hutterites. So far he is left to imagine that the sum of their belief is to be honest, forthright, reasonable people. Joking around is not something they do well with each other for fear of recrimination, however they don't hesitate with an outsider like himself.

A few more days fly by. Gibby is expecting Rachael to be pulling in at anytime. Four days later she is still not here, nor has she called.

He has confided in Henry over his concern, on the other hand, not wanting to confide too deep he keeps it superficial. "I hope she hasn't had an accident or car trouble."

Recognizing Gibby's growing anxiousness, Henry's inclination is to be helpful. "I don't know either, maybe you should ask Minister Hofer to use his phone once more, and see if you can contact her."

There are many cell phones in the colony, but they aren't personal phones. They belong to each department, and are all turned in at the end of the work day. The unwritten rule is that they are used for business only.

Gibby doesn't fear the Minister, though he is inclined to remain respectful toward the conservative values of his host by trying not appear to be frivolous or demanding. He finally musters enough manful resolve to approach the Minister.

"Sir, I know you would have contacted me had there been any messages. My friend was supposed to be here days ago, I'm worried because she hasn't arrived and would like permission to make another call."

Hofer gives Gibby a quick, hard gaze, full of concern. "Permission granted. Come on along. We'll take care of this problem."

They make their way to the Minister's office. He opens the unlocked door and motions for Gibby to use what he needs.

The call rings and rings and finally goes to voice mail. Gibby's breathing is much harder and quicker now. He feels a wave of sick emptiness in his stomach. His suspicion is that Rachael may not be coming because she has chosen not to.

His mistrust is more than a jealous paranoia. He knows enough about this paramour to realize she is an opportunist. Giving her access to nearly a million dollars in cash was probably more than she could honestly deal with.

Slowly, deliberately, he sets the phone back on its cradle. His eyes have a blank stare as the sickness is doing its best to turn to panic. His body begins to shake. He fears what is happening to him as his losses are compounding. Endeavoring to fight its desire to have him, he knows he has to work through this.

Picking up his crutches, he makes his way to the door, turning long enough to thank the Minister for the use of the phone.

With that same intense gaze Hofer reaches out to this crestfallen young man. "I understand you prefer to be called Gibby. Well Gibby, if there is anything pressing on your heart, and you feel the need to talk with someone, consider my door always open."

Gibby feels the warm flush of tears trying to force their way through his feeble attempt to remain stoic.

"I appreciate that offer. Right now I'm not feeling my best. I think I'm going to have to work on this alone for awhile."

With this same intense watchfulness the Minister put his hand on Gibby's shoulder, giving a piece of unsolicited advice, "Ask God to help you."

Gibby leaves with out comment, returning with a heavy heart to his room. He feels, alone and abandoned.

It does not occur to him to ask why Rachael would do this to him. He knows exactly why. It would be like asking a poisonous snake why it bit you after you had dared yourself to bring it into your house. Poisonous snakes bite because that's what they do. Rachael could only do what the Rachael's of the world naturally do.

Slumping into a chair, he hopes to take his mind off his injured soul by turning his attention to his discolored, horribly swollen ankle.

Tightly re-wrapping his wound, he is feeling something he has never felt in his life. It's the depression that accompanies the deterioration of the soul. "If this is what depression feels like, I hope it ends quick," he thinks.

Over the next few days, this wish is not to be. He finds himself going deeper into this seeming endless pit of black despair. Barely eating or sleeping, his depressed soul and mind bar any joy. Even his beloved machine shop offers no relief.

A good share of the Bruderhof business is raising and slaughtering pigs. After a month of sit down jobs, Gibby's ankle has healed enough to begin to put weight on it without crutches. He has had various jobs around the colony except one: today he has been assigned to feeding pigs.

All alone with this task, gives Gibby time to evaluate his past decisions. How he wanted his life to be his own apart from his family. How he had selfishly thanked his father for all he had done for him, although from that point on he wanted his life to be his alone. How he had marginalized his father and left. How his decisions have led him to the place he is today.

Watching these pigs happily swell down their feed, leads him to wonder what he could swell down to make himself this happy.

He longs for something, anything to fill the emptiness he's experiencing. He envies the happiness the pigs seem to have in the simple enjoyment of eating. No one is giving him anything, on the other hand. No human can give another the kind of food he longs for. Happiness, like rain, does not merely drop out of the sky. Both have a long history. Each person God has created must individually reconnect with the Creator as the Source of happiness. Gibby is not to be an exception.

Even though he never imagined that he would lose everything his father had given him, his imagination has not saved him. Hasn't he convinced himself that Gibby was strong enough to not let the world's allurements take him captive? Hasn't he convinced himself that he has been especially endowed with gifts from God to enable him to piss directly into the wind and not get wet?

Reflecting back, "*Hadn't there been a mental and spiritual break with the ranch before I left physically? It had been easy to blame Dillon, but then, hadn't I already divorced myself from dad's values? Maybe Dillon only proved to be the catalyst.*"

A brooding depression continues to plague him. He hardly wants to review his failed life. Not only has he lost his wealth, he has lost himself. Where he had once been able to shun any emotions, now he has no power over them. They have hooked themselves into his deepest recesses and now are pulling him, at will, in every direction.

Later that evening, out of desperation, he seeks out Henry.

"Henry I need to talk with someone, do you mind?"

"No, not at all. Let me get my coat."

With that, they start down the path leading down the lane, the lane that lead him here just a month ago.

"Henry, have you ever had a thought become so clear that it made you wonder why it took so long for you to see it?"

Henry doesn't respond with an answer, however, one can tell he's struggling to come up with something that will make Gibby feel better.

Not really needing Henry's answer, Gibby is satisfied to have someone listen to him. Someone with flesh and blood.

"Today when I was feeding the pigs, I had something come so clear. I looked at those pigs eating everything that came their way. They couldn't have been happier or more content. I envied those damnable creatures. I have thrown away all the happiness I enjoyed in my father's house. I saw no value in it. It was not until I was feeding those damned-able pigs that it became clear what I have turned my back on.

"It's now only when the pain and misery of my stupid life rises up to greet me at times like these, do I remember how generous my father was to me and all those men working for him.

"Henry, I think I've come to my senses. I want to go home!" says Gibby, laughing only as one who has found relief.

Rather than seeing his father as an enemy as he had, he now sees him as a drawing force, a power of attraction, drawing him back to his roots like a powerful magnet.

Again Henry can only look at Gibby as one who has never left home. Henry's thoughts are thanking God that he has never found a reason to leave the security of the Bruderhof, or that he has never been left destitute with out family and God.

Material, spiritual, intellectual, social and psychological needs are met in Henry's community. It's commonly referred to in German as "Ordung" or the "Order". It is an orderly, predictable existence. The basic human drives have not been deprived him, only that he subject them to God.

Gibby's heart is beating so fast, he can feel that welcome surge of adrenaline fulminating in celebration with his decision.

Even the little sayings written above the doors in the Bruderhof are coming to life. The one written over his own door, he suspects is something from scripture, but then he has no idea exactly where. Henry translates for him. It reads "Better is a little with the fear of the Lord, than great treasure with trouble."

Gibby sleeps the best that he has in a long time. Until now, waking without anxiety seems to be one of those normal luxuries of life that has been alluding him.

He's feeling well rested and at peace with his new resolve. He has yet to attend any of the "Gebet" or prayer meetings because they are in German. However, today he sat through the morning devotion with a peace that comes only when one has made a truce with God. Afterward he asks the minister for a moment.

"Sir, I cannot thank you enough for what you have done for me." Pausing for a moment to organize his next thought. " But now, I believe it's time I go home," says Gibby resolutely standing on his feet, refusing the offer to sit.

"Well Gibby, may I ask what brings you to this decision?" asks the minister. He has a pleasant, quizzical way of presenting his questions that one doesn't mind answering.

Tears begin to well up in Gibby's eyes, his voice quivers.

"I've really done my father a disservice. He always went out of his way to love me, even when, by any stretch, I was unlovable. My selfish rebellion told me I could have a fulfilled life doing things my own way. I'm a mess and I can't do anything about it. I just need to get home."

"What makes you think your father will let you come home," asks the Minister.

This question gives Gibby pause.

"I'm not sure he will take me back. I'm hoping I can just be a hired man."

The minister studies Gibby for just a moment as he recalls a similar young man in a biblical parable. He knows the outcome of that story and hopes it will be the same for this young repentant.

"If things do not work out at home I want you to know you are welcome with us," he says with the tenderness of a true father. Gibby thanks the minister once again, knowing he will not return. It's time to make his way back home.

Rubbing his hands across his bristly chin he contemplates what he has to do next. He feels like he's been a foreigner in a distant land. Inwardly he is repentant of the wild, rebellious life, lured on by the false promise that the power and money would give him fulfillment. He knows from his own experience this has been a dangerous undertaking. Sweet danger has always had its hold on Gibby. Now the hope he holds onto is that his father will accept his repentance and just give him a chance. Any chance.

The truth is Gibby has had a spiritual awakening regarding his own emerging manhood and its rightful place in God's universe. For the first time in his young life, he is looking at it honestly. Since he has been living in community with these Hutterites, their "Ordung", contrasted with his chosen life style, has left his wanting. He's beginning to see where his own misbegotten life doomed him to failure.

The following day Gibby is making his rounds, saying his good-byes. Following the noon meal he is met by Minister Hofer, Henry, Wilhelm and his wife Irene. "We have been blessed by your presence with us. You had a need, and by God's grace we have been able to share with you what He has blessed us with. The Bruderhof would like to give you the gift of a bus ticket and expense money for your trip home" says Henry.

For a momentary lack of words Gibby stands quietly. His mouth is trying to form words but no words are coming. He is truly having an emotional break down, although in a humble, healthy way. His old ways are beginning to shed off from lack of use. He actually desires a new beginning. Something these people are living has struck his soul. He longs for the peace and contentment they have.

With tears forming, he takes a moment to wipe his nose. "I readily admit the past month with you has brought me to some new insights. From the bottom of my heart, I thank you for that. I also appreciate your generosity to send me home by bus. Now I must risk the chance I may offend you. I'm going to decline your offer, hoping you'll understand. I've decided I need to make my way back home slowly and purposely, -so I've decided to walk."

Uncharacteristically of this stoic minister, he pauses for a moment studying Gibby. In a burst of emotion, he grabs both his shoulders, looking him straight in the eyes, deliberately forming his word in a bold voice declares, "Watch for God on your journey.". He again remembers the ancient story of another prodigal son's return home.

Just as uncharacteristically, of Gibby, he embraces the minister with the words, "I already have."

With that, Gibby begins to pack.

CHAPTER 17

THE RETURN
...' I will set out and go back to my father...Luke 15:20

It's the end of March. The dreary greyness of winter is giving way to the dawn of yet another spring. Nonetheless, the weather patterns remain in flux as though some dark and foreboding power refuses to relinquish its portentous grip.

Within days Gibby has said his good-byes to anyone and everyone in the Bruderhof who has touched his life.

What meager possessions he had when he arrived, have long since been returned to him. He is determined not to take any unnecessary gifts, nonetheless he has conceded to accept a backpack, a sleeping bag, some beef jerky, bottled water and a cash gift of $100.

Rebecca and a number of the other young girls have gotten together to knit him a stocking cap, a pair of gloves and a scarf, which he graciously accepts.

Leaving the safety of the Bruderhof behind, he begins his long pilgrimage the only way it can be done: one foot step at a time. Often up to ten hours a day he trudges toward home. Many nights, he falls into his sleeping bag without even making a fire. In the morning, he binds his blistered feet as best he can and continues his march with muscles still aching from the day before. Periodically, he will stop, step off the road into the woods, slump down under a tree, weak and exhausted.

Much of his thoughts turn to his fathers house. The sound of his fathers chuckle, and how his mothers hands always smelled of sweet onions as she would smooth his tasseled hair away from his eyes.

April is also occupying much more of his thoughts lately. He wonders if he has fathered a boy or a girl. He also pictures her red hair and how it always seemed to be fresh and bouncy, how she held her head to one side as she looked at him with those blue-green eyes. Oh her eyes! The hurt he saw in them as he walked away, leaving her alone and pregnant with his child, to fend by herself as best she could. Unchecked selfishness has always tried to convince its purveyor that any end it seeks is good, thus allowing its own perverse pursuits to become more and more paramount. It then readily ignores the collateral damage these selfish ends inflict on others. These chickens are now coming home to roost in Gibby's life in the form of guilt and remorse.

"Oh, dad, mom, April how can I ever make it up to you," he almost shouts, as the repetition of his foot steps continue, mile after mile, with hardly a glance at his surroundings. This is far from the sight-seeing tour it could have been under different circumstances. His mind is busy with home.

The distance he has yet to travel, and the intensity of his desire to be there often overwhelm him. It comes in the form of panic attacks. His face has, long ago, been stripped of its usual cocky, self assurance, forcing him to become more and more aware of his own powerlessness.

"Who do I belong to?" becomes his preoccupation. The Hutterites suggested that he belongs to the world, at least in his thinking. *Right now I feel*

*like a rudderless ship, defenseless against these all these pounding waves of uncer-
tainty in my life"* says Gibby to himself. He's neither frightened nor unafraid,
rather, he feels completely, and intensely, lost. It's times like these ,he truly
yearns for those seemingly simple, happier times of his younger days.

Darkness of any kind, leaves a person confused and floundering, like
a person stuck in a darkened building with no lamps. Gibby has followed
everything the world has to offer as a guiding light, only to find himself
still hopelessly lost. Darkness cannot produce light. The light has to come
from an outside source. He is slowly accepting this fact and beginning to
be tenderized enough to stop resisting a loving God whose only purpose
is to bring him home.

"God just help me get home" has recently become his daily mantra.
He can't help but reflect back to the days with the Hutterites. They knew
who they belong to. There is no question in their minds they belong to
God first, and then to one another.

With only the warmth of his fire to comfort him, and sitting alone,
night after night in a cold patch of a desolation that he alone has created,
he is discovering the resentment he still holds for his brother, will not allow him the warmth his soul craves.

The more he dwells on this, the more lost he becomes. Not able to
forgive his brother prevents him from fabricating a home without him.
The home he yearns for demands overlooking the shortcoming of all it's
members. After all, isn't this house the house of his father? Doesn't he
alone have the authority to demand requirements for membership?

Norbert has always been a fair and giving man. Even his hired men
come back and work for him year after year. Gibby finds himself envying
the relationship these men have with his father.

"My father has treated these hired guys with a decent wage. Maybe I
can, at most, ask him to simply let me work with these guys."

The beef jerky the young Hutterite girls packed for him ran out weeks ago. Nonetheless, the $100 he was given goes a long ways when parceled out at a couple dollars a day. He has eaten at least once everyday. As the weeks have gone by, he has taken on more and more of a disheveled look, bringing out enough sympathy to get at least one, good free meal a day. It seems his daily bread is being provided.

CHAPTER 18

MEANWHILE, BACK AT THE RANCH

It's nearing the end of March. The Circle G has come alive after a long winter. Norbert is rounding up all the ranch hands he laid off last fall. This is the beginning of calf and branding season. Work begins at sun up and ends at sun down.

Maybe the loss of her youngest prodigy has prompted Joanie to be more vigilant in fulfilling her role as wife and mother. On this particular occasion Norbert is her target.

"I know you don't think so Norbert, however, I think you need to let one of the buckaroos do some of the chores you're doing. I think you're getting too old to still try and do as much as you do," harps Joanie in her motherly tone.

Norbert tilts his hat back with what can only be described as a naughty grin.

"Ya but just think baby, if I keel over, you can get yourself one of these young bucks," says Norbert still grinning as he playfully slaps her on the behind.

"Norbert stop it, I'm serious. You need to slow down and let Dillon and Jed handle more of these things around here."

Norbert still not ready to take her concerns seriously, he strikes a body builder's pose as if to show his youthful muscles.

Studying him for a moment, still trying to be serious, she gives into his stupid antics.

"Your impossible! You haven't heard a word I've said," pausing for a moment hoping he'll begin to take her serious she adds, "All I want is to take good care of you. I don't know what I'd do without you."

"Don't worry babe, I'll be just fine" says Norbert conceding a bit.

Her eyes drop a little, as they do when she has something else on her mind.

"I wish we'd hear from Gibby. Sometimes I just want to drive into Vancouver and find him."

Suddenly Norbert's demeanor takes on a much more serious tone.

"The hardest thing I've ever had to do was to let that boy go," says Norbert. "No Joanie, if we want his heart and not just his body, we're going to have to wait." Giving his words a second thought he adds, "It takes longer to tenderize that part."

"I wish life could be easier," says Joanie, continuing her fussing with a basket of clean laundry.

Norbert has lived with this woman long enough to realize she will continue to grieve, and for that matter, so will he until this prodigal son makes his way back home. Their prayer together is that it will be soon.

Even with Gibby out of the way Dillon remains unsettled. His hate for his brother increases each time he sees the growing belly of April, along with his disdain for her.

Many of Gibby's sins may be against his own flesh, taking chances with fast living the way he does. But Dillon's sins are much higher up in his nature. His sins are against love itself.

Whenever someone innocently asks him anything concerning his brother, still frozen in his anger, he snaps back, "He's probably on his way to hell!"

Norbert has always loved his sons equally, realizing both their strengths and short comings. Gibby's sins are pretty base, wine, women and fast living.

Dillon on the other hand has tried to model himself as the opposite of his brother. He disguises his sins by giving them culturally accepted names. His arrogance is referred by him to be a healthy self esteem. After all isn't he the dutiful, diligent, obedient son to his father? He's sure others could use him as a righteous prototype for their own children. The bubble of anger that surfaces from far below displaying his rottenness, he excuses as righteous anger.

"I don't let people pull their shit on me." This has been the continuing mantra of many a lonely, hate-filled man.

Getting even, in a quiet secretive manner, is a way of life for Dillon. In many ways he's the archetypical passive-aggressive.

Norbert has told, neither his wife nor Dillon, that several months previous, two Chinese men had come to the ranch inquiring about Gibby and his whereabouts. They weren't clear concerning the nature of their inquiries. All they would tell him is they had hired him to fly some goods for them and he had not returned.

"You say he was scheduled to arrive back in Vancouver a week ago and you haven't heard from him," asked Norbert trying not to appear alarmed.

The first Chinese man is a young man about Gibby's age, the second is older and so far has allowed the younger man to do the talking.

Interrupting at this point, the older man said, "We are hoping you may have information that will help us locate him."

Assuring them he has not heard from Gibby, they left. For obvious reasons, this discussion left him unsettled. So much for peace of mind.

Norbert has made it a policy not to burden Joanie with problems that she doesn't need. He wisely chose to carry this burden by himself.

Now it's several months later. The uneasiness of not knowing the fate of his youngest son forces him to make the trip he has said he didn't want to make.

Leaving for Vancouver under the pretense of business, he is able to conceal from Joanie his real reason for the drive.

What he wouldn't give to have this actually be a routine business trip. Instead, he finds himself arriving in Vancouver with nothing more than an address he had finally convinced Pete Simon to relinquish.

It's to a small pizzeria. Making his way from the small parking lot in the rear he enters through the back entrance. Surprised to find a pizza parlor totally staffed with Chinese, he confronts a pretty young Chinese waitress, "I've been told that you may have seen this man," he shows her a picture of Gibby.

"Yah, I know him, that's Gibby. He usta come here all the time but I haven't seen him in quite a while."

Norbert can feel the blood forcing its way through his temples in response to what this can mean.

Just then, a man appears from around the corner of the kitchen. Norbert immediately recognizes him as the younger Chinese man visiting the ranch. The man, summarily excuses the young waitress with a hand gesture.

With another gesture, he points Norbert to an empty booth. Ironically, it's the same one usually reserved for the business dealings between Gibby, Tommy and Mooch.

The young Chinese man sits opposite of Norbert with folded arms on the table. "So have you heard anything?"

Norbert, still puzzled by all this mystery surrounding his son says, "No, but I'm hoping to find more information. If my suspicions serve me correctly, and I'm inclined to believe they do, you know more about my son then you're letting on. I'm here to find my boy and I don't intend to leave until I do."

The young Chinese man studies this fatherly investigator. He concludes he probably shouldn't antagonize him and may find him a useful ally.

Extending his hand he introduces himself as Marty Li, Tommy's cousin, which doesn't mean anything to Norbert. Norbert ignores the gesture staring intently.

Measuring his words, without going into the details concerning the nature of his business dealing with his Gibby he begins to explain how his cousins had drowned, on what had been a routine business trip, and how Gibby has mysteriously disappeared. He went on further to elaborate on how Gibby's girlfriend had been tracked into Mexico, but without Gibby.

What he doesn't elaborate on, was when they found her, she had $800,000 in cash and admitted she had stolen it from Gibby. She also implied that she wasn't interested in picking him up once she found the money, and had left him with some farm people who had rescued him from an accident. Furthermore, she claimed, she hadn't bothered to keep the information of his whereabouts. The Triad confiscated the $800,000, applying it to any short fall that may occur when Gibby surfaces.

Still puzzled by the clandestine nature surrounding his son and those associated with him, Norbert momentarily plays with his lips, running his fingers across them, suspecting this Marty fellow isn't going to be forthright with him. Taking a moment to resign himself to this obvious fact, he finally stands up, extending his hand toward Marty.

"I want to thank you for telling me as much as you have."

Marty took his offer of a handshake and returned to his kitchen thankful the meeting is over.

The weather patterns for this early spring are in a state of constant change. One day it can be below freezing, the next twenty degrees above.

As Norbert returns to the ranch, he barely pays attention to the rhythm of his windshield wipers as they try and keep up with a slushy rain. His mind is on his son.

He tries as best he can to reflect on everything Marty told him. Reading between the lines, he knows Gibby has gotten himself into something over his head. Norbert swallows hard trying to hold back the tears. The well being of his lost son is at stake.

The heart of a true father aches for any of his children who may be lost. It's a mixture of love and powerlessness. Nevertheless, his love is greater than the ache. His love is the kind that knows it can't force his son home. It's the kind of love that offers freedom. Freedom to leave and freedom to return. The door remain open both ways.

Norbert grips the wheel of his truck hard, alternating his hands as he wipes his tears. It's a long, sad trip back to the ranch.

Chapter 19

THE PRODIGAL FATHER

"... and while he was still a long way off, his father saw him coming . Filled with compassion and love, he ran out to meet him, embraced him and kissed him. Luke 15:20

"...His son said to him," Father I have sinned against both heaven and you. I am no longer worthy to be called your son. Luke15:21.

"... 'Quick! Bring the finest robe in the house and put it on him.' Luke 15:20"

Taking a long deep breath, sucking it almost to the bottom of his guts, Gibby lets it escape out into the spring mist that suffuses much of the air this time of year.

He knows he's getting closer to home as a few things become increasingly familiar. He's feeling a strange combination of homesickness and apprehension.

It's been six months since he left the security of his father's house. It may have well been six years. There remains something distant about it, on the other hand, the closer he gets, the more his thoughts turn to the familiar. His thoughts no longer see the ranch as something he needs to escape from, but rather a home he needs to return to.

For all the bright prospects leaving home may have promised, they ultimately failed him. But then failure, only in such depth, is necessary to assure that he has a sharp understanding of the meaning of coming home.

Rejecting the values of his patricians is the way Gibby would have described himself six months ago. He would readily admit today that he had left his father's house in 'thinking' long before he had physically. It's not that his father was bad, rather his leaving had more to do with his goodness. Norbert's goodness reproached Gibby. He did not wish to live up to his father's invitation to become more like him.

The questions he encounters within himself, step by step is, "What's pulling me back home? Is it to escape the famine of my life in Vancouver has produced? Do I …....? Some questions remain unanswered and unformed.

The closer he gets, the more difficult it becomes to reject these thoughts. Not because they are wrong, rather by embracing them, they promise a completeness for which he yearns. Still not able to grasp all that's happening, he knows the things that had lured him away have been used up. The world stands naked, exposing itself for what it is. The liberating guarantee it initially promised, proved to be temporary in nature, and shallow at best, always with the addendum that in order to experience all the world has to offer, the commitment to old truths and values were the lies that one needed to be free of.

His father has left a footprint of these old truths on his soul. Patience, kindness, and forgiveness: the things he rebelled against are now the things that are pulling him back home. As he begins to embrace the value of these old truths, he is sensitive to death rancorously releasing its grip, as life slowly begins to work its way back into his person.

The morning drizzle is morphing itself into an intense rain. Speeding cars going by send a cold spray swirling in odd formations. A car load of teenagers run a window down and throw the leftovers of their lunch, striking him with the remains of a chocolate malt. It quickly mixes with the dirt and grime he's acquired over the past several weeks.

His matted, tangled hair, his tattered, filthy clothing and the limp, his unhealed ankle has forced on him, have created a Quasimodo appearance about him. Coming into the sight of other unfortunates with whom he's allied, now it seems, by their responses, that he has lost any commonality with even the lowest of humans. Even these other broken fellow humans he encounters are marginalizing him. He has lost any remaining dignity that could give him rank anywhere. He now has more in common with the pigs he attended than he does with those humans who now assail him.

The hissing sound of car tires continue their assault, forcing a mixture of road grime into every crevice on his body.

"Please God, please, I don't want to be a pig anymore. I'm only going to ask dad if I can work for Jed. I've hurt him too much and don't deserve to be called his son."

His thoughts continue to ramble around and around banging against the inside of his head. "I know I can work my way back, I hope dad gives me a chance. God, I'm so tired of being a pig, please help me."

Gibby has moments of relief when he discovers that getting to a happier place means getting rid of all these things in life that prevent it. It's like peeling an onion layer by layer.

Mile after mile and layer after layer have been left behind. Even the bitterness he felt toward Dillon has been discarded as so much refuse.

Norbert has arrived back at the ranch. His face shows his disappointment in not finding Gibby. The rain pelts him as he slowly makes his way into the house. Before entering, he turns and looks longingly down the road as though expecting someone. Lowering his head against the elements, he pushes on into the house.

"Good grief Norbert, you're soaked. Get those wet clothes off before you catch your death."

Joanie is visibly perturbed as she strips him of his wet jacket.

Gibby has, at last, found his way to the entrance of his father's ranch. The rain is harder, pelting him with each drop as though it were trying to cleanse him. His body is racked with chills, but the excitement of being this close to his final destination drives him on.

With respect to his diligence to work his way back, his physical strength is failing him. With 25 percent of his body weight used up this last month his singular effort is indictable. Gibby is laying face down in a mixture of mud and rain. It covers him completely. It's quite the departure from the slick dressed, self-assured gangster life he was leading two months ago.

The rain continues relentlessly, yet in spite of its pounding efforts to cleanse him, it's failing. It has no warmth, no forgiveness, no exoneration, no ability to restore him. All it's capable of carrying out is to rack his sick body with a bone chilling cold. His deteriorated condition has left him helpless. Once again he's faced with the threat of hypothermia. He has come this far on his own, though to come up short at less than a quarter mile or as much as a 100 miles is still to come up short. In either situation he is going to require a rescuer.

Less than a quarter mile away up the road, Norbert gives in to Joanie's merciless insistence he shed his wet clothing. Now down to only a pair of boxer shorts, he makes his way to the kitchen for a hot cup of coffee.

As has been his habit, whenever he passes the kitchen window, he peers down the long driveway. Today something catches his eye. Moving a step closer to the window, he squints, hoping to reassure himself exactly what it is he's looking at.

"Oh my God!" he shouts, as he tears toward the door.

"What is the matter with you Norbert," shouts back Joanie, grabbing him by the arm.

Jerking loose of her grasp, he bolts out the door half naked on a full run, unmindful of his wife's protesting.

"Grab my coat and bring the truck," he shouts back to one confused wife.

Still on a full run, impervious to the rain, and now with bruised, bleeding bare feet, he finally reaches the object that caught his eye. It's the squalid, hard-featured, rag-tag pile of broken humanity, lying in the mud, unable to bring himself one step further. It's his lost son. He has returned home.

Like the calves that stray from their mother and become lost, Gibby needs the kind of herdsman that will leave the herd and do for him what he can not do for himself. His father is that benefactor.

Norbert's heart races now that he is sure this is truly Gibby. He's laughing hysterically as he cradles the almost lifeless boy in his arms. Sitting half naked, impervious to his own cuts and the freezing rain, he sits on the mud soaked ground rocking Gibby in his arms as a mother would a sick child, repeating over and over, "Thank you God. Thank you God." This combination of a father's love and forgiveness with the pelting rain give these waters a rare life giving quality.

By this time Joanie has arrived with the pick up truck. When she discovers the source of Norbert's flurry, she too becomes hysterical with

joy. Along with Norbert her body, soul,and mind is closed off to the severe weather they get their son to his feet. Norbert grabs the coat Joanie
brought along and puts it around Gibby's shoulders. It's his best fleece-
lined sheep skin coat. Norbert can't help but think how appropriate this
coat is to dress a lost sheep who has been returned to the fold.

Norbert's oversized coat hangs on Gibby's skeletal form, giving him
a scarecrow appearance. He's hardly able to walk, still he is well aware of
his father's loving embrace.

Joanie can't help but be the mother. She begins by ordering him, mud
and all, into the laundry room along with Norbert to strip the wet clothing off him. Within minutes he's emerged wearing a white terry cloth
bathrobe that by contrast gives his weather worn skin an even darker hue.

The cacophonous sound of pans banging together cut through all the
other sounds in the house. By the time Gibby appears she orders him into
her kitchen where she has a pot of soup boiling on the stove.

She doesn't question where he's been. The fact that he stinks and looks
like he's just returned from some hellish realm is not her immediate concern.

At the same time Norbert is relishing in indescribable joy. Wasting
no time, he races around the barns and stables announcing to anyone in
ear shot, "Gibby's back. He's come home. My son has come home." Norbert's voice is normally a rich baritone, now in his excitement it's taken
on a tenor pitch.

Seeing Jed, and without aforethought that Jed has a pregnant daughter
from this young rogue from the swine pens, he orders him to kill a calf to
barbecue, celebrating Gibby's return.

Jed, always giving deference to Norbert's wishes, grumbles behind his
back, "Yah, sure Norbert that's what I want to do. Your little idiot of a son
knocks up my daughter and now you want me to help you to celebrate!"

On an unbelievable scale, Norbert is putting together a huge celebration. Not because all his problems with Gibby are solved, but because the sadness over Gibby's undeniable lostness has ended.

"The 'old mans' got his head in the sand with this kid," a few are heard to say, as they discuss the upcoming event. "I can't believe he walked all the way from Montana," another is heard.

It's not that Norbert has his 'head in the sand' in giving this reception to this young prodigal, it's that he hasn't realized until now just how much his heart ached for Gibby's return.

"I can't believe how Norbert expects me to be happy about all this after that little peckerhead son of his knocked up our daughter and then takes off and leaves her," laments Jed to Karen.

"I know how you feel Jed, but Joanie and I have come to terms with April's pregnancy. It's going to be our first grandchild and we plan on sharing that. We've agreed that we're going to make it a happy event," asserts Karen.

"You and Joanie can do what you want, but he's going to have a lot of making up to do before I change my mind," reaffirms Jed.

Norbert has planned this party for the coming weekend. This gives Gibby time to rest up and clean up.

Taking full advantage of his parents fawning over him, he sleeps 15 hours straight. At his mother's insistence, he also gets a haircut and shave. Even though his clothes hang on him, she is satisfied they're clean.

The soiled clothing he came home in, laid on the laundry floor until his mother hooked them on a long stick and disposed of them in the big dumpster down by the machine shop. She has no intentions of trying to salvage them. The sooner they were out of her sight, the better.

Saturday has arrived at last. Norbert has hired a band, placing them in a cleaned out pole barn. The calf has been on a spit over charcoal for nearly twenty-four hours. Every neighbor and buckaroo in a fifty-mile radius has been invited. The party is in full swing.

Gibby is not particularly overjoyed with all the fuss. He still harbors a lot of shame and guilt for what he has put his people through. There are, as yet, many amends that haven't been made, a lot of forgiving that hasn't been sought.

So far, he has avoided any questions about April. He hasn't seen her yet, more over he would just as soon avoid that confrontation. But that is not to be. April has just arrived with her parents.

He can't help but stare. Her tasseled red hair is exactly as he kept her in his mind. Even though she has a bulging stomach, she carries herself poised at her full height. She's wearing a pair of cotton leggings and an off the shoulder blue tunic that further accentuates her pregnancy.

She is no more prepared than Gibby to have a face-to-face encounter. Neither has given any thought as to how such a meeting could be arranged anyway.

Noticing his stare, April is somehow pleased, yet reluctant to stare back. Her impulse is to remain coy and let him lead in this re-encounter.

Gibby's reaction is one of regret. Not regret over seeing her again, but the high cost he has paid for his low living. He is not surprised how full of life she carries herself even at full term. But then knowing her, is to know she will do nothing less.

His apologies are going to have to be a process of actions. Anything less significant would be more than hypocritical. There is no chance a simple "sorry" is going to have legs.

Norbert and Joanie are performing like a couple of perfect hosts. Old acquaintances become reacquainted. As the afternoon wares on, the din of laughter, conversation and music prevail.

CHAPTER 20

DILLON'S RETURN

"And kill the calf we have been fattening in the pen. We must celebrate with a feast for this son of mine who was dead and is now returned to life...

"Meanwhile, the older son was in the fields working. When he returned home, he heard music and dancing at the house, and he asked one of the servants what was going on. "Your brother is back", he was told, "and your father has killed the calf we were fattening and has prepared a great feast. We are celebrating because of his safe return.

"The older brother was angry and would not go in. His father came out and begged him, but he replied, "all these years I've worked for you and never refused to do a single thing you told me to do. And in that time you never gave me even one young goat for a feast with my friends. Yet when this young son of yours comes back after squandering your money on prostitutes, you celebrate by killing the finest calf we have.

"His father replied by saying, "Look, dear son, you and I are close, and everything I have is yours. We have to celebrate this happy day, for your brother was dead but has come back to life. He was lost but has been found." Luke 15:23-320

During this whole time Dillon has been on a business trip selling beef to a Japanese buyer. He knows nothing of his younger sibling's return.

Tired and weary from jet lag, and looking forward to a couple of days of rest, he makes his way off the King's Highway down the long driveway into the ranch, only to be met by at least 100 vehicles parked all along the entrance and an adjoining field.

"What the hell is going on here?" questions Dillon aloud.

Seeing a uniformed caterer carrying a large pan, he presents the same question.

"Haven't you heard, the old man's son has come home and he's throwing a party."

Dillon feels a rush of heat starting at his ankles up to the back of his neck. "A party?! I'll burn in hell before I take part in some horse shit party for that little prick," says Dillon as he turns and walks away toward the house.

While making his rounds among his guests, Norbert looks up in time to see Dillon turn his back and walk to the house. Excusing himself, he anxiously follows Dillon.

"Dillon, Dillon,"shouts his father, "Wait a minute. I want to talk to you." Only to be met by this defiant older son turning on his heels.

"Look dad, my demands have always been small. All these years I've worked this ranch, I've had your best interest in mind and always did as you asked. I don't remember you offering even a stinkin' goat for me to celebrate with my friends. Yet for this son, who swallows every dime you've ever laid in front of him, knocks up April and screws every whore in Vancouver, you kill a prize calf and invite half the goddamn province."

Norbert listens patiently without interruption to the grievances of his older son. There is no disagreement- Gibby's sins are easy for anyone to identify. He's wasted and misused everything he has come in contact with: money, time, family, friends, women and his own body and soul. There is no defense against the obvious. Gibby's sins are clear cut.

However, the lostness of this elder brother is not as easily identified. In his own defense, as he has so readily pointed out, there are many right things he has done. After all, he is obedient, dutiful, law abiding and hardworking. People respect him, admire his diligence and praise him for the many improvements he's brought to the ranch. Norbert must give him his due.

Anyone listening to his case would have to agree that on the surface he is above reproach. Nonetheless,when his proud, resentful, unkind, selfishness bubbles to the surface it exposes the rottenness below. When this is contrasted against the happiness of all the guests at Gibby's return, not the least of those are his own mother and father, it tells that his self-proclaimed virtues may be nothing more than self righteousness.

It's been said the "lostness of the resentful saint is so hard to reach precisely because it is so closely wedded to the desire to be good and virtuous."

Since Norbert has always loved his sons equally, he is doing the same for Dillon as he had a few days earlier for Gibby: he went out to meet him. In both cases the initiative has been their father's.

"Dillon, Dillon listen to me" pleads his father, "all I'm asking, is that you set aside your differences for now, and come eat with us."

Listening to his father's pleading only has the effect of causing him to grow even more rigid. Even though he professes his allegiance to his father, he feels this is asking too much of him. "After all, if people see me celebrating with this brother wouldn't they think I am one with him? Wouldn't they think I was OK with my brother's errors? How can I stand shoulder to shoulder with him and all his wrongs?

Norbert listens patiently to his elder sons concern, then adds, "I would hope not, but in your refusal to sit with your brother, you are eliminating yourself from the celebration of your brother's forgiveness."

Dillon doesn't wants to hear anything that will blunt his scurrilous opinion of his brother.

"I won't do it, dad. The next thing the little prick is going to want is to come back to work here."

Dillon pauses for a moment letting his word make an impact then continues his diatribe.

"If you kiss his ass and let him back you may as well say good-bye to me. I can't and won't work with him."

Pausing long enough to let another virulent barrage of contempt catapult toward his younger brother, "I doubt he even knows all the wrongs he's guilty of."

Norbert looks longingly at his eldest son. "How many times must I show you. All that I have is yours and that includes my care and concern for you. I'm not going to deny you anything that belongs to you," assures Norbert.

Not to be dissuaded, Dillon is shouting now, "Well he can bullshit you and mom all day long, but I'm not about to be taken in by any crap he says or does. So the answer is no.- I don't want a damn thing to do with him!"

Dillon storms off to his room and slams the door.

With a heavy heart Norbert returns to the party. He feels the same void he felt when he thought he had lost Gibby. Trying to make the best of what's left of the celebration, he busies himself with more of the details, leaving the visiting efforts to Joanie.

Sitting down next to him, Joanie senses something is troubling him. "Norbert what's wrong? What happened?"

"I'll tell you later. Right now lets be good hosts to our guests."

Norbert has been around long enough to realize life does not have a central plot, it just unfolds.

Even with the doors and windows closed, Dillon can still hear the revelers. His frustration is not subsiding. Wanting to get some relief, he decides to saddle a horse and ride the piss out of it. Without an ounce of shame, he rides full out past a group of merrymakers, shamelessly kicking dirt on them. Most excused it as the act of an unthinking buckaroo with too much to drink, not realizing this is the absent brother.

Dillon's hatred has taken a life of its own. It's so consumed him that even his poor horse is experiencing its merciless effects. Harder and harder, further and further, he rides from the object of his disdain.

By morning the only evidence of a party the day before is a few hundred tables and chairs in total disarray, garbage cans over flowing positioned on all four corners of the barn, and the ruts a hundred four-wheel drive vehicles leave on wet ground.

Norbert has already made arrangements for a clean up crew. Left over food has been divided between anyone willing to carry it off, leaving mostly barrels full of empty paper plates, plastic spoons,knives and forks.

Interrupting Norbert's administrative efforts is a noticeably concerned buckaroo.

"Boss you need to come over to the horse barn. Sompin' weird's goin'on."

Following him to the horse barn he's confronted with a lame horse, still saddled. Norbert and the buckaroo look at one another with the same look. Both recognize it as Dillon's big, black Arabian.

"He just came limpin' in," says the still confused cowhand.

Uneasy at this situation, Norbert makes his way back to the house. Joanie is busy preparing breakfast. Gibby is sitting at the kitchen table stirring a hot cup of coffee while talking with his mother.

"Dillon come down yet," interrupts Norbert as quickly as he approaches the bottom of the stairway. Not waiting for an answer he shouts up the stairs, "Dillon, Dillon are you up?"

Not receiving an answer, he rushes up the steps taking two at a time, racing down the hall to Dillon's bedroom door. The door is closed. Throwing it open he is greeted with an empty room.

Now even more excited, he shouts, "Anyone seen Dillon this morning?"

Not used to seeing this husband and father this much out of character Gibby and his mother briefly glance at one another before realizing something isn't right.

Norbert's intensity and near panic movements cause them both to respond at the same time "No why? What's wrong?"

"Dillon's big Arab just came limping into the stable still saddled, but without Dillon." With that Norbert is out the door, heading back toward the stable. He's met by Jed as he is examining the swollen leg of the riderless horse.

"From the looks of this leg, whoever the rider is, is still out there some where," says an equally concerned Jed.

"I'm pretty sure that someone is Dillon. Jed get some riders together and meet me back here in fifteen minutes," says Norbert.

By this time Joanie and Gibby, still not sure what's gotten into Norbert, show up at the stables.

"Gibby, I need you to get the helicopter ready. Dillon is out there somewhere and I'm sure he's hurt. His horse showed up without him, still saddled and lame. From the looks of things he took a spill."

Calculating nothing, second guessing nothing, for this moment Gibby is not concerned in the least with his and Dillon's disunion: his brother has a need and he may be able to satisfy that need.

Within minutes Gibby is in the air. His method is to begin with a large circle and keep tightening it until he comes across his brother.

While keeping his eye on the ground his mind harks back to the past. The resentments he's harbored against his brother are giving way to a compassion. His brother may be hurt bad and unable to help himself. He remembers himself in that same spot not that long ago. It's moments like this Gibby feels a sense of oneness with his father. It's a strange, but fulfilling sense of contentment.

Sweep after sweep, little by little, he tightens his circle keeping a keen eye open for for his missing brother.

He has been in the air close to an hour with no luck. Deciding to head toward the lake, he remembers how many woodchucks had burrowed around it, leaving just the size hole to fit a horse's foot, when something catches his eye. It looks like a human form lying on the ground. His heart races as he comes down for a closer inspection. What a moment earlier had been hope, is now disappointment as the form reveals itself as that of a half-eaten moose calf.

Still hopeful, he lifts back up to resume his search. His thoughts continue to bang around his head. Even though in the past, he has always found this kind of venture self-gratifying because it had an element of danger and excitement. Today, he is discovering that the only satisfaction he wants to receive is in the alleviation of his brothers predicament.

He remembers his father saying, "*It's easy to love the lovable who don't need much, but how difficult it is to love the obstinate who need it desperately.*"

"*Even if my brother is laying out here somewhere with broken bones, he'll still be an asshole with broken bones.*" Comes a less generous thought but none the less he can't escape the self reproach he's having for this old way of thinking.

The chopper makes short work out of making a direct line to the lake. Once again his eye catches what looks like the crumpled form of a human. It's lying about twenty five yards from the lake. Not wanting to get his hopes up he slowly lowers the chopper. BINGO! It's his brother! He's lying in a helpless heap. His fraternal feelings are rising to the surface as he battles the compulsion to jump from the chopper to his brothers rescue.

Touching the ground, flinging the door open, he is out with the reflexes of a cat, only to make the ugly discovery of his older brother's broken and deformed body lying helpless with what appears to be a broken face. Both eyes are swollen shut along with his clavicle bone sticking through his skin. In his life, he has never imagined his strong opinionated older brother in such enfeebled condition.

In an instant he's on his cell phone calling his father.

"Dad, I found him. We're on the south end of Strang Lake."

"Thank God! What kind of shape is he in," questions a concerned father. "He's alive and breathing, but he's not conscious. He's moaning a lot," reports Gibby.

In less than ten minutes the posse arrives at a full gallop with Norbert in the lead, leaping from his horse in one valiant move, he is at the side of yet another fallen son, wiping the blood from his swollen face. Norbert is oblivious to everything except this son's need. His compassion over flows for this embittered and spiritually deteriorated young man who now is close to physical death because of his raging disposition.

Risking him further injury, still having no other choice, being as careful as possible, they manage to get him into the helicopter. Needing every ounce of fuel, it's quickly decided Norbert will leave Dillon in Gibby's hands while he returns to the ranch. Then he and Joanie will commute by truck. Securing him as best they can, the almost lifeless body of Norbert's oldest is in the air making a beeline for Vancouver.

An hour and a half later he has landed on the hospital helicopter pad. Having radioed ahead, the hospital has provided a gurney and are charging him toward the emergency room.

By the time Gibby has shut down the helicopter, Dillon has been rushed to surgery. Gibby is asked to sit in the waiting room until a doctor can meet with him.

Remembering his promise to phone his father when he arrived, he makes the call. Norbert assures him, "Your mother and I are on our way. We should be there in a few hours."

Sitting alone in the waiting room, totally powerless over the outcome of his brother's injuries, he finds himself doing something he has never done in his life for his brother: He's praying for him.

In his grief over his older sibling, he discovers a generosity within himself. It's a foreign feeling that he remembers he had in his childhood..

It's a yearning to forgive. With this, he's feeling a strong intimate bond to his brother. What he is discovering is a basic truth. A generous heart can not with hold love no matter how righteous one may feel and especially withholding something as significant as forgiveness.

"Mr. Geiberson?" comes a questioning voice interrupting his somberness.

Startled, Gibby looks up to see a man wearing pale green surgical scrubs and a surgical mask pulled down below his chin. He hasn't heard himself called "Mr. Geiberson" since his days with the Hutterites.

"Yes sir, that's me," says Gibby jumping to his feet.

"We've had to do emergency surgery on your brother. It seems his fall has split his spleen. Without the surgery, he would not have lived. Even now it's going to be touch and go for a few days."

Thanking the doctor, he makes his way to his brother's room. Seeing him safely lying on clean white sheets after having pulled him from what could have been a muddy grave, gives him a sense of relief.

Even yet, with all the bandages and tubes, Dillon's tanned, swollen face looks out of place. He has tubes draining every orifice of his body. With his fate hanging in the hands of his Creator, the hospital staff continues to do their part.

It's a tragic and sad story when one is held captive by their own hate. Hate being such a powerful emotion, it always ends tragically.

"It would indeed be a miracle if when the doctor removed Dillon's spleen that all the hate and rancor went with it," thinks Gibby to himself. But for the moment his brother lays on his back in this strange environment struggling for his life.

Reaching across the bed Gibby takes the hand of his still unconscious brother and places it into his hand. Dillon is making some low groaning noises, a sound Gibby has never heard before. It's a sound that resonates half in his throat and partially in his nose "Nurse, nurse," Gibby calls out as he heads for the nurse's station.

Calmly rising from behind her station, the nurse leads him back into Dillon's room, makes a few adjustments, assuring him his brother is fine.

Gibby is having some unexpected reactions to his brother's mishap. Sitting here while staring at this person who has been his nemesis all his life, he finds a miracle has taken hold of him. He has discovered that he shows signs that he has totally forgiven his brother. Having set aside all animosity in favor of a wave of compassion that is now completely engulfing him, he is at peace.

He knows he loves his brother. He looks around the room, assuring himself that Dillon is unconscious and that the nurse has left, he forms the words, easing them past his throat and out through his lips, "I love you Dillon." Still looking around the room, convinced no one heard him he decides to try it again .With a half smirk on his face he eases out the words once again, "I love you Dillon."

Gibby's time with his brother is well spent, but short lived. Soon his parents arrive.

"How's he doing?"

The voice is that of his mother. It sounds small and distant. She looks gaunt and weak as she unconsciously removes Dillon's hand from Gibby's, replacing it with her own.

As Norbert enters the room, he stands at the end of the bed. He first looks at Dillon, then to Gibby, the room is dimly lit giving it a solemnness.

Catching the eye of his father Gibby feels compelled to say something.

"They had to remove his spleen," says Gibby, bowing his head in a sigh as though the fault had been his.

Norbert is silent. He continues to contemplate the unfolding drama before him. He has the return of one son and the departure of the other.

It remains a monumental sight for Norbert to witness the depth of his youngest son's vigil for his older brother.

He's understandably touched by this scene. One fallen son being ministered to by the brother he despises. Norbert knows the full value of time. He is always pleased to see it pass by unaccompanied by unnecessary resentments. Only the courageous know how to forgive and only the one who hates knows the power in forgiving.

"Dad, do you think he's going to make it?" Gibby asks this of his father as though he were not the only the fountain of their existence, but also its extension.

"God only knows," admits Norbert, then adds, "If hardheadedness is part of the healing process, he'll be out of here in days." It's the most lighthearted words his heavy heart can muster for the moment.

Norbert will settle for a physical healing for the present. The healing of Dillon's scorched soul is the task of a power greater than any human doctor.

Over the next several weeks, before Dillon's release, the family takes watchful turns monitoring his recovery.

The taste of death, is for some, the only method that tenderizes a hard heart of resentment. Priorities often change quickly.

Dillon's lack of compassion has given him a reputation that declares he's tough as nails. There has never been a hint that he wishes to change that kind of notoriety. He has grown accustomed to his self-imposed isolation from the rest of the family. He has vowed that he will not be like his father, especially in trying to accommodate others desires. "It's a waste of time," he declares.

Dillon is the first to admit "Work comes first." He enjoys doing a good job, let him get full credit for his virtues. Every night he has come in from long taking care of the ranch. But that's where his sense of responsibility has been brewing under all these virtues all his life. Jealousy,envy, anger, pride, selfrighteousness, sulkiness, touchiness all mixed into one bad temper.

Dillon's idea of success is not that of his father, where patience, kindness and fair play mark the integrity of a man. Rather he prefers to advance the ranch and his own career by being a tough-minded business man.

"Dad, you let people walk all over you," Dillon has been heard to say in a condescending tone.

Dillon has an almost manic reverence toward tough business practices. He is willing to do whatever it takes to achieve this recognition. "If you try to slap me around I'm comin' back swingin' twice as hard," has been his mantra.

At the same time, he longs for his father's recognition and his approval for his achievements, regardless of how he's chosen to achieve them.

Norbert loves his son and is willing to go to the gates of hell with him, but refuses to go in with him. He will only give Dillon's business performance his approval when he proves to be honorable in his dealings.

For Norbert the question remains, will Dillon now that he has been struck low, choose to fight back to his old familiar way of life, or will he now take inventory of his short comings and desire a change?

Chapter 18

A SMALL WINDOW OF MANHOOD

What makes a boy become a man? Some will say "It's when a boy assumes the responsibility of independent living." Others say "The love a good woman is what propels a mediocre man into a good man." Still others insist "It's when a man undergoes hardship and profits by it."

Norbert would agree that each of these play a role in part. He readily agrees that Joanie certainly has been a positive influence in his development. To be certain his hope is that as nature takes its course with his sons that they may also share their lives with a good woman and that they become good solid husbands and fathers. Norbert never denies that he is a Christian, bleeding heart, traditionalist.

It's been several weeks since Gibby returned home. He's made a few clumsy attempts to be where April may show up, finally managing to stumble across her in the horse barn.

"Hey, how ya doin'," says Gibby with a self-conscious grin.

April is noticeably taken by surprise as she unconsciously adjusts her hair behind her ears.

"Oh fine," she returns looking around self consciously with a look that says *"what do I do next?"*

"My mom tells me it's a girl," says Gibby rather awkwardly.

"Yah, I've named her Ingrid," says April with a tone of regained confidence.

"Ingrid?" says a surprised Gibby. Rechecking his response and not wanting to appear meddlesome he adds, "Well that's a good Scandinavian name."

"More German than Scandinavian I think. It was my grandmother's name. Anyway I like the way it sounds, 'Ingrid Landers,'" says April with an air of finality.

Hearing her add her own last name onto his child stings him for a moment. It's a reality he hadn't thought of. It's a tangle he knows he created. For now, he's going to have to live with his own blunderings and accept decisions that are being made without him.

Trying to be as cautious and courteous as he can, he addresses her with a request.

"Do you mind if I become part of her life?"

This appeal stops her for a moment. She turns and takes note, hoping to discover what truth may lie behind this petition. She catches him try and blink away a moistness forming in his eyes. Both have offended the other in various ways, so neither is the sole victim.

Nonetheless, she has been hurt beyond description. So far, in spite of her exterior bravado, she has found herself stymied and helpless to correct the wrongs she's committed, as well as those committed against her. Her solution to melting away her pain is to stay in control of herself and her unborn daughter.

Without notice something is taking a hold on Gibby. He finds himself entertaining a level of maturity that he has avoided for the past eight and a half months.

April pauses, appearing to be deepening her study of Gibby.

"I don't know,Gibby." Do you see yourself taking off again?"

Trying not to sound sarcastic or challenging to Gibby, she hopes to elicit a simple assurance of some kind of responsible support. She's not expecting rigorous honesty but at least something in that direction.

By holding her ground, she has exposed the ugliness of his actions. The high cost he's paid for his low living penetrates him as she is refusing to release her stare.

Wisely suspecting that this is not the time or place to demonstrate his own insecurities, rather exactly the time and place to be open and frank.

"Before I say anything more, I want to apologize to you for leaving you the way I did. It was wrong, it was selfish.

"I was angry with Dillon and my thinking became so narrow that I shoved you and my parents to the curb.

"I'm not trying to justify any hurt I caused you or have anyone excuse my actions. I want you to know that I'm sorry."

The moisture in his eyes have turned to tears running down his face.

While listening to his amends with a stoney silence, a torrent of emotion suddenly comes over her like a huge wave. Eight and a half months of pent up resentments are unleashed spilling out in a torrent of frustration.

"You son of a bitch! You think you can waltz in here after you ripped through my life and say to me you're sorry? What the hell is that supposed to mean? Am I just supposed to suck it up and say 'oh well I guess boys will be boys'!"

Gibby's first thought is to regard April's words as a rejection of his sincere apology and just leave. His feelings have been hurt and his thoughts are to lash back. *"Screw her. I tried my best to apologize. To hell with her. Let her live in her own resentments."*

Standing speechless before her like a riderless horse he waits for either the 'anger rider' to jump on his back and pull him one way. Or another rider called 'patience and kindness' to relocate his actions in another direction.

A second thought suddenly breaks through. *"What would Norbert do?"*

The next thought says *"These demons have to be fought with actions not thoughts."*

He can't believe these thoughts are coming from his mind. Even more so he can't believe how easily he finds himself willing to comply.

April is standing directly in front of him. Tears of anger and frustration are staining her cheeks. He slowly reaches toward her face wiping her tears with his hands, then his own, and purposely rests her head on his chest. A torrent of tears continue as he wraps his arms around her holding her as securely as he knows how. He continues to hold her even as he feels the firm roundness of her pregnant stomach heave against him with each uncontrollable sob. Correspondingly, he begins to sense a kind of intimacy with April that is strangely peaceful.

Having this small window of manhood open, he has invited it in. A change is coming about. Along with it, he is finding a new hero in his father. No longer viewing him as the enemy, Gibby has found himself embracing more of his father values.

Gibby and April spend the rest of the afternoon talking and talking and talking, even finding a few things to laugh about. He is trying to take everything slow.

He has found a particular kind of comfort with April that he didn't have with women like Rachael. Rachael was certainly a sex bomb and met that need whenever he demanded it, but when the sex was over, he was never comfortable with her. They seldom, if ever talked, and if they did, it was usually drug or alcohol induced.

Another week passes at the ranch. Healing of mind, body and spirit are not left waiting. Dillon is finally up and getting around slowly. He's tried to do a few simple chores, only before long, he finds himself back in bed.

He is spending much of his time being attended to by his mother. Norbert and Gibby are tending to the responsibilities that Dillon would normally be in charge of.

Whether it is because of his weakened condition or a major change has come over Dillon, on this particular morning he seeks out Gibby. Gibby is sitting behind Dillon's desk busying himself with some paper work.

As Dillon slowly makes his way through the door, Gibby stops what he is doing, holding his gaze. Dillon is not giving any clues as to his purpose for this visit. Gibby is fixated behind the desk waiting for something to happen. He he just doesn't know what.

Dillon's dilemma is to thank his brother for saving is life or reject him once again.

Without warning, the face of this elder brother begins to form an ev-er-so-slight a smile. Gibby, still not quite comfortable with his brother's purpose, waits for him to show his hand. Dillon stops dead center to the big desk all the while not taking his eye off his younger brother, extending his hand across to him.

"Gibby, I want to thank you for what you have done for me. I know you spent a lot of your time with me. I remember how often I opened my eyes, unable to talk with all those damned tubes sticking out of me, only to see you standing there. I'm not sure I would have done that for you and but I want to thank you.

Gibby relaxes a bit now with his brother's non confrontational demeanor. "In all honesty I struggled at times. It may not have been something I was totally comfortable with but then I remembered how dad opened his arms for me when I came home. The least I can do is to try and do the same for you, Dillon."

Rising up from his chair, Gibby takes his brother's hand. "I know I haven't been the best brother for you but I'd like to start again," says Gibby still holding to his brother hand.

Dillon nods to Gibby's request.

"Gibby, I want to welcome you home " is what Dillon would like to say but still finds it sticking in his throat. Both are satisfied with the baby steps they have taken.

What they both did or didn't say to each other is important, but it's more important to affirm the silent affirmation they have made within themselves to go forward with mending their relationship.

Both of these young men are guilty of a near-pathological, self absorption. Both have also experienced the fall out of this kind of life choice. In both cases it's had a negative impact in their lives.

Given the God given talents each of them were granted and in evolutionary terms they both are equipped to evolve into men of character.

Through a half opened door, Norbert witnessed this brief encounter between his sons. The accord between them was more than he had expected yet certainly is what he has hoped and prayed for. He knows his boys and their strengths and weaknesses. Satisfied his family is back on track, he retires to his daily tasks.

The dust on the far end of the long driveway indicate visitors. At the rate of speed the two large, black Cadillac Escalades are traveling gives the impression their mission may be more of an assault than a visit.

Gibby is the first to notice. He knows immediately who it is. It's Marty Wong and a few of his cousins. He hurries out to meet them before they are within earshot of the ranch house.

"Hey Gibby, how you doin'?" inquires Marty. The look on his face doesn't match his congenial greeting. Both his hands are shoved deep into a black leather jacket, his heads tilted at cocky angle with a cigarette dangling from the corner of his mouth.

"I've done better," says Gibby. Four men exit the other Escalade. Gibby recognizes them as the men who gave Bayliss his unwanted bath.

Looking over this emaciated, former gangster along with his tone of his voice, Marty senses a change.

"That's too bad, cause we need some 'splanin'. We ain't heard shit from you boy and we want our money." Marty's voice now matches his demeanor.

Gibby tells them about Tommy and Mooch, how his helicopter was lost in the lake and how Rachael had stolen nearly a million dollars.

"We know all about that whore you had livin' with you. We got that money. We're going to do you one big favor and apply that to your debt, so now all you owe us is 1.2 million. We also know about Tommy and Mooch. The old man took it pretty hard.

"The bottom line is this was your deal. If it got screwed up, that's your fault. All the old man wants now is the family's money," says Marty.

Gibby is feeling a true desperation. It's the kind that he will do any-thing to get relief.

"I know I owe you, but I can't pay you what I don't have. I'll work it off. I'll run dope for you wherever you want until I get it paid. Just give me a chance."

Gibby's face has the look of fear. He knows what these people are capable of and to what lengths they will go to achieve their ends. He's ready to sacrifice himself back to them if he can protect the rest of his family.

"Ya know Gibby, I've always liked you, but I'm not putting my ass on the line for you. I'll take your proposal back but don't expect anyone to be thrilled," says Marty pulling his sunglasses down over his eyes.

Getting back into the Escalades, the entourage leaves, leaving Gibby standing alone and perplexed. All that is left of them is the dust from the driveway hanging in the air, and their rancor lingering in his thoughts.

Undetected, Norbert has been observing from the window of the ranch house. Norbert didn't just fall off the turnip truck. He knows something serious is going on. Waiting until Gibby comes in, he approaches him.

"You have business with those men son?" Norbert asks. His tone of voice suggests this is more than a casual inquiry.

"Ya, sort of," says Gibby, not wanting to involve his family any more than he has to.

"You want to talk about it?" questions his father while his eyes and mind continue to search his son.

"No, it's nothing I can't handle," says an unconvincing Gibby.

Norbert has a look that cannot be mistaken. It's the look a father has when one of his children are playing with matches and gasoline. It's one of intense concern.

"I won't push you on this, but when you're ready to tell me what's going on, I'll be here to help you through it," says Norbert as assuring as a father can who loves his son.

"Thanks, dad," says Gibby, somewhat detached with other thoughts.

Looking at Gibby, Norbert can't help but hark back to his three-year-old son declaring "I can do it myself daddy" as he was about to unwisely leap into some kind of danger.

April had found wearing sweats a comfortable alternative to her signature jeans or cargo pants, no make up, and her hair pulled back in a simple pony tail.

Since Gibby's return she has rediscovered make up, curling irons and stretch leggings. Gradually, as confidence in the relationship continues the two of them are learning to appreciate each other. They are both listening to each other talk about common goals, especially in discussing Ingrid. They are building a comfortable connection. That is all fine and good but for the looming problem with the Chinese.

Gibby has been hesitant to bring this problem into his family relations much less with April. Even though he is trying to build on forthrightness, he is preferring to withhold this problem in fairness to them. It's his burden and he has no intentions of dumping it onto innocent parties. He's hoping for some kind of miracle that will get these people out of his life forever.

Meantime April is unapologetic about her desire to have Gibby be truthful.

"Gibby I trust you're telling me the truth about what your telling me. It's what you're not telling me that bothers me," says April with the full knowledge of the Chinese visit.

Finally relenting, Gibby drove April out to the cabin and spends the rest of the afternoon turning over every rock of his misspent life. He fully expects this kind of openness to be the final blow to any hopes of a relationship with April and adding only insult to injury.

April remains attentive without interruptions as she listens to Gibby's tale of woe. This is a woman who, at eighteen killed a charging wild boar with a bow and arrow. Women like April have turned aside the 1970s feminist image of bra burning to fully embrace not only a girly-girl image but also a tough willingness to take on hard ball.

At last Gibby brings his saga to the point of the Chinese men visiting the ranch.

April is sitting quietly attentive on the old couch she dragged in a year ago. She abruptly breaks her silence.

"OK big boy," she says motioning to Gibby waving an extended hand and managing a smile, "Pull me up and get me to the hospital."

She has been sitting here all afternoon feeling contractions but was not about to put off Gibby's pricking of conscience.

The reality of this turn of events shuffles Gibby's brain. He is instantly to his feet prepared to do something only not knowing what. This move is quickly short lived as yet another turn of events takes over. There is a sudden gush of water pooling directly under April.

"Oh my God! Gibby my water just broke." Her contractions are now strong and close. Assessing the situation as well as he can he says, "Lets get you to the Jeep We gotta get you to the hospital."

"I don't think I can make it, Gibby."

April has a grimace on her face that she has never before experienced its cause and one that Gibby has never seen on anyone.

"Gibby help me get these pants off quick," she shouts trying to at least begin with what she knows how to do. Not at all prepared for any of this and never before even brought to mind, he finds himself fumbling with April's clothing.

What he sees next is a scene not soon to be forgotten. There is a wet blondish red colored head beginning to make its way out from between the legs of this now vocal brand- new mother.

With nothing but instinct Gibby begins to spread her legs away from this emerging tenant. He's delivered enough colts to know he may have to assist. Waiting until her little head popped through before he reached under her arms, he gently brought her out the rest of the way.

"Oh my God, oh my God, oh my God," he exclaims over and over in wonderment. "It is a girl! Oh my God, April look at this!"

April has both a look of joy and desperation as she holds out her arms wanting Gibby to release this crying little lump on her belly. This is the little lump she has grown to love for the past nine months, but has yet to meet face to face.

With a firm hand Gibby lays his daughter on her mother's stomach. Then taking out his buck knife, he cuts the umbilical cord.

There can be no question, as one watches this mother and daughter lock eyes, that there is no power on earth that can unlock it. This miracle is a bond between mother and daughter that lasts a life time.

Instinctively this child begins to make sucking noises. Taking one of her swollen breast she places the nipple into her miniature mouth as she caresses wet ringlets of blondish red hair. "Oh Gibby, she's so beautiful."

This is the beginning of a nourishing process that will morph into many different events in the lives of this family.

This whole process has taken no more than ten minutes. All that has been a priority in their lives prior to the last ten minutes has quickly become ancient history. They will for many years conform themselves around the result of this singular event.

"Is her name still Ingrid'?" asks Gibby.

"Yah, I think so, I still like that name," says April. Pausing for a moment, "You pick her middle name Gibby."

"Give me a minute, I'll have to think about it."

Minding a pan full of lake water he's heating on the small camp stove he dips his shirt in and begins to wipe off his daughter after birth.

"I like Grace. Yah I think Grace," says Gibby with an air of finality.

April looks at Gibby then at their daughter.

"I like that Gibby. It has a nice sound to it, Ingrid Grace Geiberson."

Gibby's bathing chore came to a stand still as he digested what had just been said.

"Did I hear you say Geiberson?"

"Yes you did. I don't want to rush you into anything you don't want to do, but I was thinking, when we have her baptized we could become Mr. and Mrs. Geiberson at the same time.

"April are you sure after all I've told you, that you want to take on *this* project?" says a flabbergasted Gibby pointing to himself.

"Whatever has to be worked out we can probably do it better together. We don't need to sit around and whine. We'll survive because we're survivors," replies April.

"You know April I've always loved you, but now I'm beginning to like you. With you in my corner I know things will work out," says a grinning and happy Gibby.

Gibby can't believe how much better things are now than when he left. Unity with his father has also given him a unity with his brother and now with April.

"Promise me one thing," says April.

Gibby's grin quickly leaves as he expects his bubble is about to burst. "What's that?"

"Promise me we can live out here at the cabin."

A relieved Gibby agrees, as he surveys this new challenge, "Fine but let me fix it up first."

With their brand new addition, they head back to the ranch.

As could easily be predicted, both sets of grandparents being taken by surprise, are tripping over one another while fawning over their first grandchild.

Over the next week, Gibby begins to haul building materials of all sorts hoping he can transform 'Ole Bill Strang's' cabin into a livable dwelling.

Bill didn't have the luxury of milled lumber, consequently everything that went into building this cabin was rough. Most all the walls, roof, even the floor were made of cedar logs. Small logs, large logs, all sizes of logs.

A few improvements over the years have helped preserve the old structure. A tar papered roof and some window replacements were added at some point.

Examining the floor, Gibby realizes 'Ole Bill' had layed two-inch cedar poles tightly packed side by side, then filled in between with a heavy clay found down by the lake. It gave the floor a smooth surface as the clay hardened like brick, and kept away the dampness from merely a dirt floor.

Gibby decides he will use the poles as a sub floor and lay sheeting over the top to get rid of the dirt.

He begins the task by removing some areas of the floor that would cause his plywood sheets to lay uneven. He's amazed at how well preserved those ancient wooden poles have remained. He can still smell the cedar scent and see the ax cut marks on the ends.

The floor is primitive and needs a few pieces pulled out. After removing an odd-fitting piece in the center of the floor, he notices something odd.

"What the hell is this?" says Gibby, fingering a piece of canvas. Closer inspection reveals it continues to run under these ancient floor poles throughout this whole area.

Curious but not wanting to pull the whole floor he tugs on what is becoming clear is a canvas covering. Finally he gets a hold of a corner and gives it a good pull. It's enough to shower the room with a cloud of 150-year-old dust. Waving his hand and coughing, Gibby waits for the air to clear.

"Oh crap, I've pulled up half the floor" says Gibby. Not wanting to cause himself more work he takes out his buck knife and slits open a hole in this canvas covering. Below it, his knife hits what sounds and feels like a rock.

"Damn," he says, examining his blade, "Now I'm wrecking my knife."

He begins to scrutinize his undertaking, carefully spreading this ancient fabric, taking special care not to chip his knife blade again. This top piece of canvas seems to be a covering for something underneath that still alludes his eyes. Throwing caution to the wind, he slits a good twelve-inch hole in this superannuated covering. Spreading it open reveals some dried leather pouches. Reaching in the gap, he slides one through.

"Damn this thing is heavy," he exclaims.

Taking his knife he cuts into one of the folds on this tough old pouch. What dropped out will forever be indelibly imprinted in his mind.

'CLINK!'

A shiver went through his spine. "Is this what I think it is?"

'CLINK! CLUNK!'

More is falling out of the bag. Setting this bag aside he pulls out one by one, eleven more just like this one. His pulse is quickened at what he has, indeed, uncovered. Eleven, ten-pound bags of 'Ol Bill Strang's' hidden gold horde.

Stunned yes, but because of the possibilities this kind of discovery promises, he begins to laugh. It's the laughter that can only come when a great miracle pulls one out of a sinking hole.

While joyfully dancing around what's left of the old cabin floor, he catches a glimpse through the window of a bobbing, bouncing Escalade, purposely closing the gap between them. Behind them is a familiar sight. It's his father. He sighs a deep sigh of relief as he readily forms the words:

"Thank you Lord!"

CPSIA information can be obtained at www.ICGtesting.com
Printed in the USA
BVOW071354140912

300445BV00002B/5/P